SUBSTITUTE SISTER

KATHERINE NICHOLS

Black Rose Writing | Texas

ISBN: 978-1-68513-203-3
PUBLISHED BY BLACK ROSE WRITING
www.blackrosewriting.com

Printed in the United States of America
Suggested Retail Price (SRP) $21.95

The Substitute Sister is printed in Book Antiqua

*As a planet-friendly publisher, Black Rose Writing does its best to eliminate unnecessary waste to reduce paper usage and energy costs, while never compromising the reading experience. As a result, the final word count vs. page count may not meet common expectations.

PRAISE FOR
THE SUBSTITUTE SISTER

"This follow-up to *The Sometime Sister* delivers, not only on the suspense, but also on the lengths we'll go to for family. The book explores the depths of connection: how deeply we'll mourn the loss of it, fight to establish it, regain it, or sometimes, even die for it. *The Substitute Sister* isn't just a heart pounding suspense read but a journey of belonging as well."

–Kim Conrey, author of the *Ares Ascending* series

"The sequel to *The Sometimes Sister* delivers another intricately designed mystery to lose yourself in. I loved Grace in the first book, I love her even more in this book, and now Nichols is giving us more richly developed characters to sink our teeth into. Beautifully written, funny, and thrilling. Read this!"

–G.A. Anderson, author of *South of Happily*

DEDICATION

Without the help and support of my husband and family, I could never bring my stories to life.

ACKNOWLEDGMENTS

I've been incredibly lucky in my writing journey. As always, I have the love and patience of my husband as well as friends and family. But I have been fortunate enough to become part of the Atlanta area writing community. From the critique group I discovered as a member of the Atlanta Writers Club, I met generous authors who helped me—as George Weinstien, Executive Director of the AWC, always says—make it better.

The attitudes of these colleagues led me and my fellow female authors to form Wild Women Who Write. We are dedicated to encouraging women to tell their stories. Our podcast, Wild Women Who Write Take Flight, serves as an outreach for their voices. Without these women—Gaby Anderson, Kim Conrey, Kat Fieler, and Lizbeth Jones—my characters wouldn't be half as much fun.

Two special friends dedicated time and effort to helping me develop and edit this book. Walter, aka Todd, Lamb and Beth Villemez. They made a difficult task much easier.

Both *The Sometime Sister* and *The Substitute Sister* are tributes to bonds women form. Without a sister of my own, I've learned about these relationships through observation. My daughters show me how sharing with a sister changes lives. My friends teach me DNA is only one way to define family. I'm forever grateful to them for making me a part of their special sisterhood.

I'd like to thank talented photographer, compassionate counselor, and great friend, Madonna Mezzanotte, for my headshot.

And much credit goes to Black Rose Writing for making me feel like a real writer.

DON'T MISS
WHERE THE SERIES BEGAN!

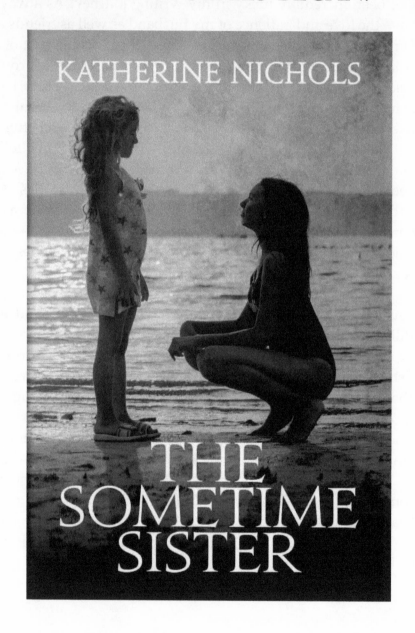

KATHERINE NICHOLS

THE
SOMETIME
SISTER

THE
SUBSTITUTE
SISTER

CHAPTER 1: GRACE

Four years had passed since my ex-fiancé murdered his wife, who also happened to be my sister. Families can be complicated.

Although the man who tricked us both into loving him wasn't the one who choked the life out of Stella, her death was on him. Losing her cluttered my life with complications and contradictions. For example, mornings. Once straightforward moments of the day, they became the cruelest of hours. Regardless of the horrors from the night before—images of my sister's broken body lifeless on the rocky beach, or her face when she struggled for her last breath—those few minutes after waking, I forgot she was gone. I shrugged off my nightmares as guilty remnants of hurt and anger toward her for stealing my soon-to-be husband. Comforted by the knowledge I had all the time in the world to offer her my forgiveness and love, I would close my eyes and be me, Stella's big sister.

Then a vague feeling of dread descended. It wasn't the throbbing pain of an unwelcome memory. It was the same fresh slash of agony I experienced when I first received the news she was gone.

And just like that, morning, the sneaky bitch she had become, did it again. Promised a day free from crushing guilt and delivered never-ending reality.

After a long while, I caught on, and the beginnings of my days stopped threatening to end them. With the help of my complicated family, I accepted the impossibility of reclaiming the before times. Grief was a part of me, but it didn't have to define me. I was the only one who could do that. So, I embraced what I had and cherished my happy memories.

This decision was the first of many made by the new Grace Burnette McElroy. I still had trembling night terrors but recognized them for what they were, a reflection of our tragedy. Morning no longer possessed the power to derail me.

On this sunny June day, I headed to the mall, remembering how much Stella loved to shop. My resolve to return to normal was holding strong, until I stopped at Nordstrom's makeup counter, where a tsunami of doubt almost knocked me off my feet. The capable, if wounded, woman I'd become lost the ability to make a simple decision.

Should I go with Plum Delicious or Just Peachy? Then I saw Raspberry Rage. My problem would have been ridiculous if it hadn't been oddly frightening. When I tried to choose, I didn't remember how to do it.

Determined to regain control of whatever region of the brain was in charge of matching skin tone to lipstick color, I reached for the sample tube, and it happened. A prickle of electricity rippled the hair on my forearms.

"Stella," I gasped.

"Are you okay?" The saleswoman's voice reflected concern, but her perfectly lined lips remained in a well-constructed pout.

"Am I what?" I stared at the streak on my palm, Naughty Minx. Advertised as the red guaranteed to bring out the vixen in every woman, it reminded me of a *National Geographic* spread, where a grinning tiger looms over its bloody prey. I swiped at the crimson trail with my finger, smearing it over my wrist.

Without stepping closer, the beauty clinician tossed me a tissue and asked again if I was all right.

Stronger now, the current traveled upward. I turned away from the woman and sped to the shoe aisle.

And there, in front of the summer sandal sale sign, stood my sister. Her sun-streaked hair swinging as she fled toward the exit. I followed, dodging pre-teens in the junior department and white-haired ladies picking at discount jewelry. Desperate to catch her, I pushed past a young woman shoving a protesting toddler into a stroller and an elderly man with a walker.

But when I reached the mall entrance, she was gone. I wanted to call her name, louder this time, but knew she wouldn't answer. Dead women seldom do.

.   .   .   .   .

My ghost-sister sighting unnerved me. I lost interest in choosing between accenting my sexy side or bringing out my girlish glow and went straight to my car. After turning on the engine, I rested my head on the steering wheel for a few seconds, then called my husband and was sent to voicemail.

"Hope everything's going okay. I miss you." I gave my best imitation of a carefree wife, not a wild woman losing her mind.

Although Justin understood the complicated relationship Stella and I had, even he would have trouble making sense of what happened in the department store. Or what I thought had taken place. Just hearing his voice comforted me, but lately I sensed a distance between us. Not as if we'd lost our connection, more like our cables needed tightening. It was as if he were hiding something from me. Whispering into the phone and leaving the room for late-night calls, being difficult to reach or vague about his whereabouts. Things he'd never done before.

I attributed the change to the challenges of balancing parenthood and careers while keeping our love life interesting, nothing some time together wouldn't fix. On a day like this. when I so badly needed to talk to him, his absence hit me as evidence of a worrisome shift in our relationship.

I addressed myself in the rear-view mirror. "There you go, looking for trouble when nothing's there."

Stella once warned me my problem was not believing I deserved a man who would treat me with love and kindness. She said I rejected them before they got the chance to dump me.

Her words returned when I fell for Justin. I listened to them and accepted my good luck in finding a husband like him. I mustered the courage to believe he was just as lucky to have found me.

But self-confidence never came easy for me. And seeing my dead sister shopping for shoes didn't make it any easier.

CHAPTER 2: GRACE

I drove on autopilot to my mother's home in the suburbs. The early June traffic moved easier in Atlanta. With the buses full of screaming students and SUVs containing harried parents late for drop-off removed from the picture, drivers experienced only the usual slowdown, resulting from an overheated vehicle or a fender-bender.

Built in the seventies and scorned by the children who grew up in them, houses like the one where I spent my childhood were back in vogue. Mom threatened to sell hers and move into a fifty-five and older community, but we knew she wouldn't.

On this sunny summer Saturday, Emma Grace, my four-year-old daughter, sat on the steps blowing bubbles with my mother's longtime boyfriend Mike. Rather, he blew the bubbles, and she caught them on her tongue. The moment I stepped from the car, she darted toward me, dimpled arms outstretched.

Despite the dark hair inherited from her father and her silvery-gray eyes the exact shade as mine, a genetic gift from my grandmother, she was the image of my sister.

"Did you miss me?" I scooped her up and kissed her neck. Her sweaty little body was airy light with the warm, yeasty smell of post-toddler. She giggled and held me close for a few sweet seconds, then squirmed to be let down. We walked hand in hand to the porch, with its wicker chair, geranium pots, and *Did you call first?* welcome mat.

"Mikey made bubble monsters, and I ate them." Emma Grace was the only person in the world who could get away with calling Mom's tough-as-nails Marine Mikey.

"You're home early." He hugged me before opening the screen door. "Grandma's fixing lunch."

He picked up Emma as we entered the living room. Other than an overpriced console table Mom bought on a whim, nothing much had changed. The same sagging sofa cushions Stella and I used for fort building were there. And the creased leather wingback chair not fit for sitting maintained its place beside the fireplace. Sometimes, I expected to see my sister lying with her feet propped up on the sprung couch, reading *Cosmo* or *Glamour* or some other piece of great literature.

The three of us went to the kitchen, where Mom stood at the stove, squeezing orange goo over a steaming bowl of macaroni.

"It's mac and cheese," Emma explained. "I love mac and cheese."

"Who doesn't?" Mike eased her to the floor. "Let's wash our hands. Then you can help me set a place for your mommy."

After three years, I continued to marvel at being called *mommy*. My sister appointed me as Emma Grace's guardian when the child was born. I often wondered if she sensed she wouldn't live to see her daughter grow up.

Before the ink was dry on our marriage license, Justin and I adopted our niece. We celebrated by going to Seagrove, the same beach where Stella, our whimsical cousin Lesroy — named by his hateful daddy Roy who deemed him too weak to be a junior — and I spent so many happy summers.

Emma raced to the water's edge, burrowing her tiny toes into the sand. At the first ripple of the tide, she ran to the shore, her wild hair flying, the same way her mother when she fled from the foamy water countless times before.

"Are you okay, Grace? You look a little pale."

Mom always thought I looked a little something–stressed, tired, thin. But that day she was most likely correct. Seeing a dead woman on a shopping spree can take the color right out of a girl.

Named after Marilyn Monroe, my mother bore scant resemblance to the shapely blonde bombshell. After the death of her younger daughter, anguish turned her into a skeleton, one who wandered from room to room mumbling to herself. She lost so much weight the doctor threatened to hospitalize her.

But it wasn't his warning that rescued her from that terrible dark place. Emma Grace did that.

Even she couldn't dispel the thick black cloud that overshadowed our family, making us fearful the mention of my sister might poison the air with sorrow. And we never spoke the name of Emma's father.

Mom plopped a glob of the gooey cheese mixture into the Peter Rabbit bowl, a relic from Stella's childhood. Mike put the little girl in her booster seat and fastened a lacy bib around her neck.

My daughter undid the bib, dropped it to the floor, and proclaimed only babies wore them, and she was not a baby. Her grandmother shrugged and scooted her closer to the table.

"We've been doing some thinking." She paused to guide a spoonful of noodles toward Emma, who wrested the spoon away and moved it toward her lips. "Careful, sweetie. It's hot." She hovered as her granddaughter touched a noodle with the tip of her tongue before taking a bigger bite. Satisfied no imminent danger existed for the child, she resumed.

"You know Mike has asked me to marry him on several occasions."

"Five to be exact," he added.

I hadn't realized the number was so high but remembered the last time he promised never to mention the subject again. If she wanted him, she would have to do the proposing.

"Anyway." Mom ran her fingertips over his hand. "I was always afraid to say yes. I didn't have much luck with your father. But I worry about our little girl being around us when we're uh, when we're like this."

"You mean when you're living in sin?" I offered.

"Shh!" She blushed and covered the child's ears with her hands. Mike and I laughed, but my mother was dead serious. I put on a more suitable expression and nodded for her to continue.

"I told Mike if he still wanted me, I would marry him."

"Not the romantic proposal I hoped for," he said, rubbing her shoulders. "But I accepted."

Overcome with the realization of how much he loved this beautiful, exasperating woman, I raced to him and wrapped my arms around his waist, startling Emma, who tipped over her bowl, and watched its contents splatter onto the floor. Mom leaped to her feet, grabbed a dish towel, and wiped up the mess, while fussing at me and Mike for scaring her grandbaby. Not the least bit intimidated, Emma laughed at the commotion.

"We want a small ceremony, just family and a few friends." She glanced at her intended, then cleared her throat. "And we'd like to have it in the church, but only if you're okay with that."

The *church* was the one where we had my sister's funeral on a cold December afternoon. My mother, propped up on each side by Mike and Lesroy, led our sad little procession down the aisle.

The urn with Stella's ashes held the place of honor next to the pulpit, where the young minister struggled to comfort our family. Not an easy feat considering the many unresolved emotions surging below the surface of our Xanax-induced calm.

I wasn't enthusiastic about revisiting that chapel, but if it made her happy, I would do it.

"That sounds like the perfect spot to have your wedding." And maybe it would be a circle of life situation: The same place that marked the end of my sister's short life would herald the beginning of a new one for them.

Emma licked the bottom of her empty bowl and wriggled from her seat. She almost got away, but Mom grabbed her and wiped her face and hands. The child squirmed in protest, but my mother prevailed, then appeased her angry granddaughter with a cookie. Emma clutched it in one hand and tugged Mike's sleeve with the other, requesting he read her a story. He acquiesced, and the two retired to the den, now more of a playroom.

Mom finished cleaning up the mess and asked if they could keep the mess-maker for a sleep-over. I hated to be separated from my daughter overnight, but after the mall experience, I couldn't shake my unease.

Despite a childhood filled with tales of spirits and the supernatural, provided by our imaginative cousin, I never believed in ghosts or ghosties as Lesroy called them. Stella had died, and she wasn't coming back. I had the evidence to prove it: an eight-by-ten glossy of her lifeless body outlined in the golden sand, the same terrible image that haunted my dreams years after her death.

Now, it came to me less often. But the terrors I faced while uncovering the reason someone dropped my sister on the shoreline as a feast for the crabs were never far away. They drove me to search the internet for news of anything related to Ecuador, the exotic country where my sister was murdered. I kept my obsession a secret from my husband.

I sorted through sites devoted to promoting travel in the region. Rich cultural heritage and incredible architecture, surfer-laden beaches, hot springs, stunning mountain views, local markets, and smiling people. I had experienced their bounty.

But I had also witnessed the darker side of the country — corrupt officials, drug smuggling, cops for hire. No different, I supposed, from my own. For my purposes, I needed the low-down on individuals who thrived on brutality and had no respect for law or life.

Adelmo Balsuto, Emma's father, had been one of those men. He insisted the love he shared with my sister changed him and proclaimed he would no longer be a part of his family's business. I suspected her death ended his transformation. If not for the child she left behind, I couldn't imagine a world in which he would continue along a peaceful path without her. I hoped the knowledge his daughter was safe and loved would satisfy him. And as the years passed, I allowed myself to believe in this happy-ever-after ending.

During the last year, I let my guard down. And while I knew there had to be a logical explanation for her manifestation, I was equally certain Stella had come to warn me. Of what, I hadn't a clue, but if it was important enough for her to show up in person, there would be nothing happy about it.

CHAPTER 3: GRACE

I tried to remember the last time Justin and I had two entire nights alone together. Earlier in the spring, we sent Emma to Mom's when I had the flu. But lying in bed burning with fever instead of desire didn't count. Before then, it had been our second anniversary almost three years ago. My initial reserve at the idea of deserting my daughter changed into schoolgirl-giddiness at the prospect of snuggling with my handsome husband.

Miss Scarlett, the seventy-pound Doberman Stella and Ben deserted when they ran off to Ecuador, greeted me with subdued enthusiasm. Her stubby tail wagged furiously as she sidled up to me, nuzzling my crotch with her long, slender nose. She stopped and stared behind me.

"Sorry, sweet girl. She's staying at Nana's."

My regal canine understood more words than most dogs and divined that her beloved mini mistress wouldn't be coming through the door. Her ears folded, and she whimpered. From the moment we brought Emma home, Scarlett claimed her. The dog slept in her room and seldom left her side. She loved me and my husband, but she adored our girl.

I reached out my hand to scratch the sweet spot below her muzzle, and she accepted the gesture, closing her eyes and groaning while I checked my text messages.

Hey, babe. This system's screwed up worse than I expected. We're going to have to work most of the night. Promise I'll be back tomorrow for dinner. Give Emma a kiss and tell her to pass it on. Love you.

Under different circumstances, I would have enjoyed an evening to myself. After my mall experience and the increasing frequency of his late hours, my previous inkling something was off with us returned.

As if sensing my uneasiness, Scarlett leaned against me. "That's right, baby girl. At least we've got each other. Let's go outside."

Instead of her ecstatic happy dance, she stood quietly while I clipped the leash on her collar.

I intended to take her on a long walk, but the weather forecasters had been accurate with their warning this southern June would set record temperatures. Today threatened to be one of the worst so far. Even the wooded area behind our house, shaded by old oaks and tall pines, offered little relief from the stifling heat and thick humidity. Gnats swarmed my face, and when I tried to bat them away with my free hand, I smacked myself in the eye with a doggie clean-up bag. Luckily, it was empty.

"I think we'll cut this short," I said to my companion. From her heavy panting, I assumed she agreed a return to air conditioning was a good plan.

We had just emerged from the gravelly path when I saw a car idling two houses down. It was a beige Toyota or Honda and looked familiar. I slid my sunglasses lower on my nose, trying to get a clearer look. The windows were tinted, but the one on the driver's side was open about a fourth of the way. From my angle I couldn't make out any details about the driver. Scarlett strained on the leash, a ridge of her smooth hair forming a dark line down the middle of her back.

"It's okay, girl. Come on. Let's go."

She resisted before giving in and following me onto the sidewalk. I heard the low murmur of the engine as we hurried toward home. Then she stopped. My right ankle turned at an unnatural angle, and I emitted a yelp, not so loud that it attracted the neighbors, but powerful enough that the driver must have heard because the car lurched forward while I struggled to regain my balance.

As it sped past, I caught a quick glimpse of profile. A shiver identical to the one I felt at the makeup counter ran up my back. Whoever it was wore a dark baseball cap and oversized sunglasses. I sensed it was a woman in what I confirmed was a Toyota Corolla.

Scarlett and I paused at the edge of the road, while I watched the vehicle disappear. Beside me, the dog stayed frozen, ears pointed and stiff. The dull throb in my ankle snapped me out of my trance, and I bent down to survey the damage. Since the stabbing pain had subsided, I surmised I had only twisted it.

"Think I'm going to make it," I said to my companion . The hair on her back was no longer raised, but she continued to whine until we reached the door. Once inside, she scrambled to the front window, where she stood guard. I wrapped ice in a dish towel to put around my ankle. The combination of pain and heat made me dizzy. I pressed the cool cloth to my forehead before hobbling to the den. Settled in on the sofa, I turned the channel to Cesar Milan's *Dog Whisperer*, Scarlett's favorite show.

Today's guest, an unruly Jack Russell, wouldn't stop barking at his shadow. We watched as the diminutive trainer transformed the paranoid pup into a proud, confident canine.

Unlike the tiny terrier, my paranoia held strong. Scarlett dozed on her pillow beside me. I lowered the volume and replayed the events of the day. The certainty I could have been close enough to my sister to touch her if she hadn't vanished into the busy crowd. The strange vibe from the vehicle I thought I had seen before.

"Don't be ridiculous." I spoke aloud, causing the dog's right ear to twitch. I switched to my inside-my-head voice.

You didn't even get a good look at whoever was behind the wheel. And Stella wouldn't be caught dead driving an economy car.

I winced at the unintentional cruelty of my words.

"You are losing your edge, Grace Burnette McElroy. Instead of worrying about non-existent threats, you need to get your ass in gear Google-style and find out what's going on in South America."

A twinge in my ankle slowed me on the way to my desk in the sunroom, where I operated my free-lance writing agency. I might not have been physically agile, but my brain crackled with energy.

Sources with information about Ecuador's recent history brought back memories of its volatile nature. The country's original role as a transit route for coca became the perfect spot for money laundering. A corrupt president with a strong-armed penchant for being involved in drug trafficking himself transformed the country into a haven for organized crime, with the Balsuto family leading the pack.

Although the government's innovative policy decriminalizing gang affiliation allowed members to pursue more positive outlets, such as social activism and cultural advancement, I wondered what effect it had among the kingpins.

"What do you think, Scarlett?" I nudged the sleeping dog, who had relocated and settled underneath my desk. She moaned and rolled over. "Come on. You know how I value your opinion. Could it be good news? Like maybe all those nasty people started creating native art or reforming education and aren't interested in killing or maiming each other anymore?"

She sat up and shook her head until her ears rattled.

"You're right. I'm being naive. Adelmo Balsuto isn't the kind of man to tutor disadvantaged children. And he would never give up something as precious as his and Stella's child."

A cramp in my shoulder reminded me how long I'd been sitting at the keyboard. I flexed my ankle, pleased the pain had subsided, and stood to stretch. My stomach rumbled. I glanced at the clock — almost eleven and, other than chips and salsa and limes, I hadn't eaten since lunch.

"Not sure about you, but I'm starving."

Without Emma and Justin to consider, I enjoyed the freedom of cereal for dinner or midnight snack or whatever I wanted it to be. Like the half-sleeve of frozen Girl Scout Thin Mints I devoured while gazing into the darkness, wondering if someone stared back.

I thought of Adelmo's craggy, handsome face and how his deep brown eyes overflowed with sadness when he spoke of losing Stella. And how quickly they became dead and cold at the mention of finding the men who took her from him.

Unsuccessful at determining which Adelmo I might encounter, I had been at the mercy of his whims. But I was a different person from the Grace he knew. The woman looking into the black night in search of danger didn't care whether she faced a loving father or a crazed man grasping for what no longer belonged to him.

I had become one of the deadliest creatures on earth. A mother protecting her child.

CHAPTER 4: GRACE

The chorus of "Copacabana" blasting from my phone startled me out of my reverie but not my resolve.

More than a welcome distraction, Lesroy's ringtone reminded me I wasn't the only one determined to protect Emma. Uncle Lessy, as she renamed him, would give his life to keep her safe.

"Hey there, Gracie. What's up with my favorite cousin?" His exaggerated drawl, with its musical quality, slowed my breathing and made me smile.

Without thinking, I responded, "Not much," then corrected myself. "That's not completely true. I mean, technically, there's not anything. And you know, I can get a little anxious sometimes. So, Emma's with Mom and Mike, and Justin's out of town, and it's just me and Scarlett hanging out, but she's such a lightweight, and I hate to drink alone. Plus, someone was casing the house, or that's what it looked like. So, how about coming over and keeping me company?"

"Whoa, there, cuz. A little anxious is your tagline, but you said *was*? They're gone, right? If not, I'm calling the cops."

"No. Don't do that. It drove away when I got close. Probably somebody stopping to check directions or to answer the phone."

"Okay, no police. Let me get my shoes on. How fast should I drive?"

"Under the speed limit, please. You can't afford another ticket. And it's not an emergency. If you and Vincent have plans, I'll be fine."

Vincent Sanderson was the very hot contractor who had been my cousin's faithful companion for over four years. Not only tall, dark, and awesome, he was funny, kind, and super patient. That last characteristic proved essential in dealing with my cousin. Lesroy wasn't undependable or flighty. He just didn't quite see the world the way the rest of us did.

"Vincent's working on a remodel somewhere in east Atlanta. Turning wood into gold, so he won't be home until late. Heading out the door."

Relief surged over me, and I almost choked on unexpected tears. "There will be margaritas with Amaretto waiting for you."

"That's great, but there's something you're not telling me, isn't there?" Before I had time to deny it, he added, "You saw her, too, didn't you?"

. . . . .

I was admiring my icy concoction when Lesroy rang the bell, then used his key to enter. Scarlett's deep-throated growl shifted to high-pitched yelping at the sight of my slender, but well-muscled, cousin. At first, the dog terrified him, but he forged a bond with her during my journey to Ecuador in search of my sister's killer. He kneeled as Scarlett bounded toward him and placed her forelegs on his shoulders.

"You're a good girl, aren't you," he cooed while fending off an onslaught of wet kisses. "Yes, you are." She slid down, flopped over, and presented her belly to be scratched. When he stood, she rolled to her feet, whining in resignation over the end of their lovefest.

"And you're a good girl, too, aren't you?" He pulled me into his arms, hugged me tight, then rubbed his knuckles against my scalp.

"All right, already." I wriggled free and marveled at how he never aged. Older by over a year, even as a kid he seemed younger. Now, his hair had grown a little shaggy, but that added to his boyish demeanor. Only the sorrow lines between his eyes showed the signs of damage from losing Stella. Like me, he adored her, and her death devastated him.

My sorrow had a different face. I lost my sister and my identity. No longer a sibling, I struggled to redefine myself. Being a wife and mother helped, but I became an emotional amputee. Instead of agony from a missing limb, the loss of my sister sliced into my soul.

I almost convinced myself that my longing for her brought about her appearance at the mall, but there were no warnings from beyond the grave. Until Lesroy posed his impossible question. Despite his fanciful nature, as an adult, he had become more substantial. His casual revelation that he, too, had seen Stella unmoored me.

"Sit while I get your margarita."

"Bring the pitcher. We're going to need it." He sat on the loveseat, Scarlett at his feet.

Once we had drinks in hand, I began. "So, where did you see her?" I still had trouble speaking her name.

"You go first."

It was unusual for him to be reticent, and I worried he was trying to trick me. After Stella's death, he insisted I talk to a therapist. Since he hadn't mentioned it in months, I hoped he had given up. Was this another ploy, pretending to have seen my sister to get me to spill my guts, only to use my craziness against me as proof I needed a shrink?

I decided to trust him, to tell him everything from the tingling sensation to exiting the store and the strange car in front of my house. During my account, he remained silent instead of interrupting me every few seconds to ask a question or make a snarky comment, the way he almost always did whenever I told a lengthy story. When I finished, he stared at the limes floating in the golden-green drink.

I waited for him to speak, but the silence grew too heavy, and I blurted out, "Now it's your turn."

"Slow down. Tell me more about what she was driving. Was it a beige Toyota, one of the smaller ones?"

"Yes, a Corolla. Hold on. How did you know the color?"

"Because I've seen that car parked on your mother's street before. Once about a couple of weeks ago and again when I stopped by last Monday to pick up a butt cake pan to take to Mom."

"For God's sake, Lesroy. It's a bundt cake. Not a butt cake."

"Do you want to talk culinary arts or hear the rest of the story?"

"Sorry. Please, continue."

"Anyway. I didn't think much about it. Figured it was a neighbor or a Jehovah's Witness. But the second time, I got a look at the driver and almost peed my pants." He drained his glass and refilled it from the pitcher.

Coming close to peeing his pants was a mundane response to seeing Stella's ghost. After his reaction to my baking correction, however, I deemed it prudent to keep that to myself. But when he began taking deep, leisurely swallows of alcohol as if I wasn't there, I had to speak up.

"So, you saw her? Stella?"

"Of course, I didn't."

"But you asked me if I'd seen her, too?"

"I didn't mean Stella. Honey, she's dead."

"Are you kidding me? I can't count how often you've come over squawking about seeing the spirit of some long-gone resident floating up the halls in one of Vincent's remodels. Or all the times you insisted that old house on the corner was haunted."

"Jeeze, Grace. Have I taught you nothing? Those cases were different. They were the ghosts of people trapped between worlds because of unfinished business. You made sure Stella's spirit could rest in peace."

"So, what the hell were you talking about?"

"My person was much younger and taller than Stella. And she was wearing a baseball cap, which you are aware our girl would never have been caught dead — Well, you get the point."

"So, she might have been the girl at the mall?"

He nodded.

"Why would some strange woman be hanging around Mom and me? Oh, God, Lesroy. Please don't tell me this could have something to do with Adelmo?"

"Let's not jump to more crazy conclusions. From what you told me, I can't see him sending some blonde chick to do surveillance work for him. Does Justin have any whacko exes?"

"Of course not. And even if he did, we've been married almost three years. Why would she wait this long to come after me?"

"Good point. How about a former client dissatisfied with whatever it is your hot husband does?"

"Now who's ridiculous?"

"Regardless of whether it makes sense, there's one thing that's clear."

"Why don't you help me out with that because absolutely nothing is clear to me."

"Isn't it obvious? You have a stalker."

"Talk about a leap in logic. There has to be a reasonable explanation. Remember the theory about how everyone has a twin somewhere? Somebody that looks so much like you it's hard to tell the difference. And I didn't even get a good look at her. And there are tons of beige Corollas out there and lots of drivers in baseball caps. Thanks to Jose, I'm way better. So, drink up and let's change the subject. You heard Mom's wedding news, right?"

Lesroy clapped his hands. "Mike called last night. Thank God those two are finally legalizing their union. I can't wait to take her shopping for dresses."

"Shouldn't I be the one to do that? I am her daughter, after all."

"Only if it's going to be an Amish ceremony. But you can come along if you promise to smile and nod."

I shrugged. Nobody had ever complimented me on my fashion sense, plus the tequila had mellowed me out too much to protest.

A twinge of nausea struck at the same time I refilled my glass, so I stopped at one and a half. Lesroy poured himself another and another.

When the margaritas ran out, so did my cousin. Rather than risk driving home in his altered state, he summoned a rideshare.

"Vincent will be so proud of how responsible I'm becoming," he slurred. "And it won't hurt to have another car in the driveway, in case your stalker gets freaky."

"Who's jumping to conclusions now?" I punched him on the shoulder, then kissed his cheek. But I bolt-locked the door before he stepped off the porch.

CHAPTER 5: GRACE

I hadn't argued with him, but the idea Adelmo had something to do with the appearance of Stella's doppelgänger stuck with me.

Like the country of Ecuador, my sister's lover was a study in contradiction. Gentle and kind in a seaside garden fluttering with butterflies and hummingbirds, he charmed me into believing we shared the desire to bring her killers to justice. I hadn't understood what he really wanted—not until I saw Ben Wilcott's bloody, broken body in Adelmo's trailer.

Ben, my brother-in-law and ex-fiancé, ran off with Stella weeks before our wedding. I never stopped loving my sister, but I refused to forgive her. And even when I knew about the escalating danger of her situation, I did nothing to help her leave the man responsible for her death.

His involvement with drugs and Ecuador's loose extradition policy attracted him to the beachside town of Montañita. Once a hippie-surfer spot, it offered consistent waves for surfers and plenty of smoking opportunities for hippies. It became home to an eclectic group of expatriates from all over the world.

Although it seemed to be the perfect place to relocate, neither he nor my sister flourished there.

What if Lesroy was mistaken about Stella's spirit resting in peace? Did that mean her appearance had little to do with sisterly love and more to do with vengeance? Maybe she wanted to give me the chance to look at her beautiful ghostly face and utter words of forgiveness. No matter how desperately I needed to believe in a world with Stella in it, I couldn't. I did, however, recognize the reality of one where Emma's father showed up to demand the return of his daughter.

Adelmo kept their relationship and baby a secret because of his family's criminal activities. Their role as exporters of cocaine brought with it enemies—the kind who had no qualms about taking down innocent bystanders along with their rivals. Kidnapping and torture of wives and children were rare but not unheard of. He feared acknowledging my sister and her child would put them in danger. So far as I knew, he remained in hiding. But there was always the risk he might come for Emma. Unless, instead of being on the run, he was dead.

· · · · ·

I awoke to the sound of my own guttural cries and struggled to free myself from sweaty, tangled sheets. Scarlett nudged my arm with her nose and gave me a look of canine concern.

"I'm okay, girl. Just a bad dream."

My dog sensed my lack of candor and used her back legs to propel herself onto the bed. When I switched position to avoid being kissed on the lips, she molded her body to mine and draped her leg over my hip.

"You're right. It was awful."

It had been weeks since Stella starred in one of my distorted dreams. Last night, she returned. Unlike the top ten of my pop nightmares, this was a chartbuster. It made the others seem like Mediterranean cruises, without drunk teenagers and competitive buffet line participants. Far worse than the scenario where she and I sat together watching Emma play in our childhood backyard when a cloud caught us in mid-laughter and blotted out the sun. When the light returned, they were gone. And not another familiar favorite, where I stumbled over Stella's body as I searched for shells on the beach.

In this new medley of terror, my sister lay between the sand and the water. Instead of milky unseeing eyes, hers were closed in a parody of slumber. When I kneeled beside her, those blue-veined eyelids flickered. I cried out to the gathering crowd, "She isn't dead. Stella is alive." Then I turned to her and discovered the movement I had taken as a sign of life was only the shadow of a seagull flitting across her frozen features.

The content of last night's horror show might have been more disturbing, but the message was the same. The future I had imagined—watching my children playing with their cousins while their mother and I laughed for no reason—died alongside my sister.

I leaned against Scarlett for a second before pushing myself into a sitting position. My need for Justin matched the throbbing in my head. After the restraint I showed the previous evening, the intensity of my headache and the wave of nausea that sent me racing to the bathroom shocked me. After what seemed like an eternity of violent retching, I stood and turned on the tap, letting the stream run into my open mouth. I gulped until I gurgled.

I popped a few antacids and stumbled to the kitchen.

"I'm not up for a walk just yet, but when you come inside, your kibble will await you."

She gave me a reproachful glance before sauntering through the door to our fenced-in yard. I filled her bowl and vowed to make it up to her later.

Back in bed, I covered my eyes and waited to see if my sickness would return. I thought about Justin and the volatile nature of our early days.

Hired as a hitman by my mother to take care of the men who killed my sister, he was Mike's Marine buddy. My soon-to-be stepfather realized the enormity of Mom's loss had driven her lust for blood. Afraid she might find a real killer or an FBI agent posing as one, he asked Justin to fake being in the murder business.

Our first encounters had been fiery, fueled by the combination of my blinding grief and our mutual passion. We were still hot and steamy, but we now had the luxury of time and the bond of love.

He understood that grieving was a lifelong journey and had generously agreed to walk it alongside me. We created a peaceful rhythm together—a balance of his security company and my freelance writing—cemented by our devotion to our daughter.

For the last few months, I had begun to question my career choice. The work was fun, and most of my clients were great. But I wondered how long I could continue selling bras and cars and quality quilts. When all the catchy jingles and colorful brochures would send me over the edge.

I wanted to do more—create something that might help people for whom fancy underwear or a shiny new vehicle or expensive bedding didn't cut it. I considered writing about my sister because it would be an opportunity to do more for those who were in a similar situation, minus the murder and exotic location. People whose loss had outpaced forgiveness. And there was the possibility telling what happened to her would bring me peace.

But where would I start? Should I begin with her as a child, mercurial and fairy-like? I could write about the way her laughter filled the house. How would I describe that electric smile of hers, so wide it threatened to split the atmosphere? Or her evolution into a shooting star with the power to dazzle or destroy? And there were no words to explain the light that shone so brilliantly it blinded everyone, including me, to her true value.

I worried it might not be fair to expose her memory to strangers. To reveal how she used her loveliness to betray me. I concluded that the real story of my sister was one of transcendence, a picture of the woman who emerged from all her faults into something even more beautiful. But her incredible transformation came too late to save her. Instead, it put her at the mercy of selfish, greedy men too small spirited to qualify as evil. And it left behind a daughter who would never meet the spectacular person her mother became.

While debating my ability to tell her story, it struck me it might not be Stella's truth I didn't want to expose. No matter how careful an author is, it's impossible to avoid becoming part of the narrative. Secrets and weaknesses slip out. Was I protecting my sister or myself?

Now I feared that reluctance played a role in causing me to see a girl who wasn't Stella, possibly a girl who didn't exist at all. The Toyota had been real, but that didn't mean its appearance had anything to do with me. And my cousin's insistence he had seen the same car twice at my mother's? Well, that could be Lesroy being Lesroy.

Despite my attempts to stifle it, another thought came to mind, a possibility I wouldn't let myself believe. In this scenario, Stella's ghost didn't live in the mall or behind the wheel. Her angry spirit resided in me. But whether her fury resulted from my refusal to write about her or my fear of revealing too much about myself remained to be seen.

CHAPTER 6: GRACE

I awoke to a chorus of Garth Brooks singing "Friends in Low Places," my mother's ringtone.

"Hey, Mom," I said as perky as I could muster, hoping she wouldn't suspect I was sleeping during the daytime and assume I had thyroid cancer.

"I'm not your mommy. You're *my* mommy." My daughter giggled at the absurdity of my mistake, making me laugh along with her.

"And there's nothing else I'd rather be. What's up, buttercup?"

More snickering, followed by a recap of her time with her grandparents. She had fallen asleep to the Disney channel, colored in bed with Grandma, made pancakes with Mikey, and was going to go swimming in the giant blow-up pool in the backyard.

"That sounds like so much fun."

"Yes," she said and left me hanging, toddler-style, with no goodbye.

Mom took over. "She's been so good, and I know you hate being away from her, but we want to take her to a movie and the church dinner. Could we please keep her another night?"

After Stella's death, my mother immersed herself in religion. Lesroy and I suspected it had more to do with showing off

Emma Grace and Mike but were glad it kept her off the streets. More important, it kept her off the phone.

An unexpected wave of relief washed over me at the prospect of being able to stay in bed. I considered the possibility I might be coming down with a stomach flu.

"Gee, Mom," I spoke with fake reluctance. "I already miss her, and Justin will be disappointed."

"Well, I suppose we could plan it for another time."

"That's okay." Dammit. I'd been too convincing. "He'll understand."

Too happy to question my sudden change in tone, she offered to drop Emma at daycare on her way to poker with Aunt Rita the next morning.

I forced myself to get dressed and take Scarlett for her walk. Lesroy must have come over earlier to pick up his car, and there was no Corolla at the curb. No one at all was out in the heat.

"Let's go home and sit under the sprinkler. Doesn't that sound good?" Noncommittal, my walking companion squatted, then tugged at her leash, and led me back to air conditioning.

The shift from sizzling hot to frozen tundra made me woozy enough that I had to lean against the table in the foyer. The dizziness passed, but I was still lightheaded.

"I'm starving. And how about a treat for you?"

Scarlett's ears twitched as she pranced toward the kitchen.

I took out a chew bone from the jar and tossed it to her before rummaging through the cabinets for something that wouldn't bring on another round of vomiting. I settled on cheese and crackers with ginger ale and was chewing cheddar and checking emails on my phone when the smooth harmony of NSYNC's "Thinking of You" announced a call from Justin.

"How are my favorite girls?" he asked.

"Missing you like crazy. Where are you? Please don't say Dallas or Fort Worth or wherever you ended up."

"I'm exactly where I wanted to end up. At the airport parking garage on my way home to you."

·　　·　　·　　·　　·

"Let's keep this from Emma, but I could use a little alone time with my sexy-as-hell wife."

Chilled by the gust of air from the vent, I pulled the sheet up and snuggled closer to him, worries of a growing rift almost forgotten.

"It'll be our secret." I nibbled his earlobe. He groaned, and I trailed kisses along his neck.

"You'll be the death of me, woman. But I can't think of a better way to go."

Much later, we ordered Thai and ate it on the sofa, where Justin explained the intricacies of cyber security.

"Enough of that boring stuff. What did you do, other than moon over me while I was gone?"

"Somebody's pretty full of himself." I punched his arm. "How do you know I wasn't having hot sex with the pool boy?"

"For one thing, we don't have a pool. And the way you attacked me? Not the actions of a sexually satiated female. So, what did you do?"

Reluctant to share what happened at the mall, I told him about Mom and Mike's upcoming nuptials and Emma's expertise with bubbles. He found both equally delightful.

"And Lesroy came over. Vincent was working late, so we consoled each other with my famous margaritas."

"Your cousin has a sixth sense when it comes to free alcohol."

"True, but this time I invited him."

I shared my experience with the car and Lesroy's assertion he had seen it twice before at Mom's. And I included my cousin's theory that I had a stalker. I didn't mention the girl at the mall, who might not have been there at all.

When I finished, he gathered our plates and carried them to the kitchen. I don't know what reaction I expected at my news, but it wasn't a burst of domesticity.

"Justin, are you washing dishes?"

After a minute or two, he came back and sat close to me.

"So, do you think you have a stalker?"

"I didn't at first. Now, I'm not so sure."

"Did Lesroy have any opinions on who it might be?"

"Not really. I mean, we couldn't come up with anyone."

"Sounds like he's overreacting. But no harm in being cautious. I can work from home, and I'll get one of my guys to drive by when I can't. You keep the pepper spray on hand, right?"

Despite having removed it from my purse after Emma mistook it for perfume, I nodded.

"Good. I'm sure there's nothing to worry about."

Only there was. Because the sense that he was keeping something important from me had returned, compounded by the growing guilt of my own secret.

·   ·   ·   ·   ·

Other than coming up with a sidewalk sale promotion featuring a petting zoo for a client who owned a small children's bookstore and had an even smaller advertising budget, my day had been unproductive. The fleeting expression on Justin's face when he said I had nothing to worry about continued to bother me. Had my look been similar when I hadn't told him everything?

I picked up Emma early to take her for ice cream. When I reached her pre-school, a group of screeching children were racing around the playground. Kids leaped from bright red swings, ran across rope bridges, and climbed inside a three-story tree house. I spotted my daughter in the sandbox with her best friend Wyatt. Interrupting her during recess was a very bad idea, so I sat in the car and watched as the two of them constructed castles.

Images of the elaborate structures Lesroy and I built before Stella was born came to me. Our palaces were made of sturdier stuff—Gran's quilts piled on broken furniture salvaged from the neighbors' discards, stones from a nearby creek. We spent hours planning ways to reward our loyal subjects and defeat our enemies. After my sister arrived, we settled for tamer activities to be close to her. By the time she was sturdy enough to join us in our kingdom, we had lost interest in make believe.

A series of chimes signaled the end of play period, but Emma and Wyatt had become tone deaf. Both had closure issues and hated to leave a task unfinished. When a young woman appeared and began rounding up her charges, Wyatt got up and dusted sand off his pants with the meticulous mannerism of an elderly gentleman. My daughter leaped to her feet and shook herself like a wet dog, the same way Lesroy had done when we were children at the ocean side.

I walked to the gate to tell the teacher I was there, and we chatted while the kids lined up behind her. Determined not to embarrass my child with an inappropriate display of parental enthusiasm, I waved in her direction.

She squinted before running to me. Once again, she filled me with joy at knowing I was the reason for the goofy grin on her face as she wrapped herself around my knees.

I bent to pick her up and caught a flurry of movement at the fence. Half hidden by the flowering lilac bushes, a woman in a pink baseball cap stood, squinting into the light. She stepped back and whipped her head to the right, then bolted toward the surrounding woods. I scooped Emma into my arms and held her close as clouds covered the sun.

CHAPTER 7: NATALIE

I'm one of those people who reminds everybody of someone else. A little over five eight with straight dark-blonde hair and greenish-blue eyes, attractive enough but nothing special. Strangers approach me to ask where we met before and are disbelieving or disappointed when I explain we haven't.

If questioned about what I do for a living, I say surveillance and flash a mysterious look, an expression I've practiced in the mirror hundreds of times. I tell them my work is classified, which is more of a misdirection than a downright lie. My actual job is with a temp agency because Natalie Burden is a temporary kind of girl.

I am in the espionage business, though, in a highly specialized capacity. But I never divulge my area of expertise. Because if I did, I would have to admit to them and myself that an agent with only one person of interest is less spy and more stalker.

·　　·　　·　　·　　·

By the ninth grade, I learned that if anything nasty happened — and it probably would — nothing I did or didn't do would stop it.

This often resulted in what my therapist would have referred to as "high-risk behavior designed to establish my independence." But I just liked doing crazy shit: driving fast, ditching school, bad boys.

By my senior year, I became an expert on taking those kinds of risks, which was how I discovered my mother had been keeping secrets from me.

The first night of spring break, a little over a month from my graduation day, I told her some girlfriends and I planned to go shopping at the only decent-sized mall in Chattanooga.

Instead, I spent hours smoking pot and drinking beer with my boyfriend Dylan and his so-called Death Metal band, Tony and the Tumors—there was no Tony nor any tumors, as far as I knew.

We were in Dylan's garage listening to a new song he'd written, "Spit in My Eye," a diatribe against the media corrupting our senses and how we sit there and take it. To be honest, I couldn't take it—or anything else they played—unless I was stoned, and then I couldn't remember what the hell any of it meant. A real conundrum, so I took the easy way out and fell asleep on the ratty sofa. Passed out is more accurate.

When I came to, my boyfriend snored and snorted into my neck. I rolled away from him and dug my cell out of my back pocket: 1:15. Shit! Almost two hours past curfew.

"Dylan." I grabbed his shoulder and shook it.

In middle school I used to sneak into my mother's closet drawer where she kept a bunch of smutty, torn-bodice novels. I zipped through those suckers, hoping to get a head start on understanding what the big deal was about sex. Other than discovering about a million different ways to refer to a man's genitals, I didn't learn much. But I noticed the writers spent a lot of time describing how turned on they got watching their sleeping lovers.

None of them had ever woken up next to a snoozing Dylan, mouth open with a shiny line of drool winding its way down his chin. I felt no fluttering in the pit of my stomach or the least bit of burning hot desire racing to my girl parts.

"Wake up!" I yelled into his ear, wondering when his mother had stopped asking if he washed behind it. He groaned and inched away from me, but I punched his arm hard, and he regained consciousness. "We've got to move. Now." I stood and nudged his butt with my booted foot.

"Okay, okay," he muttered and stumbled to his feet. We picked our way over the bodies of his bandmates and climbed into the beat-up Dodge van his parents had given him. It was almost 2:00 when I made him stop about a block from my house.

"Do you have to go in right away?" he asked, while trying to unzip my jacket.

"What part of two hours past my curfew do you not get?" He hung his head and sighed. I removed his hand from my zipper and kissed him on the cheek. "I'll text you tomorrow." He reached for me again, but I opened the door and hopped out.

If I was lucky, my mother had fallen asleep, and I could slip through the basement window undiscovered. Then I saw the light in her room and knew I was screwed.

Fingers crossed, I hoped she'd drifted off while reading. I eased through the opening, snuck up the stairs, and tiptoed past her room. My doorknob squeaked, and I froze at the sound of her voice. Crap! But she wasn't talking to me.

"Oh, no, Char, that's awful. I'm so sorry."

I wanted to ask *sorry for what*? But then I would be busted for nothing because Mom would most likely terminate the call and refuse to discuss it.

And if I asked Char or Charlotte, my mother's sibling, she would act as if she didn't understand what I meant, part of the sister pact the two of them shared since they were kids.

When I was little, my aunt came over once or twice a week, occasionally with Uncle Dwight, who would ask me something lame like how's school or did I have a boyfriend, then fade into the wallpaper. Char had personality enough for them both. Her bubbling laughter flowed throughout the house, carrying us all with it.

In the past few years, her visits dwindled. I guessed it was about some disagreement over the way Dad treated her. From time to time, I overheard short phone calls between the sisters but gave up on finding out why we didn't see her more often.

If they were talking this late, something horrible must have happened.

"I never asked, but I always thought he left because of them."

I figured he was my dad, who bailed the year I turned twelve. It had been around dinner time, and I was on the living room floor, crouched over a map of Africa when shouting disturbed me. I put on my headphones and kept looking for Zimbabwe.

My father burst out of the bedroom, coat in hand. He paused long enough to pat me on the back on his way out the door. In the story I told my therapist, he bent down to tell me he loved me. In reality, I had the music cranked up so loud I don't know if he spoke to me at all.

Identifying Dad as the partial subject of the conversation offered no clue who Mom referred to as the reason for his disappearance.

Either she hung up or she was whispering too low for me to hear. I planned to wash off my smudged make-up and brush the stale taste of weed and White Claw from my teeth but made the mistake of flopping onto my bed and fell asleep in my clothes. During the night, I got up to change into a Janis Joplin t-shirt and a pair of sweatpants.

I woke with a pounding head and an enormous sense of righteous indignation. I had always believed Dad's departure related directly to me. If there was friction between them, they hid it well, so well it was like that corny line from an old movie about completing each other. Together, the two of them had no need for me.

All those times I heard her crying at night after he walked out on us made me want to scream at her to shut up and forget about him, so I could do the same. But she wasn't the one I was angry with. I was furious with myself for driving my father away. Like most adolescents, I couldn't imagine a world where everything and everyone weren't revolving around me. So, I overlooked what should have been the obvious conclusion that their problems might have nothing to do with me. My egocentric attitude caused me unnecessary pain. Now it hampered my ability to narrow down on whatever my mother was hiding.

Thoughts of that miserable night made me mad all over again, this time at the way she sidestepped my questions and insisted Dad would be back, that he just needed some space. Her misguided attempts to protect me strengthened my belief I was the one he wanted distance from.

But now would be different. I was no longer a kid trying to navigate the Dark Continent. I didn't need her to save me from the truth. And if she hesitated, well, I would hit her with hard evidence.

I never felt as confident as when I took the stairs two at a time that morning on my way to confront her. And I have never experienced the same level of confidence since.

CHAPTER 8: NATALIE

Uncle Dwight was passing out peanut butter crackers and Cokes when Aunt Char jumped from her seat.

"That's him. The surgeon who operated on your mother." She grabbed me by the arm and dragged me across the waiting room.

"Doctor Magnus," she called out to the lanky stranger who had been playing God with Mom's brain for the past six hours.

My uncle said his wife had a voice that could bring the cows home without a bell. The doctor, however, seemed not to hear her. He picked up his pace and sped by the nurses' station. Too bad for him, my aunt hadn't missed a Peachtree Road Race in over twenty years. She released me and sprinted by him to the exit door, where she spread her arms to block his escape.

"Hold on a second there. You just finished operating on my sister Olivia Burden." She pointed to me. "Her daughter and I need a few minutes of your time."

His jaw tightened, but he turned to me, his face unreadable.

"It's really too early to tell. Your mother had a hemorrhagic stroke. Because of the severity of the bleed and the lack of clarity about how long it took to get her to the hospital, she will likely have difficulty with speech and daily activities. We will have to conduct more tests before recommending the next course of action."

My aunt peppered the doctor with a series of questions. What problems might she have with speaking? Which tests and when?

It was clear her persistence annoyed him. I lost focus when he mentioned the delay in getting Mom to the emergency room.

"Is there anything you do know? Like how to find your ass with a flashlight."

Dwight slipped up behind her and wrapped an arm around her waist. Dr. Magnus stepped back.

"It seems as if the doctor has told us all he can. Why don't we get something to eat and balance out your blood sugar? Then we can swing by later and maybe get in to see Olivia."

"To hell with my blood sugar. I need a goddamn drink."

· · · · ·

No one blamed me for Mom's stroke. But I knew the truth. Staying out late with a boyfriend whose greatest attribute was his ability to set my mother's hair on fire, skipping school, barely passing my classes — all were designed to punish her for sins she hadn't committed.

It wasn't as if I left a banana peel on the tile and waited for her to take a fall. My crime was worse. My war of attrition drained her of physical and emotional reserves and left her vulnerable to the shock of Charlotte's call.

As penance for my past behavior, I put my questions aside. While guilt might have overridden my desire to discover the contents of their conversation, I didn't forget about it. Not when I sat by her bedside talking incessantly about what celebrity was getting a divorce and what couple from *The Bachelor* would be headed down that road before the next season. And not when I washed her face with a warm cloth or plumped her pillows or brushed her hair.

Questions lurked in the jumbled shadows of my mind like jungle cats ready to pounce. But my blazing misery drove them away.

I also kept Dylan at bay until I dropped him in it. It wasn't his fault. He tried but he was too scrawny to lean on, and he was even less coherent straight than stoned. Perfect for making my mother fear he would steal her daughter's virginity—to be fair, it was a gift—besides being a musical deviant, my boyfriend served his purpose well. With no one to torment, I no longer needed him.

My teachers expressed their confidence I would maintain my C average with or without completing the last three weeks of the year and urged me to walk at graduation. I chose to receive my diploma in the mail and taped it to the wall in Mom's hospital room.

After two months in the rehab unit, other than relearning how to feed herself and go to the bathroom on her own, she made little progress. Although I was certain she recognized me, she never said my name or much of anything else we could understand. Her doctors discussed releasing her, and Char insisted she would stay with us until we were back on our feet.

My aunt was true to her word. She drove an hour each morning to sit by her sister's side while I worked at the temp agency. Each evening, she made the same drive home. I slept on an air mattress by Mother's bed.

One spring day six months after the stroke, I woke to an unfamiliar, familiar sound.

"Charlotte, why are you on the floor?"

Sleeping Beauty had returned from the land of the dead, a mixed mythaphor, but who cared? I scrambled to my feet.

"It's me, Natalie." I threw my arms around her and burst into tears.

"Natty, baby. What's wrong?" Since I turned twelve, I hated when she called me by my childhood nickname. Today, I didn't care what she called me. She stroked my hair until I was cried out.

"You've been sick, Mom. But you're getting better."

Her empty stare made me question my optimism, but I was determined not to give up.

"Remember, you fell in the kitchen?" I hesitated to say the word stroke because I didn't want to remind her I was the one who caused her head to explode.

"It's a little frenzy for me. Could I have some, uh, what do you call it? Something to make my throat not dry?"

"Water? You want water?" I began pouring from the pitcher on her bedside table. She dribbled when she drank, but I was too excited to care. Mom was back. She might not know the difference between frenzy and fuzzy or the word for water, but her hollow look had vanished.

"Say again how I got here. All I can remember is a little boy humming out the window."

I suspected I looked like a dimwit as I tried to bring up the memory. Like Daddy's old hound, who in her golden years forgot how to fetch, I couldn't find the stick. Then it came to me, an off-key lilting murmur. "You mean Billy Baxter?"

The youngest of five boys in the family, he lived next door when I was nine until we left the neighborhood and moved into the home my mother still occupied.

"Right, the only one of the brood with those bright red curls. Your grandmother said it was the exact shade of the mailman's. That woman." She ran her fingers through her tangled hair, stopping at the spot where the nurse shaved her head.

I drew a blank on the carrot-topped mailman but recalled the humming boy. Before I decided whether to remind Mom it had been years since he serenaded us, she covered her face with her hands. A gurgling sound escaped, and her shoulders shook.

I sat on the bed beside her and rubbed her shoulders. This outburst of emotion frightened me. "Don't cry, Mom. Everything's going to be okay."

She raised her head, and tears spilled down her cheeks.

"I'm not crying," she said after catching her breath. "That boy's bathroom performance still cracks me up."

"His what?"

"You remember. He'd sit on the toilet forever, humming away."

Then it came to me. The only thing separating the Baxter house from ours was a narrow grass pathway. If we both had our bathroom windows open, we heard the flush.

"Oh, my God. You're right. Poor kid." I laughed with her at the memory of the two of us taking bets on when Billy would finish his business and head back out to play.

When my aunt arrived, she found us humming tunelessly in tribute to the boy with the world's slowest moving bowels.

"What the hell?" She dropped into the chair by the bed, her eyes welling with empathy tears.

"What's got you crying? Did somebody die, and you forgot to tell me?"

Char wiped her eyes, looked at me, and started laughing. Pretty soon, I was giggling along with her, while Mom stared in confusion.

"For goodness sakes. People would think you two were the ones who had a stroke."

CHAPTER 9: NATALIE

Mom's stroke took a chunk of her memories and made it difficult for her to create new ones. After that morning, though, she improved in tiny increments, so small we hardly noticed. Yet they astonished her doctors. While she might never read again or do the Sunday crossword, she recognized friends from the accounting firm where she worked before her collapse. She still forgot Uncle Dwight's name, but lots of people did.

Her insistence I apply to college reassured me of her return to her parental role. When Aunt Char took up the cause, things seemed almost normal. The two of them harangued me until I registered at a state school close to home. Neither approved of my choice, but they accepted it as better than nothing.

My straight-A's first semester thrilled them. Instead of explaining the material was basically a repeat of my senior year, I encouraged their celebration. It made me happy, too, because not worrying about my academic career let them focus on Mom's recovery. Trips back and forth to therapy kept them occupied and freed me to revisit my quest for information about who and what propelled my mother into her deadly tailspin.

I recalled my determination to confront her, to see her expression when I demanded she tell me what upset her the night before. Surprised at how little it mattered now, I vowed to find the answers on my own. As with so much of my life, I realized my path to discovery crossed with the crooked road my father had taken.

The temp agency had access to records not available to the public, so I began a search for Jack Burden in Chattanooga and discovered plenty of Johns and Jacksons but only a few plain Jacks. None of them matched Dad, so I included North Georgia and the Atlanta area.

No luck. Frustrated, I checked again, scrolling down the long list. My eyes blurred, and I dropped too far down, landing on Inez Burnette. Below her name, I saw it. Jack Burnette. Not my father, but I clicked anyway.

Within minutes, I had his driver's photo, place of birth, military status, and marriage license, followed by a divorce decree. Jack Burnette was indeed my dad, but it wasn't my mother, Olivia Morgan, he'd been married to and divorced from. This wife who ended up an ex was Marilyn Hawthorne Burnette.

Finding info on Marilyn was easier. I went straight to the record of her divorce from my father and found what I hadn't known I was looking for. Grace and Stella Burnette, the two children in her custody — my sisters.

Did that make me Natalie Burnette, and had dear old Dad literally saddled me with the burden of being one of his daughters? The man loved a good joke, and I appreciated his sense of humor, but he crossed the line between funny and downright mean.

And if he married my mother under a fake name, what did that say about their union? Being illegitimate might make me more interesting, but it left me with more questions than when I started.

Before I could explore my newfound identity and get out of the English equivalent of a telenovela, the manager emailed another assignment, and I put my quest on hold.

At home, a pot roast, courtesy of my aunt, warmed in the oven. Her note reminding me of the visit to the physical therapist in the morning lay on the counter. Mom and I ate at the table—my mother, chewing with deliberation; me, picking at strands of glistening meat.

We sat beside each other watching reruns of *Friends* until she dozed off. After I helped her to bed, I dragged myself to my room.

The full moon cast shafts of light across my black comforter—a small rebellion against the woman who wanted me to snuggle under roses and lilacs. I lay there, thinking what a shitty daughter I was, of all the ways I had devised to make her miserable.

My favorite included going all day without talking to her. When I got bored with giving her the silent treatment, I set emotional booby traps for her. I asked her opinion about an outfit or a boy. Then rolled my eyes when she offered the incorrect response and stalked out of the room in disgust. Of course, there was no correct answer. It was a question like "What number am I thinking of? Wrong!"

One incident especially stood out for me. I sat at the kitchen table pretending to work on algebra while I texted Dylan. When Mom came in, I shoved my phone under the math book and frowned in fake concentration, hoping she wouldn't start asking a bunch of dumb questions.

She stopped beside me, a blank look on her face, and said, "Darn it. What in the world was I looking for?"

"How would I know what—"

Before I could lecture her on not interrupting me when I was studying, she was gone. It wasn't her first example of forgetfulness, nor was it worrisome. I knew adults often lost their way.

But Dylan and I spent much of our time together competing over whose parents were more irritating. Since I only had one, I doubled down and turned the smallest parental infractions into humiliating stories. I texted, *It's official. My mother is totally certifiable.*

Shame at my arrogance overcame me. I felt disgust at the way I smirked at what I determined were signs of old age. Never would I wander through the house mumbling in confusion over an unknown purpose. But now and then, it was as if I were one of those forgotten objects.

I understand how foolish it was to imagine I'd been abandoned by people who were clueless about my existence. If I hadn't known I belonged to a sisterhood, wouldn't they be in the dark, too? Unless their mother told them about me and they chose to leave me out of their lives, turning me into that elusive object no one remembers to find. Or worse, they never even thought to come for me at all.

CHAPTER 10: NATALIE

I woke to the smell of something burning and bolted toward Mom's door. Determined to be as independent as possible, she insisted on dressing herself and making her bed. So, it was no surprise to find her room empty, but it still scared the crap out of me.

My heart stopped pounding at the realization the house hadn't been engulfed in flames but resumed when I noticed the trail of smoke coming from the kitchen. Visions of my mother wandering away from a hot stove or lying on the floor while grease popped and sizzled over her lifeless body sent me bounding down the stairs. Relief slowed my heartbeat when I found her upright, dodging scalding spittle.

"Damn it! I should wear one of those hazy mat suits when I cook sausage."

Once I would have ridiculed her jumbled word salad. Today, it made me almost giddy.

"Here, Mom. Let me finish for you, please." I expected a protest, but she smiled and stepped out of my way. I eased the fork out of her hand, slid the pan from the burner, and speared slices onto a plate.

"The least I can do is make some toast." She handled the task with no hiccups, and we ate bacon and lettuce sandwiches for breakfast—neither of us had thought to buy tomatoes.

When Aunt Char arrived, I told them I had a research project for my sociology class and would spend the day at the library.

"Your Uncle Dwight and I want to take your mother out for dinner. You're invited, but it won't hurt our feelings if you'd rather hang out with your friends. You know, get a little crazy."

I doubted our ideas of how I might reach a state of craziness were in any way similar and had lost touch with friends over the past two years. But an evening on my own sounded incredible.

"Well, I'll try not to get too out of control, but if you really don't mind —"

"Of course we don't," Mom chimed in.

I kissed them goodbye and scooted out the door.

·　　·　　·　　·　　·

If I tried to map my life before the stroke, it would turn into a geographical maze. Not the fun corn kind either. More the scary type from a horror movie, set in a remote spot, where creepy kids chased after you with axes.

Like most tales of terror, mine started out normal enough with sunny beach photos of four-year-old me, tugging at the crotch of my one-piece bathing suit. Shots of my parents and me posing in front of aquariums and amusement parks. But the narrative took a downward turn with fewer and fewer happy images.

Although we seldom went to the mountains, my memories contained sharp-faced inclines and dark, smoky clouds. They loomed over me as I cowered in a canyon waiting for the other parental shoe to drop. My time with Dylan was a murky marsh, and now with my mother it seemed an endless desert.

It made no sense at all, but I believed uncovering the mystery of my sisters had the power to turn that barren ground into a blossoming plateau. With so much riding on the right keystrokes, everything, including the location, had to be perfect.

When Mom was in the hospital, I spent most of my time sitting beside her. When I needed a break, I wandered through downtown Chattanooga. Like many Southern cities, my town redefined and recreated herself in both the past and present. In school, I had learned all about the shameful pride of being on the losing side of a fight to keep rich white people rich and white. My sixth-grade social studies teacher teared up when she told the story of the fall of the city and how it marked the beginning of the end for the Confederacy.

Chattanooga might have lost the war, but her wealthy, fair-haired elite came out winners, as did their kids and grandkids. The proof of their victory lined the streets I strolled along on lonely afternoons and evenings. Laughing couples spilled out of successful local breweries and restaurants, making my aloneness sharper. On cold, rainy days, I ducked into shops and bookstores, wishing for the strength to be passionate about all that creative stuff. I took comfort ducking into the aquarium, where I stood underneath watery passages and faced down dead-eyed sharks with stares of my own.

On one of my lonely walks, I came across an oasis in the middle of my dry, dusty life. Wildflowers Tea and Wellness Shop. Despite my aversion to Eastern philosophies with their inward eyeballs and relentless meditation, the Zen atmosphere didn't annoy me. Exposed brick walls with row after row of herb-filled jars promising everything from amped-up energy to mellow mindfulness intrigued me.

I couldn't decide which end of the medicinal spectrum I should pour from to make my research more fruitful, so I ordered a chocolate Chai latte, then set up in a corner as far from the windows as possible.

I checked Facebook first. Grace's last post was from over three years ago, and none of the earlier ones included photos.

No selfies or drunken nights out with girlfriends or kissy faces to boyfriends.

Next, I searched for the third sibling and found Stella Burnette Wilcott. Instead of an active site with pictures of what she had for dinner or random sunsets, I landed on a memorial page. My newly discovered sister had been dead for over three years.

I turned away from the screen, sipped my uninspiring drink, and hoped I had somehow made a mistake, that I had the wrong Stella Burnette. As I scrolled on, I became certain she was the right one.

I saw my half-sister jumping waves in bikinis and dancing in grown-up prom dresses. She rode on speedboats, her blonde hair flying. She fluttered between worlds on surfboard and danced in the sand. Always in motion and never facing the camera, none of these photos offered a clue to what permanently stilled Stella.

Nor did her obituary provide information about her passing. From date of birth and death, I computed she died at twenty-seven, only five years older than me. The article listed Grace, her mother, an aunt, and a cousin named Lesroy as survivors. They failed to mention our escapee-dad.

The omission tightened my chest and clouded my eyes. Living without my father had given me an emotional limp, barely perceptible but an impediment to healthy relationships. This sister loss was more agonizing — like the phantom pain amputees have. Only in my case, the missing limb had never been there, but the torment was real.

I moved through the heartbreaking confirmation of Stella's death and beach and boating scenes where she seemed to have spent the last days of her life, then came to family photos taken in a cooler climate. The first group was from decades past. A toddler zipped from chin to toe in a snowsuit stared at a boy sticking a carrot nose on a lopsided snowman. In another, two little girls sat on the lap of the Easter Bunny, the smaller one clinging to her sister as both leaned away from the leering grin that exposed the rabbit's enormous teeth. The size of the laps decreased as my sisters got bigger—Santas, giant pumpkins, princesses—but the pose remained the same. Stella leaning into the protection of Grace's arms.

When I pushed my chair back to stretch, the shop was empty except for me and the wellness guru behind the counter. A chill came over the room, either from my tepid tea or from being kept from the warmth of family. I wanted to run from the images teasing me with the hopeless prospect of belonging but couldn't make myself close the screen.

Then I saw it, the first shot of Stella directly facing the camera. I zoomed in and gasped. Her blue-green eyes shone from a heart-shaped face. Other than her long blonde hair, sun-streaked and lighter than mine, I could have been staring at myself. Not in a magic mirror proclaiming I was the fairest in the land, more a funhouse version. Because despite the similarity of our pieces, the finished puzzles weren't the same. She was gorgeous and ethereal; I was pretty enough but very much of this world.

Both of us had dipped into Dad's genetic pool, inheriting his ivory complexion and fine bone structure. Her cheekbones were more prominent, emphasizing the hollows below them and giving her that hungry look women envied, and men were drawn to—without realizing why. At first, I thought we shared the same smile, but Stella's was different—full-lipped and knowing, yet innocent. Hers was almost too perfect, as if she practiced it in her own mirror.

I wondered if I would come to resemble her more when I got older. The possibility of having the power of her beauty should have excited me, but it didn't.

Instead, it was the overwhelming understanding I had become a part of something bigger than me. I'd inducted myself into a secret sisterhood. Now I needed to find out if revealing myself as a member would result in the comfort of acceptance or the devastation of rejection.

CHAPTER 11: NATALIE

The smooth surface of the river shimmered with reflections of the multi-storied condos alongside the riverbanks. Where dilapidated warehouses had once been scattered like broken blocks, trendy shops attracted tourists and locals.

I put my window down and joined the line of traffic waiting for the Southern Belle to glide under the bright blue Market Street bridge. Chattanooga's best known tour boat, the top deck of the majestic lady was littered with folks enjoying the authentic riverboat experience promised in the brochures. Typical of most tourist attractions, it was a tribute to the past. Everyone liked to imagine a past when genteel ladies with flowery fans batted eyelashes at lucky suitors. But people like me and my mom would have been paddling upstream on Huck Finn's raft.

My only time onboard Big Belle had been four years earlier at my high school graduation party. The sunset was spectacular as we left the dock. And I'm sure the colorful city lights continued to dazzle. The poisonous purple hue of vodka and grape juice spewing over the deck is the only color I remember, though. In one of his few gallant gestures, Dylan held back my hair as I puked my guts out. The boy wasn't all bad.

Today, cars inched forward as the boat cleared the bridge, disturbing the mirror-like surface. Sunlight threaded the churning water with gold. Thinking about the horrors lying below made me regret not skipping more of my ecology classes.

Especially the lecture about an assortment of chemicals, plastics, and corpses—both animal and human—that mingled on their way to the Ohio.

"For God's sake. Do you have to turn everything into an internal documentary?" I asked myself and determined to take a more shallow view of life.

But nothing could disguise the stink of sewage from a system that depended on volume and rainwater to clean itself. As my high school English teacher would have said, something was rotten in the state of Denmark. Or in this case, the city of Chattanooga. I closed the windows.

A beat-up van like Dylan's pulled next to me at the light. Fearful I might have summoned him with my compliment, I scooched down in the seat before turning to get a better look. It wasn't him.

I thought about the last time we were together after a gig somebody's brother's cousin's friend set up at what turned out to be a biker bar. The clientele was too drunk to understand the band's liberal lyrics but not drunk enough to ignore how terrible they sounded. When a lumpy guy covered with dense graying hair and a full throttle tattoo on his sloping belly started throwing beer nuts, I insisted we hit the road.

Dylan and his buddies whined all the way home, but I pointed out we were lucky to escape before they moved from hurling snack food to lobbing beer bottles. We dropped the band members off at a club where the bass player knew the bouncer, then smoked half a joint I dug out from underneath some rubbery french fries in a Dairy Queen bag.

"I'm starving." I rummaged through the glove compartment, but all I found were a loose piece of spearmint gum, an open pack of lint-covered cherry lifesavers, and a moldy cheese curl. If there had been a chocolate covered anything, I might not have dumped him that night. But his lack of ability to provide for me was the last straw.

I don't remember the exact date of our breakup, but it was in the middle of December, the year they buried Stella. Even though my mother didn't find out about the funeral until it was long past, I blamed her for keeping me away from the event. I'm not sure I would have had the nerve to show up, but I kept on fantasizing about being there.

Then and now I took comfort in replaying my reunion with Grace on this giant screen in my head, like the one at the drive-in movie Dad took me to when I was a kid. I guess it wouldn't have been a reunion since you can't reunite if you hadn't united in the first place. Whatever. The details were fuzzy, but the story always ended with my new-older sister throwing her arms around me, delirious with joy at discovering that once again, there were two Burnette sisters. It became this incredible fairy tale. Only instead of stepping into the magic slippers, I stepped into Stella's spot and made everything right.

There was, however, a price to pay for that happily ever after thing. Disney glossed over the Grimm version of those stories, but I knew better. Cinderella found her prince, but her stepsisters lost several toes and eventually had their eyes pecked out by crazed birds. Boys who changed their minds about never growing up discovered Peter Pan was a homicidal maniac with strict rules about keeping everyone in a state of perpetual adolescence. And the little mermaid lost both her voice and her mobility. But I decided to give the saga of the beautiful Burnette sisters a perfect ending.

Before I could conjure up a satisfying conclusion, I pulled into the lot in front of the Fallen Five Monument and parked. I walked along the riverside path until I reached the giant wreath of honor suspended from five white pillars. From a distance, the wires attached to the enormous golden bird's nest disappear and the whole thing looks as if it's floating between heaven and earth.

The city built it for the five soldiers killed by a lone shooter while they were working in a recruitment center. It happened about the same time Mom had her stroke. All I remembered was being surprised at how young the guys looked. I wondered if shooting men who were trying to get people to sign on to do some shooting of their own was the point. Turned out there wasn't really a point at all.

I sat at the base of a column and stared up at the metal bands slowly revolving in a never-ending circle. The sun lay low on the river. It shot weak beams of light that were bright enough to illuminate the cut-out words on the rounded blades. *Heroes forever* and *Thank you for your sacrifice* and *Never Forget*. Was it possible those phrases eased the pain of the families left behind? Or was it worse to realize that beautiful but cold monument would outlive the ones they loved?

When I got home, I was no closer to answering those questions than when I emerged from the shadows cast by the hanging wreath.

•   •   •   •   •

Whether the spirits of the men lying beside the swirling river or my increasing fear of being an unwelcome guest in what should have been my own life influenced me, the burning need to follow up on my sister-quest faded. I still felt guilty over the way I had treated Mom and didn't want to do anything that might add to her pain. So, instead of resuming my obsessive search for information, I stepped away from it and concentrated on being a better daughter.

Except for work or school, I stayed close to her. I resisted the urge to force Mom's sentences to completion and nodded encouragement when she finished on her own, even if she often made little sense. We went to movies where she dozed off and spilled her popcorn within the first thirty minutes. We mall-walked at a poky pace that would once have driven me crazy. I drove her to the mountains, and we took pictures of waterfalls and streams she wouldn't remember when we got home.

Late at night, I creeped into her room to make sure she was breathing. And early each morning, I rushed to the kitchen, so her breakfast would be ready when she made her heavy descent down the stairs. After we ate, I waited until she showered before getting dressed myself. And I brushed her graying hair before I left. More than anything, it was those iron-like veins of mortality that terrified me.

If not for my aunt's more practical approach to aging, I might have remained a prisoner of fear and guilt.

"Sweet Baby Jesus, Olivia," Char proclaimed after popping in on a Saturday morning in late spring. "I bet you can't even remember the last time you had your hair done? You look worse than Granny Morgan with a hangover."

Mom opened her mouth to protest, but my aunt had already turned to me. "And I hate to say anything negative, but you're not exactly cover girl material either, honey." She grabbed my ponytail and shook it, then wiped her hand on her jeans. "A lesser woman might not be up to the challenge. But Auntie Char's got this."

I don't know how she got us in on a Saturday afternoon and didn't want to ask, but four hours later, we emerged from Ina Jean's Salon of Allure transformed. No longer steely gray, Mom's shining locks were silvery white and smoothed into what Ina called an inverted bob. One of the younger stylists with a nose ring and a rainbow pixie-cut snipped off the tip of my greasy ponytail and replaced it with a shoulder length style lightened by caramel highlights. Ina Jean herself styled my aunt's auburn curls. A squadron of manicurists painted all sixty of our nails varying shades of pinks and fuschias.

"You must feel five pounds lighter after shedding that horse's tail. And, Olivia, you are so beautiful I could just cry."

"Aunt Char's right, Mom. You both are absolutely gorgeous."

A load heavier than my thick hair lifted. Thanks to Ina Jean, the burden of my mother's mortality no longer weighed me down. And I was ready to find out what had caused the obvious rift between my sisters.

Although my confidence in Mom's odds for surviving had increased, I worried that questioning her about the Burnettes might cause a setback. So, I returned to Stella's memorial page, searching for the missing pieces of their story. Among the many consolation comments, I came across the name Ben Wilcott and googled him.

I found a mention of his elopement in a local paper. The article referenced both the groom and the bride's employment with a law firm — Ben as an attorney, Stella as receptionist — and a description of the beachside town of Montañita where the two settled. That explained all the beach pictures. His absence in them indicated Grace hadn't been the only one who had been cut out of my sister's life. But why? I almost overlooked the newspaper blurb that predated his marriage to Stella: Ben's engagement announcement.

Other than the bride's mother, no parents received credit in the couple's presentation. I skimmed the rest of the brief announcement and if not for the photo, might have missed it. This time, it wasn't Grace or Ben who had been removed from the picture. It was Stella.

CHAPTER 12: NATALIE

I sat there, still staring at the photo of Ben and Grace, trapped for eternity in a stiff embrace, when Aunt Char burst through the front door with Uncle Dwight a few steps behind her. Leaping to my feet, I shut my laptop faster than if I'd been caught watching porn.

I braced myself for one of my aunt's premium hugs and submitted as she pulled me to what she called her "bountiful bosom."

She loosened her grip, and I slipped from her arms.

"I wasn't expecting company. Mom's sitting out back, but I can get her if you want."

"Who are you calling company? And don't bother Olivia; we're not in any hurry." She grabbed my arm and squeezed it. "Honey, you are getting way too thin. You're one step away from a double Ensure milkshake. See here, Dwight." She spun me toward him. "This child is skin and bones."

He shrugged and patted his ample belly. "I'd say she looks fine. Might try to drop a few pounds myself."

Stunned at this mild act of rebellion, I stuttered my thanks and waited for the explosion. My uncle never contradicted his wife. I assumed he'd given up cultivating opinions of his own on his honeymoon.

Instead of restating her assessment of my physique, Char stood with her mouth open. Her inability to speak shocked me more than Dwight's act of defiance.

"Well, that loose gutter I promised your mother I'd repair isn't going to fix itself. I'll leave you ladies to it." He touched my aunt on the shoulder, then ambled to the kitchen and out the back door.

After a few more seconds of unnatural silence, Char shook her head and dismissed the exchange. "Humph. Let's get some iced tea and have a little chat."

A chill shot up my spine, sending me to the dark place of deadly diagnoses. Please, not more grim news about my mother's future or whether she had one.

I followed my aunt to the refrigerator and watched as she whipped out our never-ending pitcher of sugar-laden liquid.

"Just water for me," I said.

"Are you sure? How about some milk?"

I wrested the glass from her grip and filled it from the tap.

"All right. But your mom and I made oatmeal cookies yesterday, and we're going to have some."

"Please, Aunt Char. What is it you need to tell me? Did they find a brain leak? Is she about to have another stroke?"

"Slow down, honey. It's nothing like that." She patted my hand before taking a bite. "Best damn oatmeal cookie in the state if I do say so myself."

I sighed and bit into the chewy concoction. Experience told me my aunt would get to her story on her own time. The sense of relief and cinnamon flooding through my system made it easier to wait her out.

She washed hers down with a swallow of tea and dabbed her lips with a napkin before speaking.

"I've been trying to figure out a way to tell you this without coming across as useless as teats on a bull. I expected you would bring it up the night of the phone call and was going to explain the situation to you. When you didn't mention it, I figured you might have forgotten. Dwight said I should stop lallygagging and get it all out in the open. So here goes."

She cleared her throat. "Your mom found out about your daddy's other family a few years after they got married and told me. She said she overheard him on the phone saying he was real sorry to a woman he called Marilyn and badgered him until he spilled it all. He was offering his condolences to his ex-wife because her mother had died. Finding out your daddy had all that crap in his background broke her heart."

I wanted to scream *What about me? Didn't I deserve to hear the truth about my other family?* But I was afraid if I interrupted, she might stop talking.

"We decided not to say anything to you. You were so young, and your dad couldn't have cared less about following up with the daughters he left behind. He said he'd been gone too long to start up a relationship. Olivia insisted he felt so guilty about deserting them he was ashamed to show his face. I told her the selfish son of a bitch had an allergy when it came to taking personal responsibility. Either way, it didn't make sense to tell you about the girls. Your mother acted like she forgot they existed, so I never brought it up. Not until I got the news about Stella."

She explained the Atlanta paper ran a feature story on how Grace traveled to Ecuador to find out what happened to her sister. A friend who lived in the city saw the picture of Stella and freaked out because she mistook my half-sister for me. After reading the article, she realized her mistake and called my aunt, who told Mom. They agreed it was time to come clean about my surviving sister. But she got sick, and Char was afraid I wouldn't be able to handle any more stress.

"And poor Olivia didn't remember anything at all. Not just the phone conversation or Stella's death. She forgot who Jack was. Not all that bad, but it left me in an awkward position. I wanted to break the news to you, but we'd planned on talking to you together. Without your mother, it seemed wrong. Dwight said I was making chickenshit excuses, and he was right."

I tried to remember a time my aunt had admitted her husband was right about anything, but nothing came to mind. I wondered if this shift in dynamics might somehow be related to my father's first family. Or had I simply misjudged their relationship?

"But it was more than that," she continued. "Being your mom's little sister wasn't easy. She was smarter, prettier, all around nicer than me. Not terrible, though, kind of like walking a tightrope with a safety net. In elementary school whenever I got one of those talks-too-much notes, she forged your grandma's signature. When I missed curfew, she plumped up pillows under my covers and pretended to talk to me whenever Mom listened at the door. And she always left the window open for me to crawl back in."

Char reached for another cookie. "I knew nothing bad would ever happen because my big sister would always be there to protect me. She made me invincible. When she got sick, it hit me for the first time how vulnerable we both were. At least I had the chance to love her. Honey, I have no idea what might transpire between you and Grace. But it's not fair to keep you from finding out. I should have told you sooner. So, go ahead and cuss me out if you want to. I deserve it."

Part of me liked the idea of flinging curses at her for keeping such an important secret from me. My more rational side warned me that while I would enjoy doing so, it wasn't going to help get information. I had to discover whether Grace knew I existed.

"I'm not mad at you. Please, just tell me about my..." I stumbled over what to call them. In my mind, they were my sisters, but the words caught in my throat. They were too intimate, too full of promise. "All you know about the Burnette family. Like what happened after Stella stole her sister's fiancé?"

"The article didn't say." She popped from her seat and knocked her almost empty tea glass over. "I am such a klutz." After making a big deal of cleaning up and getting a refill, she sat down again.

"So anyway, that's about it."

I knew my aunt too well to accept her statement.

"Aunt Char, I find it hard to believe you wouldn't have been curious about sister-on-sister drama. Spill it."

"Okay, okay. I have to admit it intrigued me. No way could I imagine stealing Olivia's boyfriend, what's less the man she planned to marry, not even if he was Brad Pitt. And especially not that jug-headed, bug-eyed daddy of yours. I expected your mother would be interested in finding out more, but she insisted on leaving it alone. And I would have. When she had the stroke, though, I decided it was my responsibility to you to find out as much as I could."

She sighed as if the weight of having to dig for juicy gossip, even if it was attached to a tragedy, had been almost too much for her. I didn't buy it but played along to keep her talking.

"And I appreciate you going to all that trouble for me."

"For you, no trouble at all, just tricky. First, I called my friend in Atlanta to see if she found out anything. Her cousin is a fashion editor for the Marietta paper. He hooked us up with his ex-boyfriend, who's a caterer. And honey, he was the nicest man. We started talking about how Covid destroyed the buffet line. He said it should have been axed ages ago, what with people breathing and sneezing and grabbing cheese with their grubby fingers. I asked him what he thought about those little shrimp and grits kabob thingees. He told me they —"

"Aunt Char," I blurted. "Please, get back to the part about Grace and Stella."

"All right, already. But don't come to me begging for help with appetizers when someday you're planning your wedding, God willing." This sigh was several seconds longer than the first.

"He had all the dirt because Grace's mother canceled less than a month before the big day. Poor guy said it made him sick to have to keep her deposit. He used to date the florist's assistant, who told him the intended groom and the sister ran off to some country not likely to extradite rich Americans. His flower shop got lots of orders for Stella's funeral. That's when he heard about her murder. What she did was downright slutty, but she didn't deserve to die for it."

I wanted to ask why Grace had gone to Ecuador, but Mom and Dwight came in from the garden. It was just as well, since I suspected the only one who had the answer was my surviving sister.

I can't explain why I was so certain hearing her reason would help me understand not only her, but myself. But it was why I became an expert in surveillance stalking.

And if I hadn't started tailing my sister and her niece, I would never have discovered I wasn't the only one lurking in the shadows.

PART TWO

CHAPTER 13: GRACE

Emma squealed with delight as we raced to the car. She wasn't as delighted when, in my panicked state, I strapped her in so tight the belt pinched her chubby thighs.

"Mommy, you're hurting me." She struggled against her restraints, and I saw tears welling in her dark eyes.

"I'm sorry, baby." I adjusted the straps, slammed the door, and ran to the other side.

I locked the doors, turned the key in the ignition, handed Emma a juice box from the stash of snacks I never left home without, and stepped on the gas pedal hard enough to leave a cloud of dust behind us.

I needed to tell Justin what was going on, but before I could instruct Siri to call him, Emma kicked the back of the seat.

"Stupid thing won't go in," she grumbled as she stabbed at the foil.

"Let Mommy do it," I offered, extending my arm at a painful angle while checking my rearview window. The juice box flew onto the passenger seat, where I retrieved it, jammed the sawed-off straw into the top, and hyper-extended my elbow returning it to my disgruntled child.

I wound in and out of tree-lined streets in the opposite direction of home, trying to come up with a way to fill Justin in on the woman at the playground that wouldn't paint me as completely paranoid or worse, delusional. Seeing her in the sunlight convinced me that instead of my sister's avenging spirit, she was a solid flesh and blood entity. One who only looked like Stella. Whoever she was, she had been staring at our daughter and had been so focused on her she hadn't noticed me. Yet something startled her enough to make her disappear into the wooded area.

I turned onto the main road, constantly assessing the cars behind me to see if any were familiar. If someone followed me, they were darn good at it.

Unless—I smacked my forehead in frustration—they didn't need to follow me because they already knew where I lived.

•   •   •   •   •

When I pulled into the garage and rounded the car to extricate Emma, she was totally out—arms flung to the side with a plump fist clutching her smushed juice carton. A green blob of what I hoped was finger paint oozed from folds of baby fat below her chin. I marveled at her complete surrender, her trust in those who vowed to keep her safe. It weighed on me I might not be up to the task, couldn't protect her from whatever dark forces threatening to steal her from the people who loved her?

"Bullshit. I pity anyone who takes on my badass sister."

I whirled around, searching for the source of encouragement. Of course, I already knew the voice had to be in my head. But it sounded too clear and strong to be a product of my imagination.

"Mommy, bullshit is a bad word. You owe Daddy a dollar."

•   •   •   •   •

Emma read to a row of dead-eyed dolls of varying sizes and colors while I stayed close to her. My hands still shook from seeing my familiar-looking stranger at the playground and the even stranger encounter with my foul-mouthed sister, real enough that my little girl heard her. I didn't want to panic him, but I needed to talk to Justin.

He answered on the second ring. "Hey, babe. You caught me sitting here thinking about you."

"How soon can you be home?"

"What's wrong? Is Emma hurt? Are you okay?"

"Nothing like that, just something at the playground. Rather someone."

"I'm on my way."

In less than thirty minutes, Emma greeted him at the door.

"Mommy ordered pizza, and it's not even Friday," she proclaimed, as he picked her up. "And she owes you money for using inpropropriate language."

"*Inpropropriate language*?" he repeated and tossed her into the air. "Is that worse than inappropriate?" he asked when she stopped giggling.

"Yes. Much more worse."

"Mommy and I will have to have a serious talk—after pizza."

I set the table while the two of them washed their hands, then grabbed beers for us and milk for Emma.

She chattered about the fort she and Wyatt were making when I interrupted them. My stomach twisted when she mentioned she wanted to go to his house for a playdate this weekend. I distracted her by letting her dump more parmesan onto her plate and ignored her when she cleaned up the excess with her tongue.

Justin raised his eyebrows and asked, "So, you had an eventful afternoon?"

I nodded before clearing our plates and wiping sauce and cheese off our daughter. "How about some cartoons before your bath?"

"Cartoons? Really?"

She raced from the room. In seconds, the theme song from *SpongeBob* sounded throughout the house.

"It's going to take another beer for me to handle that rectangular doofus. Can I get you one?" Justin asked.

"Sure," I said, wondering where to begin with my story. I reminded him of Lesroy's stalker theory. For him to understand why seeing the woman at the park unnerved me, I would have to backtrack with the mall sighting.

"Okay," I began, but he cut me off.

"Before you start, I need to tell you something. Something I should have told you weeks ago."

I watched as he scraped at the label on his bottle. I thought of those late-night phone calls and his unusually long hours and how certain I'd been he was hiding something from me and shuddered. Was my husband, the love of my life, trying to tell me he was seeing someone else? My throat constricted with the memory of the pain and humiliation I experienced when I discovered my fiancé had run off with my sister. But Justin wasn't Ben.

He drained the rest of his beer and set it down hard enough to cause Scarlett to sit up and stare at him.

"You know Harry and I have been staying in touch?"

His mention of Mike's friend was so random it took me several seconds to recall the man who had been invaluable in helping us navigate Ecuador's complicated legal system. Without his kindness, I doubted we would have made it home safely. It didn't surprise me they'd been talking. It did puzzle me Justin hadn't mentioned their conversations.

He didn't seem to expect a response. "Well, he's been keeping his ears open about the Balsutos. Last month, he heard Adelmo had returned to Ecuador to be with his family at their compound. Apparently, his remaining brothers and their kids want to go legit. Using drug money to buy rental property and laundromats and farmland. Harry isn't sure of the impact Adelmo's return will have on their efforts, but if they've gone back to their old ways, no one is talking about it."

"Does that mean the people he ran from stopped looking for him?"

The horror of the filthy trailer demolished by lightning flashed in front of me. The nightmare place my sister's lover took Ben to exact his own kind of justice for taking the woman he loved. When Adelmo walked into that hellish building, Ben would never walk out. I had been less disturbed by the knowledge than I should have been. What did terrify me was his killer had escaped, and I would have to live with the certainty that, unless one of his many enemies got to him, her biological father might come to claim Emma Grace.

"Or he found them first. Whatever happened, it seems he's running the business again. At least until a few months ago when he and a young man authorities think might be the son of Adelmo's brother who got himself killed a few years back were spotted boarding a private jet." Justin reached across the table for my hand. "Harry said he can't be certain, but his sources suspect the plane was headed to a small airport in Miami. No one has seen Adelmo, but they sighted the kid at a hotel outside of Savannah."

Too disoriented to be angry Justin hadn't shared such important information, I returned to the mystery woman at the park. I might not know who the woman stalking me was but she wasn't Adelmo's nephew. And if that young man had been sent to check up on me and Emma — or worse, to kidnap my daughter — who the hell could she be?

CHAPTER 14: GRACE

After I explained to Justin it wasn't one of the mysterious Balsuto men who had been stalking me, we had no viable theory as to the identity of my mystery woman. We agreed it would be unusual for two people to have such an unnatural interest in our lives, but I couldn't let go of the idea the blonde in the baseball cap was connected to Adelmo. My husband grudgingly admitted the possibility.

More important, we pledged that even though our motives had been reasonable—he didn't want me to worry unnecessarily, and I didn't want him to think I was losing my mind—there would be no more secrets.

"What about the nephew? Is he on his way to Atlanta?"

"Maybe, but Harry's team doesn't have a positive ID on him. If he's an employee, he might be negotiating a business deal in Savannah."

"But that's not his take, is it?" My eyes clouded at the memory of the scene I'd caused at the airport when I sobbed my goodbye to the man we'd come to depend on to keep us out of danger.

He hesitated before responding. "No, it's not."

High-pitched peals of laughter reminded me Emma was on her second episode of her favorite show.

"It is so past her bedtime." I moved to get up, but he beat me to it.

"You relax. A little Emma time is exactly what I need right now."

His falsetto rendition of "Let it Go" from *Frozen* replaced crustaceans singing and was followed by shrieks of protests and giggles.

"No, Daddy, no," she shouted as she ran toward the stairs. "You're drilling my ears."

He sang louder.

Relaxing was out of the question after Justin's revelations, so I decided to take another look at the Balsutos.

I began by investigating recent drug activity in Ecuador to see if Adelmo had been serious when he swore my sister made him want to be a better person. I grabbed my laptop and searched for cartels, cocaine, and marijuana in the area.

There were plenty of sites and articles connected to Ecuador's efforts to end drug exportation and several gory accounts of shoot-outs and murders. But I found nothing about Adelmo or anyone associated with him.

"What the hell did you expect? A directory of criminal specialties?"

I hadn't expected there to be any mention of Adelmo's journey to Miami but hoped to find something about his flight or return to his own country. It shouldn't have surprised me in a place where the press was categorized as "not free" that Ecuadorian newspapers could be bullied or bribed into omitting information. And even if there had been a listing of bad guys, the Balsutos would have taken great pains not to be on it. Their involvement went back far enough for them to have had years to make over their image by hiding the dirt underneath legal businesses.

Harry's people might not have confirmed the man traveling with Adelmo as his nephew, but family mattered to him. No way would he include an outsider on such a sensitive mission. Hopefully, his reason for coming to the States only involved business. If, however, he had come to reclaim his—no, *my*—daughter, I needed to know what his companion looked like in case I had to stop him.

Eva, Adelmo's nanny and Stella's only true friend, told me about his younger sister who had been kidnapped and killed by a rival gang. There were other siblings, but they would be too old and cautious to be part of the Facebook era. I doubted their children would embrace a medium that made it easier for enemies to track them down either. The grandchildren were a different story.

I searched through public records from major cities in Ecuador, slowed by my limited Spanish and Google translate. Among death notices, I saw Adelmo's mother outlived her husband and three of her seven children. She was survived by the remaining offspring, including Adelmo and eighteen grandchildren.

Eva should be able to supply me with their identities and the schools they attended. But asking her to talk to me about one of the most dangerous criminal enterprises in the country would put her in danger. If the people who were looking for Adelmo found out, they might assume she knew where he was hiding, if he was alive. And that wouldn't be good for her.

I clicked on private schools in the country, not sure what I expected to find. It wasn't as if they would publish student names along with the glossy promotional photos. Boarding schools made the most sense for kids raised in a remote rural area. There were several highly ranked multi-lingual ones.

I thought of Adelmo's flawless English when he spoke to me of getting revenge for Stella's murder. His words flowed effortlessly, as if he were reciting a sad but lovely poem. I shivered as I remembered the jarring contrast between the warmth of his tone and the cold fury reflected in his eyes.

At the time, I had been unsure whether to feel terror or gratitude. I still wasn't.

If not for the memory of those eyes, I might have missed the young man standing in front of a trapezoid monument with an enormous brass globe on top. I enlarged the photo to read the name of the building *Cuidad Mitad el Mundo,* City in the Middle of the World. When I zoomed in, I saw the boy was younger than my first impression of him. His dark hair framed a square-jawed but handsome face complete with a grin suggesting a private joke between him and the photographer. And while his eyes were neither cold nor angry, they were almost identical to those of my sister's lost love.

I experienced a quick jolt of elation dampened by the even quicker realization the kid in the picture could be anyone. Despite that reality check, I held onto the belief he wasn't.

"So what?" I asked myself, as I closed my laptop. "There must be thousands of students like him."

"Who are you talking to?" Justin rescued me from my growing disappointment. "It's not your sexy boyfriend hiding in the closet, is it?" He flopped down on the bed and began bouncing up and down, pounding his chest gorilla-style. "Nobody messes with my woman," he said as he moved closer.

"You're the only man for me. The pool boy doesn't count, right?"

He roared, then leaned over me and nuzzled my neck. I wrapped my arms around him, but he pulled back.

"Not so fast, my lady. Your presence is requested in the princess's bedchamber for a bedtime story. Make it a short one."

• • • • •

Frantic barking brought me out of a thick sleep. I rolled away from a still sleeping Justin and checked the time. It was only a little after ten, and the dog was going crazy—alternating between low-throated growls and thundering bellows.

"Scarlett," I whisper-shouted as I threw on my robe and ran to the hallway. "It's okay." My half-hearted attempt to calm her had the opposite effect, probably because she sensed I didn't really believe it myself. My sweet-tempered watchdog never freaked out like this.

She glanced over her shoulder but remained at her post, yelping and scratching at the front door.

"What the hell, Scarlett."

"Jesus, Justin! You scared the crap out of me."

Then I noticed he had a gun. I despised having it in the house although he kept it in a safe with fingerprint recognition security. If he was willing to risk my ranting about how much I hated having firearms in the home, this must be serious or worse, dangerous.

"Stay back," he commanded at the same moment we heard a deep, guttural cry. He darted to the door, and I followed, grabbing Scarlett's collar as he opened it.

I held tight when she tried to pull away from me. We could hear sounds of a struggle, a crash as if something or someone heavy dropped onto the porch. Justin eased a few inches closer to the noise, and Scarlett broke from my grip and lunged past him.

Within seconds, she had one of the intruders pinned face down on the ground, her jaws clamped on the sleeve of his right arm. Justin ignored him and bounded in the direction of pounding footsteps. At the end of the driveway, he stopped, turned full circle, then raced back to the porch.

"Don't move," he said, gun pointed toward Scarlett's captive.

"I couldn't if I wanted to," he mumbled as he twisted his head to the side. "This is a hell of a welcome for an old friend."

"Harry?" I shoved Scarlett aside to get a better look. "Oh my God, it's Harry!"

CHAPTER 15: GRACE

After examining Harry for injuries, we found he only suffered scraped knuckles, a scratch across his cheek, and a ripped jacket. Justin made coffee while Scarlett and I checked on Emma, who had slept through the commotion. When we joined them in the kitchen, he explained how he ended up sprawled out on our porch.

"I tried to call from the airport but got sent to voicemail. Figured I'd drive by to see if you were home. When I slowed down out front, I saw him. A guy dressed head to toe in black, skulking around the side of the house, peeking in your windows. So, instead of stopping, I eased my way to the back and slipped out of the car. Then the hound of the Baskervilles started that ungodly barking and spooked him."

Scarlett, who had maintained her position between me and Harry since releasing him from her jaws, whined and scooted closer to me. I scratched behind her ear, and she moaned. "She's really a sweetheart."

"A sweetheart who'll rip your throat out." He shifted in his chair, and the dog sat at attention. "Hey, no worries. It wasn't personal; you were only doing your job. But I'll just back up an inch or two in case you decide to make it personal."

He scooted farther away and continued.

"Anyway, the big guy turned toward the street, but I cut him off, and he bolted for the house. I caught up with him on the porch and grabbed his shoulder. The sonofabitch broke away and knocked me flat on my ass. Then that hell demon pinned me to the ground."

Justin set a steaming mug of coffee for Harry and poured one for himself. "Anything for you, babe? Hot chocolate? Decaf? Wine?"

"Whiskey. I need whiskey." I stood and opened a cabinet over the oven.

"That's my girl." He grinned as I put the bottle on the table.

"Pappy Van Winkle. A woman after my own heart," Harry said.

I gave each of them a generous amount in their cups and a smaller portion in a glass for me.

"I don't want to sound like I'm not happy to see you, but I doubt you traveled all this way to take me up on my offer to visit anytime."

He cleared his throat and looked at Justin, who nodded. "She knows as much as I do."

"Truth is, I've been getting homesick, and I haven't seen my goddaughter since she was a little bitty thing. And all this stuff with the Balsutos got me thinking now might be the right time to make sure she recognizes her Uncle Harry."

"Oh, she's well aware of who you are. We keep your picture on her dresser. Most nights, you're at the top of her prayer list."

"Glad someone's putting in a good word for me." He blew on his coffee before taking a sip. "Have to admit, I thought Adelmo was long gone. I never wanted the guy to turn up dead. But having him alive, with no idea where the hell he was or what he might do, was worse. When he showed back up, I wasn't sure if it was something to worry you guys over. When I heard he was headed for the States, I figured worried wouldn't begin to cover it. So, I got in touch with Justin and kept up with the rumors about where Balsuto was going and who he'd brought with him."

He reached for the bottle and added whiskey to his cup.

I took advantage of the break in his narrative.

"Didn't you hear it was his nephew? Could he have been the one outside the house?"

"That's what the local guy who told me said. But Adelmo has more than one nephew. The guy I ran into could be part of the family, but he moved like an older man. And the Balsuto men—the ones I'm aware of—barely stand over five ten or so. This dude was huge, at least six three or four and heavy."

"If he's not involved with them, who is he? And why would he be watching us?"

They exchanged glances. Justin took my hand.

"It's possible the man Harry fought with has nothing to do with any of this. He could be your run-of-the-mill thief who happened to be in the wrong place."

"That's about as likely as my winning the Georgia lottery tomorrow without having bought a ticket." I slid my hand from his. "Remember our promise to be straight with each other? So, what do you really think? No. Wait. I'll go first. The man tonight isn't part of Adelmo's crew. He's one of his enemies, trying to find a way to get to him. And that way is through Emma."

. . . . .

Too tired to make sense, we agreed to continue our conversation in the morning. Justin and I insisted Harry spend the night. I got him settled in the guest room, and Justin double-checked locks on doors and windows before turning off the lights. We left Scarlett curled up on the rug by our daughter's bed.

"I don't feel good about sending Emma to daycare." Shivering despite having pulled several blankets over us, I moved closer to my husband. He wrapped his arms around me.

"I agree. I need to see what I can dig up about this new guy while Harry looks into Adelmo and the kid. I'll put one of my security guys on the house."

"What about Mom? If she suspects something's going on, she'll come barging over and flip out. Or worse, whoever might be after Emma could know about her and Mike and go after them." I slipped from his arms and sat up. "Oh, God, Justin. I hadn't thought of that. We should call them now and warn them."

"Hold on a minute." He pulled me close. "Just because Harry didn't catch him doesn't mean he wasn't spooked. My guess is he'll lay low for a while. But you're right. Your family needs to know what's going on. We'll head there first thing tomorrow and fill them in. It won't be a bad idea to have a military man like Mike on our side." He kissed me on the cheek and held me tighter.

"Are you forgetting Mom?" I asked.

"Oh, my dear God, no. I never forget your mother. I'd face three or four Marines rather than get between that woman and her granddaughter."

His warmth didn't stop another chill from coming over me as I recalled the image of Mom outlined by the porch light when she faced down Lesroy's daddy. I didn't see the shotgun until after Uncle Roy scurried down the steps and she slammed the door, then turned to face me.

More shocking than the memory of my mother slumped against the wall, cradling a weapon almost as long as she was tall, was remembering I hadn't been the least bit shocked.

●　　　●　　　●　　　●　　　●

Sunlight slipped through the closed blinds and across the dark wood floor. I turned to reach for Justin, but he wasn't there. A murmur of male voices startled me, and I hit the ground running to check on Emma. I was halfway to the hallway when the events of the previous evening returned to me. Reassured by the knowledge Harry and Justin were there to keep us safe, I took the time to slip into leggings and a sweatshirt and run a brush through my hair.

Emma's door was ajar, but she was still asleep with Scarlett tucked under the quilt beside her. The dog raised her head, then rolled over and went back to sleep.

The bitter-rich aroma of coffee led me to the kitchen, where the men sat at the table

"Sleeping Beauty herself." Harry stood to pull out a chair for me. The sight of him in baggy shorts and Hawaiian shirt was familiar and comforting.

I sat and stared at the clock above the refrigerator: 6:20. Justin placed a steaming mug in front of me.

"Dear God. How long have you guys been up?" I stirred cream into my cup and waited for it to cool.

"Only for about an hour. This guy of yours came down a few minutes ago. I told him he was getting soft."

"Soft, huh? I'm not the one who got his ass kicked last night."

"That's a bad word, Daddy. You owe us a bunch of dollars." Emma stumbled to me and climbed onto my lap. She stared at Harry a minute, then cupped her hand over my ear and whispered loud enough to alert the cavalry. "Who's the stranger?"

"He's not a stranger, baby. He's our best friend Harry. The one from the picture in your room." I buried my face in her sleep-dampened hair and breathed her in before she wriggled away.

"Oh, he looks different in real life. What's for breakfast?"

"Emma, say good morning to Harry," Justin urged.

"Good morning to Harry." She yawned and stretched her arms high in the air, exposing the toddler version of a beer belly. "I'm hungry."

Harry guffawed. "I was just asking your daddy where he keeps the flour and eggs. I don't like to brag, but I make maybe the best pancakes in the world. Ask your mom."

"It's not bragging if you're telling the truth. Is it true, Mommy?"

I assured her Harry wasn't one to mislead her when it came to food, and she insisted on helping him by covering herself and the counter tops with flour and eggshells.

"I bet my daughter isn't the first female impressed by your culinary skills." I said after Justin took Emma upstairs to help her get dressed for Scarlett's morning stroll.

"You'd be surprised by the scarcity of women I've lured into my kitchen." He smiled when he spoke, but there was an off note that could have been loneliness. The entire time we'd been in Ecuador, I hadn't asked him anything about his personal life. Our schedule had been so hectic and I had been too devastated by my sister's death to care about making deep connections. But Harry became a friend.

And I was about to reward the poor guy by introducing him to my mother.

CHAPTER 16: GRACE

By 8:30 I showered, set up a meeting with my family, and, after much discussion, allowed Emma to pick her own outfit: a stretched-out two-piece bathing suit underneath mermaid-shaped pajama bottoms covered with a gauzy purple tutu.

The conversations I had with Mom and Lesroy had gone as expected, which meant not so good. I told them we needed to discuss some things concerning Emma's future, but they weren't serious. Neither bought it.

"If we're talking about my granddaughter's well-being, it most certainly is serious. Please tell me you and Justin aren't thinking about running off to another drug-infested hell hole putting yourself in danger and turning Emma into an orphan."

I assured her it was nothing like that, even though she seemed to have conveniently forgotten she was the one who sent me to the only drug-infested hell hole I'd ever been to.

Lesroy didn't handle the situation any better. "Dear God, Grace. Is it a brain tumor? That would explain the whole seeing-dead-people thing."

"It's not a tumor, damn it. We want to make sure Emma will be taken care of if, well, you know."

"I do not, but you can count on me." He sighed. "I understand Aunt Marilyn would have a hissy fit if you didn't give her full custody in case you and the hunk pass over the rainbow bridge at the same time. But Vincent and I won't allow the poor child to turn into a neurotic Burnette woman. And we will guarantee she develops a keen fashion sense. Well, I will anyway. Speaking of my flannel-clad sweetheart, is it okay if I bring him along?"

I hadn't intended to include Lesroy's partner in the initial meeting. I planned to let my cousin fill him in later. It wasn't because I didn't trust Vincent. It was more about steering clear of the intricacies of their love life. More specially, I was trying to mind my own business when it came to their complicated relationship, especially after the heated exchange Lesroy and I had about six months earlier.

·   ·   ·   ·   ·

With Justin out of town and Emma at Mom's, I looked forward to sleeping in. A few minutes after seven, the frantic buzzing of the doorbell put an end to my dream. Wrapped in my fuzzy robe, I stomped to the kitchen and peered out. Lesroy stood with one eyeball pressed to the peephole and his index finger still pressing the buzzer.

"For God's sake!" I yanked open the door.

"Good to see you, too." He held up a white bag. "I come bearing gifts."

He breezed past me, leaving the sweet smell of warm doughnuts in his wake.

Scarlett emerged from the bedroom, wagging her tail. She made a muzzle-lunge for his crotch, but he had become familiar with her favorite method of greeting and side-stepped her signature hello.

"I thought we agreed you have to buy me dinner first." He extended his free hand as a consolation prize. Scarlett sniffed, then licked it before sauntering out her doggie door.

I motioned him toward the kitchen table and excused myself to go to the bathroom. When I returned, he sat with a box of Krispy Kreme doughnuts and two cups of coffee.

"Check it out," he said, pointing to the pastries. "I brought cream-filled with chocolate icing, vanilla with sprinkles, jelly-filled, and plain." He picked up a big, puffy doughnut and bit into it. Jelly, raspberry from the look of it, squirted and dropped onto his paper towel. He scooped it up and licked his fingers.

Despite growing up with an abusive father who disappeared when he was ten, my cousin maintained a childlike sense of wonder. As a kid, he created incredible comic strips starring me and Stella as super-heroines. He filled the walls of his rooms with Stella Star, a fierce, beautiful warrior princess, and The Grace, an equally lovely, but gentler protector of the weak. Ironically, I couldn't protect my fearsome sister.

Compact and muscular, Lesroy had the body of the gymnast he was in high school. Too free-spirited to commit to a lifetime of disciplined training, he abandoned his Olympic dreams his freshmen year in college and took up epic partying. But he never gave up on art, which led him to being the owner of a graphic arts design company.

The morning of our fight, he crackled with electric energy. His hand hovered over the chocolate cream, but I snagged it first.

"So, did you stop by just to destroy my diet?" It was my turn to send a spurt of filling flying, this one landing on my chin.

"Actually, we are having what I envision as a Krispy Kreme celebratory announcement."

He brushed a dark auburn curl off his forehead and grinned. "At least, it could be an announcement. Maybe it's more of a possible announcement or an intention." He picked up his coffee and swirled it. He held his cup higher and looked pointedly at mine.

"Look, buddy. I'm operating on a serious shortage of sleep, so you're going to have to…"

"Pick up your mug, Grace. I want to propose a toast."

I obeyed.

"Here's to Lesroy Tucker, who has been officially asked to become a legally married man."

"Oh, my, God. That's absolutely freaking wonderful." I jumped up and threw my arms around his neck.

"Easy, cousin. I belong to another. Or I might."

I released him and stepped away. "What do you mean *might*? Please tell me you said yes."

"Not exactly." He slumped into his chair.

"So, what did you say to the dreamboat of your dreams, the one you've been waiting for all your life, when he professed his love and devotion? When he offered to make an honest man out of you?"

"I told him it was the best offer I'd ever had and, uh…" He mumbled the last part.

"And, uh, what?" I urged, trying to keep the irritation out of my voice.

"I asked if I could have some time to think it over."

"Jesus, Lesroy. That's worse than when someone says I love you after having the most mind-blowing sex you've ever had, and you tell him he has a terrific personality."

"Thanks for the support, cuz." He stood and slammed the top of the doughnut box shut. "Of all people, I expected you might understand. But I guess now that you've got the perfect life, you've forgotten how it feels to be afraid."

I wanted to throw his words back at him. How could he say my life was perfect without Stella? I started to ask him what the hell frightened him. But, of course, I knew.

My father answered the call of the road when he disappeared. His RSVP'd to a different kind of invitation. Both remained absent from our lives. He almost lost his mother to anguish and grief. I almost lost mine to bitterness and anger.

And we both lost Stella. The risk of losing the ones he loved terrified him.

Before I had the chance to explain I understood, he grabbed the rest of the pastries and stormed out the door.

The next time I saw him, he acted as if nothing had happened. He never mentioned the subject of his marriage again. His wanting to include Vincent in our family discussion seemed like a good omen to me. But I would keep my mouth shut.

CHAPTER 17: GRACE

"Mommy," Emma's voice penetrated the fog of my thoughts. "I asked you how much more longer."

"Sorry, baby. We're almost there."

She shot me her special brand of side eye and kicked the seat. "You always say that."

I had a sudden terrifying glimpse into what life with a teenage daughter might be like. The sight of the lipstick red Mustang convertible in Mom's driveway drove those thoughts from my mind.

"Is that who I think it is?" Justin parked beside the snazzy sports car.

"Yep. It's Aunt Rita."

Emma leaned forward and emitted a high-pitched squeal. "Auntie Rita Roo."

Rita Tucker, my mother's sister, was named after Rita Hayworth by my starstruck grandmother, who chose the name Marilyn Monroe for her eldest, and Mom never let her younger sibling forget who the bigger star was. Once a gorgeous redhead, Rita had been battered and bullied into a sepia-toned version of herself by Uncle Roy. After his disappearance, color began to slip back into her life. Now she overflowed with shades of red and purple and orange. The Mustang was part of the overflow.

I finished unbuckling Emma's belt, and Justin helped her down, ambling behind her as she bolted for the door.

"Aunt Rita must be something else," Harry said from the front seat.

"Nice way to put it," I said.

Emma was inside before we made it to the porch.

"Well, if it isn't Harry Davenport. You old so-and-so." Mike bear-hugged his friend into a wrestling hold for a few seconds, then released him and slapped him on the shoulder. "What brings you to our little corner of the world?" He looked over Harry's head at Justin. "I guess I'm about to find out, aren't I?"

Without waiting for an answer, he said, "Hurricane Rita made landfall, and tropical storm Emma is coming on fast," he announced. "Hope you're hungry because Marilyn just nuked a bunch of Trader Joe's breakfast junk. Toasty tortillas and something with avocado and eggs. Why anybody would do that to perfectly good scrambled eggs is beyond me."

I eased by him and left the men outside. In the kitchen, I found Emma flailing her arms, while spinning round and round between Mom and Rita—her version of an aquatic fashion show. She stumbled and both women dove in to keep her from bouncing into the refrigerator. They merged into an impromptu group hug.

I brushed away unexpected tears from the corners of my eyes as the three of them clung together, laughing and swaying. The sisters had gone through a lifetime of rough patches, some worse than others. There had been years when they barely spoke and several when almost every conversation ended in a shouting match. Yet here they were, wrapped around mine and Stella's child.

The thought of my sister hit me with longing sharp enough to stop my breath. I looked past them and out the window to the backyard where the two of us had spent much of our lives together. Our rusty swing set had been replaced by a fancy wooden fortress fit for a princess. But when I closed my eyes, it was back. The feathery ends of Stella's long blond hair tickled my face as I pushed her. The higher she flew, the closer she came to the sun.

"Mommy, look. Grandma squashed avocados all over the toast."

My daughter shook my arm and pointed to the table, covered with an assortment of gourmet items straight from my mother's favorite store.

Before I could comment on the feast, my cousin's voice drifted down the hallway. "We're all here now, Aunt Marilyn. Let's get this party started."

"Look who we found," Mike called out.

My cousin bounded past him, bouncing on the balls of his feet. His earlier concern over the possibility I had convened a family meeting to announce a terminal illness seemed to have evaporated. Vincent trailed behind him, hesitating at the entrance to survey the room. He had learned to be wary of—as Lesroy referred to us—a gaggle of Burnette women.

"There are my darlin' boys." Aunt Rita rushed toward her son and his partner with her arms extended. She stood on tiptoe to kiss Lesroy on the cheek before hugging Vincent.

"Pick me up, Uncle Lessy," Emma demanded. He responded by tossing her into the air, catching her, and whirling around like a human helicopter.

"You're going to drop that baby on her head the way your momma must have done with you. Put her down." My mother waved a spatula at them, and he docked Emma safely into her booster seat.

"There's something different about you, Vincent." Rita took a step back to check out her son's sweetheart. "I know," she crowed. "It's your new haircut."

She turned to Lesroy. "Why can't you get a haircut like Vincent instead of looking like a time traveler from the seventies?" She tucked his wavy hair behind his ears and most likely would have continued assessing areas needing improvement but stopped when Justin and Harry entered the room with Mike following them.

"Morning, everybody." Justin squeezed Mom's shoulder. "I'd like to introduce you to a good friend of ours." He stepped aside and nudged Harry toward the middle of the room. "This is Harry Davenport, the man who saved our, uh. He, uh, kept us safe in Ecuador."

Mom thanked him for being there, Lesroy asked him if he worked out daily, and Rita glanced at him from underneath her lashes and smiled.

Harry blushed, either from being the immediate center of attention or from his proximity to my aunt. "I feel like I know all of you already."

"Who's hungry? It's getting crowded in here. Mike, why don't you get out some TV trays, and we'll set up in the den. Rita and I will stay in here with Emma."

Rita, who hadn't looked at anyone but Harry since he walked into the room, gave my mother one of their sister-looks. An outsider might not have noticed the quick exchange of glances— my aunt's dark and sharp, Mom's blankly innocent. But I saw it and suspected they were communicating about more than who would be eating with Emma.

"Don't be silly, Marilyn. I bet Miss Mermaid would love to have a picnic with the Paw Patrol gang."

"Paw Patrol," my daughter shrieked and leaped from her chair. "I'm going to watch Paw Patrol."

This time the sibling squint went from Mom to Rita, who ignored it and returned her gaze to Harry. "You must be exhausted after your trip. Why don't you sit down in one of those comfy recliners while I fix a plate for you?"

Within seconds, the kitchen was empty except for me and Mom.

"Is there a reason you thought it would be a good idea to include Rita in our meeting?"

"I didn't invite her over, and I can't imagine Lesroy would have. You know how she is, Grace. She's got a sixth sense for showing up where she isn't wanted and making everything about her. I tried to get rid of her, but once you and Emma showed up, there was no way she'd leave. And did you see how she was looking at the poor guy? That woman has always been man hungry."

Rita had gone a little wild after Lesroy graduated high school. She rode with an aging motorcycle gang, had a relationship with a racecar driver at least ten years her junior, and almost ran off with a real estate mogul from Miami. After serving time with Uncle Roy, I understood her desperation for fun. As for Harry, a stateside fling might do him some good, so long as he didn't end up wanting more than a hot, but short-lived, romance.

"He's a big boy who can take care of himself. And Rita would probably find out about everything anyway. So, we might as well just get this over with."

She grabbed my arm and said, "Wait a second, honey. Before you start, please tell me you're okay — you and Justin both."

Her eyes clouded, reminding me of those endless days after Stella's funeral when I wondered if any of us would see the world clearly again, without a thick film of grief. I grabbed her by the shoulders and pulled her close.

"We're fine, Mom," I whispered. "But there have been some strange things going on. They could be nothing, but in case they're not, we want everyone to be on the same page."

"All right, then." She nodded and moved out of my arms. "In the words of your goofy-ass cousin, let's get this party started."

·　　·　　·　　·　　·

It was almost one when Justin strapped a protesting Emma into her car seat. Goodbyes have never been her thing, especially when they involved leaving her grandparents' home. Before we reached the highway, her head was lolling on her shoulder, a thin line of drool dangling from her chin.

"That took longer than expected," I said, referring to our ordeal at Mom's, not the amount of time it took my daughter to pass out.

Justin and Harry tried to give an abridged version of what happened in Ecuador, but every five minutes or so, Mom asked if anyone needed coffee refills or more cookies. She ignored us when we insisted we didn't need a thing and dashed off to the kitchen. Rita couldn't stop asking if Harry was comfortable and commenting on how brave he was. Lesroy demanded details on Adelmo's criminal background and had to breathe into a paper bag after hearing about the death of the Balsuto sister. Each incident required repetition and patience.

"We sprung a lot of scary stuff on them. I knew Mike would handle it like a pro, but your mom surprised me. After she stopped popping up and down, she was a trooper."

I had shared the story of my Uncle Roy's disappearance with Justin but glossed over the part my mother and grandmother had played in it. While the complete account might not have shocked him, it could have given him serious doubts about the wisdom of marrying into the Burnette family.

Harry nodded and added, "I was worried about your cousin's reaction, but once he caught his breath, he bucked up. And that momma of his, she's something else. I wouldn't want to go up against her."

I bit my tongue to keep from saying going up against him was exactly what my aunt had in mind. He'd find out soon enough.

Justin gave everyone a copy of the picture I found of the nephew and instructed them to be on the lookout and call the police if they saw him.

Mike volunteered to enlist the help of his fellow American Legion friends. Harry liked the idea, and the two set up a dinner meeting at the hall to coordinate their efforts.

Lesroy sent Emma home with enough drawing paraphernalia to keep her occupied while I answered emails and worked on an article for my client and friend Cara Frazier. Owner of Cara's Sweet Caress, a lingerie boutique catering to well-endowed women, she hired me to work on a campaign for the opening of a second location in Woodstock, Georgia. She was also the one who helped me find a new normal after Stella and Ben eloped and once again after I lost my sister. She deserved my full attention, but thoughts of men peering at us with cold-hot fury in their eyes plagued me—eyes like those of Adelmo Balsuto when he vowed to get justice for the woman we both had loved.

His concept of justice included the torture and execution of my ex-fiancé. I told myself his actions horrified me, that I could derive no pleasure from the lingering thought of the man responsible for my sister's murder, sitting bloody and battered in the hellish trailer, moments before his death. Yet, not once had he appeared in the nightmares still haunting me.

"Mommy, my show is ready."

While I had been reliving some of the worst events in my life, Emma had been decorating the room with her artwork. She took my hand and led me to what she called *exbibit* number one, a drawing of three not-quite stick figures. The artist gave me an impressive bosom, and Justin's shoulders were frighteningly broad. The child between us had Emma's dark curls and smiled at the elegant dog leaning against her.

I commented on her striking color choices—my hair was streaked with the same pink as the sky and Scarlett's coat was deep purple—and we moved to the next *exbibit*. She provided a running commentary as we went from Mom and Mike, Lesroy and Vincent, dolphins leaping offshore at the beach, and finally, to Emma and Wyatt in the sandbox.

"Mommy, are you even listening to me?" My daughter's exasperated tone cut through the buzzing in my ears that started when I stepped closer to get a better look at the two friends at play.

Emma captured Wyatt's lopsided grin and replicated the shirt he wore down to the dinosaur stitched on his pocket. Her teacher hadn't been exaggerating when she said my child had an artist's eye for detail. She included the pattern of the chain link fence and the sun beaming on the pink cap and blond ponytail of the woman behind it. Emma's version wasn't a full-on view of her face the way I remembered. It was of her profile as she looked up at a giant dressed in black. He was the one focused on the children in front of him. My little artist had given him a scraggly beard and sunglasses. There was no sunlight shining on him. Instead, he was surrounded by charcoal-gray scribbles.

Emma barely made it through her meal and bath before falling into bed. She was asleep before Justin reached page two of *Goodnight Moon*.

We were looking at the drawing of the watchers by the fence when Harry returned from dinner with the troops. We showed him the picture, and he agreed it confirmed the theory our little girl could be the target of surveillance.

"The good news is Mike has some really solid guys who can't wait to get started on Operation Emma. That's what they're calling it."

He provided names and descriptions of the men who would tail us and of the overnight team positioned a half block from the house beginning tomorrow night.

I wondered if we might not be overreacting, then remembered the thug Harry wrestled to the ground outside our front door.

As if reading my mind, Justin said, "I know having this many people involved is overwhelming, but…"

"But nothing," I interrupted. "When it comes to keeping Emma safe, the more the merrier."

We decided to celebrate with more of Justin's pricey bourbon. The guys were pouring their second drink when his phone rang.

"Probably about the job in Boston next week," he said and stepped into the hallway.

Harry took the time to ask a few questions about Aunt Rita. I was in the middle of trying to explain how she became a widow when Justin returned.

He ran his fingers through his already disheveled hair—his trademark tell for whenever he was worried.

"That was Mike."

"Oh, my God! What's happened?" I stood and rushed to him.

"It's okay, Grace. Everybody's fine. Well, I guess not everybody. Mike called on his way home to see if the girls needed more wine. Apparently, they had more than enough to catch some poor guy peeking into your mom's back window. Rita spotted him. The two of them came up with the plan for them to go out the front. They sneaked up behind him and pepper sprayed him to the ground, then cracked him on the noggin with a flashlight. Next, they duct taped the peeper to one of the steel posts in the basement. He's there now in his underwear with a seed bag over his head."

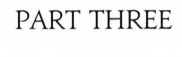

PART THREE

CHAPTER 18: NATALIE

Over three years passed between Mom's stroke and my descent into Stalkerville. The days and weeks and months reminded me of the time Dylan and I did magic mushrooms at the park.

Some moments froze with the sharp clarity of an icicle before it puddles at your feet. Mom's face when she learned to tie her shoes, my hand in hers on the elevator up to her doctor's office. Others drifted in and out of a thick, dark haze. Sitting outside her room, listening for the shuffle of her slippers or the closing of her closet door. Staring at nothing, waiting for my life to begin.

I didn't wake up on a specific morning, no longer afraid this would be the day my mother sank back into herself again or I lost her forever. The fear subsided along the way in tiny pieces until it became small enough to stick in a drawer instead of it stuffing me into one.

I relaxed, and that was my first mistake. My second was assuming there would be no harm in returning to my search for the truth about my sisters.

As with most self-destructive tendencies, mine began with a simple premise. I discovered as much as possible about Grace's trip to Ecuador—very little since she refused to talk with reporters, which meant they had to rely on secondary, anonymous sources. So, I determined the next logical step would be to meet the woman. But the idea terrified me because, from the little I had been able to find out, it appeared my sister was some kind of superhero.

I should have cut myself some slack. I mean, seriously. In less than a year, my mother had a stroke, and I discovered my father had a second family, complete with two daughters, my sisters only minus one now. Combined with the knowledge my remaining sibling was practically a goddess—of revenge or justice I had yet to discover—all that crap would have been overwhelming for a normal person. It paralyzed me.

I went on autopilot: I worked, knocked out the rest of my core courses in a mini-semester, and watched Mom. And I still had time to fantasize about meeting Grace.

In my favorite, I simply show up at her door.

"I'm sorry to bother you," I say shyly.

But I never get any further because she recognizes me and rushes forward to embrace me. Too overcome to speak, we stand together, tears streaming down our faces.

In another, slightly more melodramatic version of sisterly reunion, I pretend to be a potential client and set up a meeting in a coffeehouse. I enter and Grace leaps to her feet.

"I always knew something was missing in my life," she exclaims, closing the distance between us in mere seconds.

We huddle together in the middle of the café while customers smile and nod their approval. Once again, lots of tears are involved. No matter how hard I tried, though, my mind refused to create follow-up, after-revelation scenes.

I recognized my attempts to claim a place in Grace's life as what they were: pathetic make-believe from the outside sister. So, I fixated on "if onlys." If only I'd known about Stella and Grace when we were younger, things would have been different. After all, if changing one tiny detail in the fabric of time had the power to reroute the course of history, wasn't it likely knowing about me would have drastically altered the story of the Burnette sisters? If only I'd been there for Stella, maybe she would have never gone away at all and would still be here.

I even considered bypassing Grace and introducing myself to her mother. Since we shared no blood ties, I doubted learning about me would be a big deal. Regardless of how many hours I spent cyber-stalking the house on Google maps, I couldn't picture myself strolling up her walkway.

Eventually, I decided inserting myself into the Burnette clan now might not be such a great idea. At an earlier point, I would have been surprise sister number three. Possibly, they would have welcomed me into their family or rejected me completely. Either way, it wouldn't have seemed as if I were trying to slip into Stella's place, like some lame bench-warmer, taking advantage of a star player's fatal injury. The substitute sister, who was only a painful reminder of the enormity of the family's loss.

I accepted it would be better for everyone if I backed away from my obsession, let the Burnettes go. But the problem with obsessions is they don't give a shit about anything but themselves. And neither did I.

I referred to my research notes and came across Graceful Solutions, the site of my sister's freelance advertising business. I called the number, planning to disguise myself as a potential client. But when she answered, I panicked and hung up.

After weeks of inaction, I revisited the website and scrolled through the list of clients until I saw Cara's Sweet Caress, a fancy lingerie shop, promising "support and sensuality" for well-endowed women. Since I'd never been considered endowed at all, I skimmed over most of the content written for Cara Frazier's customers and almost missed the announcement for the grand opening of a second store in Woodstock, Georgia, wherever the hell that was.

The event was scheduled for tomorrow, with Graceful Solutions coordinating it. I had nothing on my agenda for that

Saturday or any others. Map Quest told me Woodstock was only about an hour and forty-five minutes from my house. I pictured myself hidden by a rack of generously proportioned camisoles, catching a close-up look at my sister. Clueless about what I would do after seeing her, I thought, screw it, then made plans to leave early the next day, telling Mom I was going to a nearby outlet mall.

I was so ridiculously excited it took forever for me to fall asleep. Every time I closed my eyes, I saw Grace's face. Eventually, I fell into the half sleep world, where I couldn't distinguish between dreaming about being awake or really being awake, wishing for sleep. Either way, I was exhausted when the alarm went off at seven.

Even though the open house didn't start until eleven, I hit the road by eight. The weather forecast warned of approaching storms, but they held off until I arrived at the outskirts of downtown Woodstock a little after nine thirty. The town was smaller than I expected, with railroad tracks running through its center. A strange conglomeration of old buildings with antique shops and tearooms and big fancy loft condos over trendy, new shops, the little city was like some mad scientist mixed antebellum South with a healthy dose of new South, and the whole thing exploded. I liked it.

After parking in an empty church lot, I ate the biscuit I bought from a drive through fast- food joint. The sign said they were as good as momma used to make, but I got it anyway. By now the rain was coming down pretty hard, so I sat in the car trying to come up with a way to approach my sister without totally scaring the shit out of her. At five minutes before eleven, the downpour had lightened to a drizzle. I wound my ponytail into a bun, put on a light-weight navy windbreaker with a hood, and slipped on square sunglasses. I caught my reflection in the window and hoped no one would call Homeland Security.

The green awning above Cara's Sweet Caress was identical to neighboring shops, but she had painted the trim work a pale pink. Below the overhang in the same pastel shade, the store name was printed in lacy letters. The door stood open, probably to accommodate customer overflow.

I stepped inside and was immediately engulfed by two pairs of ginormous boobs. The accompanying women were sturdy, but they carried the bulk of their weight in their chests. If either one of them had committed a crime, I would have been unable to give a description to the police artist because of those aggressive bosoms. For the first time, being a 34 barely B didn't seem so bad.

When I wriggled out from between those massive breasts, my hood came off and my sunglasses slid halfway down my nose. I straightened them and looked for a good spot to survey the group of frenetic shoppers.

"You are going to love the way this fits," one buxom lady exclaimed to her equally chesty companion. "Those girls will be standing at attention in no time."

I envisioned the prow of a ship but kept my thoughts to myself while I scanned the crowd. From my vantage point, I could see approaching customers as they passed between the headless lingerie-wearing torsos in the display window. And then I saw her. Her hair was shorter than in her online pictures and lighter, and she was thinner. But she was definitely Grace.

I moved too quickly to take in much of what she wore, a pale green blouse, tucked into slim leg jeans. Snatching a handful of bras from the nearest rack, I ducked into the fitting room before the attendant saw me. Above the din of enthusiastic women, I heard the salesperson who promised her customer military precision boobs call out my sister's name.

The number and physicality of the customers made the shop seem larger than its actual size, which is why it surprised me how fast the two reached the register just outside the dressing room.

"Wow, Cara. This turnout is better than we hoped for."

Her voice was softer than I expected and deeper. I could imagine its soothing effect on a child who had fallen from a bike. Or a woman who had taken a frightening leap of faith. I wanted her to say more, but the store owner launched into an account of how wonderful the campaign had been and of how she couldn't have done it without my sister.

Another customer interrupted the tribute. Grace must have slipped away because I never heard her speak again. When I worked up the courage to exit the dressing room, she was gone.

.   .   .   .   .

On the drive home, I distracted myself by pretending to be a travel writer, a career I briefly considered after my geography project on Zimbabwe. I abandoned the dream when I learned about all the shots I would have to get before heading to exotic locations. As an adult, I sometimes thought about giving it a try. Now it wasn't needles I feared but the idea of relying on myself in a strange country when I could barely do so in a familiar one.

I paid close attention to the road signs, imagining I had been assigned the task of creating an itinerary for an Arabian warlord touring the South. Today, I would work on transforming his trek from Woodstock to Chattanooga into a magical journey full of insights into the American psyche.

As the head of a fighting tribal unit, my client might enjoy a trip to Kennesaw Mountain, the site of a bloody battle between Sherman's Union soldiers and Joe Johnson's Confederate troops. The same elementary school teacher who teared up recounting the South's temporary setback at Gettysburg oversaw the yearly staging of our school's version of the Battle of Kennesaw Mountain. Sensing my lack of interest in Southern mythology, she put me on the Yankee side to serve as cannon fodder. I got to lead the charge and die early while my fellow Yanks attacked and fell back until their final retreat to Atlanta.

My daddy explained around four thousand men died in the fight over real estate and the right to enslave other men. When I asked my teacher if she thought it was worth it, she told me the Yankees lost three times as many troops as the South, so, of course, it was.

Next stop would be at the Calhoun outlet malls because what goes better with bloodlust than running shoes? After meandering through cookware and leather goods, we'd head for Ruby Falls and Rock City. My first and only trip to the falls had been with my fourth-grade class. I must have been dozing on the day we learned the waterfall ran below ground. I hyperventilated in the elevator on the way down to the bowels of the earth and spent the rest of the trip breathing into a paper bag.

On second thought, we'd skip the water works and concentrate on rock formations.

While debating whether to end the tour on top of the big rock or take the sheik and his harem into Chattanooga, I almost passed my exit.

CHAPTER 19: NATALIE

Disgusted with my pathetic performance at the lingerie shop, I tried, once again, to convince myself to give it up.

I dated a guy in my lit class because his hair reminded me of a picture of a British Romantic poet in the textbook, but his idea of romance was fumbling around on the sofa while chilling with Netflix. I joined the forensic team but dropped out when I learned instead of looking at blood samples and dead bodies, we would be debating crap like Apathetic Youth, a redundancy, and An Overmedicated Society — duh.

I doubled-down at work and got promoted to an assistant something-or-other with no pay increase. At night, I read to Mom, who pretended to fall asleep before sneaking downstairs to watch TV. I cooked dinners and invited Char and Dwight. My aunt brought a casserole of her own on those occasions, and my uncle brought bourbon.

One Friday afternoon, I came across a documentary about Malala, the Pakistani girl shot by the Taliban for speaking out against their treatment of women. As the closing credits rolled, so did a suffocating sense of shame. I asked myself WWMD — What Would Malala Do — if she found out she had a sister who might or might not have known she existed.

The answer was obvious, and I was inspired. Not enough to take the plunge but enough to take some action, like sitting outside a stranger's house hoping to catch her walking the dog or playing with her dark-haired daughter. On my more motivated days, I drove to Grace's mother's, where a child blew bubbles and danced.

·   ·   ·   ·   ·

The problem with the slow stalk is you get both complacent and impatient. At first, pretending I was part of their life was enough. I imagined they were waiting for me to come through the door before starting dinner or unwrapping birthday presents. When I closed my eyes, I could see the child dimple up at the sight of me. If I listened hard, I heard her giggle and call out "Aunt Natty," in a clear, high voice. I began to believe I belonged in their world.

I didn't stop parking my car down the block or around the corner, but I worried less about someone noticing it or me.

When Grace saw me, I was surprised at the way her body stiffened. Her reaction irritated me, and I sped off thinking, "Come on. Can't you sense it's me, your own sister?"

My frustration made me cocky and a little angry. Why didn't she understand it was time for some sisterly bonding? Some shared activity, like going out for drinks or taking a yoga class or getting our nails done. I needed to do something with her, not observe her do stuff with other people. For inspiration, I followed her when she ran her weekend errands.

And that's how we ended up shopping together. Not exactly together but definitely in the same store. While she stood at the makeup counter, I passed close enough to see the hideous slash of red lipstick on her wrist.

"No, Grace, no. It's nasty," I thought. But when she jerked her head around in my direction, I wondered if I'd spoken the words and sprinted to the shoe department.

Then I bolted for a side exit and wove through the crowded mall and into the parking lot. About two-thirds of the way home,

I came down from my adrenaline high. Instead of the expected crash, though, a different energy took over. Like one of those crazy saints after receiving a sign from God, I had a renewed sense of purpose.

My sister might not know it yet, but we had a connection. Without seeing me, she had been aware I was close by, and the need to be near me overcame her. Once again, I screwed up what could have been our moment. If I hadn't run away, had faced her, we might be sitting together right now, sharing stories, laughing, crying.

"And I'm doing it again." I said and slapped my palm on the steering wheel. "Slipping into a sappy Hallmark movie, not living in the real world."

I asked myself what would Malala do or Sister Theresa or Joan of Arc. I nixed Joan because of the burning alive thing and rephrased the question.

"What should Natalie Burden do?"

For the first time in my life, I had an answer that didn't make me small. Natalie Burden would accept the sign she had been given. She would ensure Grace Burnette understood their connection. And she would make it stronger. And then she would stop talking about herself in third person because it made her sound like a lunatic.

.   .   .   .   .

An email from my college counselor delayed me from acting on my newfound resolve. Dr. Beth Eastman requested I contact her to discuss credits needed for graduation and for what I planned to do in the future. Her summons came as a double surprise as I hadn't thought about graduating and didn't know I had a counselor. As for the future, I couldn't imagine sharing my intention to aggressively pursue becoming a part of my sister's life.

I considered ignoring her and taking my chances on the personal sort-of-a-plan I'd been kind of following. I had checked off pre-requisites and wandered into an assortment of literature classes that would lead me to a degree in English—equal parts harmless and vague. If my math was right, I had enough credits to graduate next fall. Since I had taken the bare minimum of math courses, I decided a quick check-in with Dr. Beth wouldn't hurt. I was also curious about her ideas for my future.

The counseling department took up the entire third floor of the student union building. The set-up reminded me of the counselor Mom insisted I see after Dad deserted us. Instead of tables overflowing with children's books and wooden puzzles, the waiting room offered a variety of tattered magazines that looked like they were from the previous decade. My therapist had filled the walls with paintings of jungle scenes, featuring deceptively innocuous-looking lions and tigers. Neutral colors dominated this academic space, almost as if the designer had feared including anything that might agitate already over stimulated clientele.

The woman behind the cluttered desk in the middle of the room provided the only splash of color. Burgundy glasses perched on the end of her long thin nose and matched the merlot highlights in her short, curly hair. She wore a fuchsia sweater with a silk, floral scarf draped around her neck.

Whether it was the contrast between her flamboyant style and her somber expression or the flood of emotions from my previous therapy sessions, when she glanced up to ask how she could help me, I went blank. She repeated the question, louder and slower, as if she suspected I might have an impairment. Maybe a problem with hearing or a lack of intellectual capacity.

Fearful she might launch into a chorus of American Sign Language, I stammered my name and the reason for my visit with Dr. Eastman.

"Yes, of course." Her smile transformed her from stern schoolmarm to kindly grandma, and I exhaled. "She's expecting you. It's the third door on the right."

I knocked and a woman instructed me to come in. If not for the sign identifying the office as belonging to Dr. B. Eastman, I would have been certain I'd stepped into the wrong room. Behind a desk laden with computer, file folders, and stacks of paper, sat a woman who looked as out of place as I felt.

She had smoothed her dark, shiny hair into an updo, giving her the look of a starlet from a black and white movie. Long, sooty lashes framed her enormous chocolaty eyes. When she focused them on me, I moved forward without thinking.

"Natalie. Is it all right if I call you Natalie?" She didn't wait for an answer. I suspected she never had to because few people ever denied her requests. "Please, sit down." She pointed to a chintz armchair, where an oversized briefcase took up the entire seat. "Just toss it in the corner."

The bag, as she called it, was a rich brown leather with a tiny drawing of a horse-drawn carriage with the name Hermes etched below it. Obviously, not an object to be tossed anywhere. I cradled it in my arms before easing it onto the rug and leaning it on the leg of the coffee table.

"My ex-husband gave it to me. Like him, it's ridiculously expensive for no reason at all." Her smile revealed the whitest teeth I'd ever seen.

I wanted to ask if he'd given her those, too, but there was no need to piss off the woman holding the power over my plans for the future.

"I'm so glad we've finally gotten the chance to meet. I feel terrible I didn't follow up on my earlier emails asking you to come in."

Passive aggressive much, I thought, then wondered if I should tell her the truth—about how I often went for weeks without checking my email and deleted stuff without reading it or registering where it came from? Would that make me sound as crazy as referring to myself in third person? And why did I even care about Dr. E's opinion?

If she noticed my discomfort, she didn't let on. "But better late than never, right? Especially since it seems you've been doing perfectly fine on your own."

She slid a folder out from the stack on her desk and opened it. We spent the next half hour going over what she referred to as my extraordinary record. While I hadn't excelled in several of my core requirements, I had made up for it in my English courses. She shared praise from professors I had during the days of my mother's recovery.

I barely remembered them because of my involvement with getting Mom back to herself. According to my newly discovered counselor, I was some kind of idiot savant, delighting my teachers with insights that seemed obvious to me.

"And if you take another history course next semester, you'll graduate with a double major. I doubt if I could have come up with a better plan of action."

I considered explaining to her my path had been more one of inaction. I liked reading about kings and queens and beheadings. The Spanish Inquisition and the French Revolution had been a perfect match for my mood during those dark months of dread. So, I kept signing up for classes that explored the amorality of the human race.

Since it would have been unnecessarily cruel to burst the beautiful doctor's bubble, I let her ramble on with suggestions for my last semester and watched as she entered them into her computer. When she finished, she printed a copy of my schedule and beamed at me while I pretended to be delighted.

"I'm so glad you're pleased with our choices. But I have another reason for wanting to talk to you." She paused for dramatic effect, I assumed, and raised her perfect eyebrows.

When she didn't continue, it occurred to me she expected a verbal reaction.

"Another reason?" I injected as much enthusiasm as I could into the question. The truth was she had begun to get on my nerves with her unrelenting good humor.

"I've discussed your situation with the head of the English department, and she agrees you're an excellent candidate for an advanced degree. I'm sure we can find funding for you."

I expected more suspenseful silence, but she appeared too excited to pull it off.

"Here's a packet I prepared for you with all the information. The website for the application for admission and for financial assistance is in the pamphlet. I highlighted the section on our work-study program, which offers a substantial opportunity for earning while you pursue your masters and doctorate."

She held out the folder, and I stared at it for several seconds before taking it.

"Wow, this is a lot." I didn't have to fake my surprise.

"Yes, it is. You have until the middle of second semester to submit your application, and I'm available to go over everything with you anytime. This is a wonderful opportunity, Natalie. I hope you know you deserve it."

After assuring her I would look at the material right away, I thanked her and backed out of the office.

"This must be a mistake," I said to myself on the ride to the first floor. "Like there's another Natalie Burden."

As I walked to the car, I realized Dr. E's folder was quite thick. Her comment about how I deserved this opportunity came back to me. It was almost as if she had expected me to react this way. That was impossible because she didn't really know me at all. But what if she did? What if I was the right Natalie Burden and I deserved it?

I was tempted to read the packet before I headed to work but decided to wait for a better time and place to discover whether I might possibly be worthy of being a Burnette sister.

CHAPTER 20: NATALIE

I spent the next four hours slogging through files and following up on agent requests. When I finished my shift, I remembered nothing about them and hoped I hadn't clicked on *reply all* in response to the administrative assistant's snide comment about her boss. I planned to stop at the library to check out a possible opportunity of a lifetime but the bright red and green umbrellas outside the Chattanooga Brewing Company distracted me.

Like many Southern cities, the craft beer craze hit my hometown hard. At least twenty breweries opened in the space of a few years. CBC was one of my favorites because of its history. Founded in 1890, it grew into a six-story building that took over an entire city block. The brewery produced over 150,000 barrels of German beer a year. Prohibition put an end to the good times until almost a century later when two crafty guys brought it back to life.

Out front, couples of all ages filled most of the smaller tables, and a group of college-age kids claimed a long wooden table closer to the street. The combination of lovebirds leaning into each other to talk above the laughing and squealing coming from the boozy crowd didn't offer the ambiance I needed for quiet contemplation, so I walked inside.

Light from the floor-length windows captured the magic of that hour when the sun was fading but still bathed the room with its dying glow. I scanned the area and picked a table in the corner. A waitress, friendly but not intrusive, appeared before I settled in. She took my order for a giant pretzel and a pint of Hot Mama, a spicy little number brewed with habanero peppers fresh from the local farmer's market.

I wiped the already spotless tabletop. Then removed the folder from my bag and placed it in front of me. But I didn't touch it. Not because this wasn't the perfect spot for considering my future. Because seeing it lying there reminded me I had forgotten the most important part of the future: my sister.

But were the two mutually exclusive? Wouldn't I be a more useful and interesting addition to her family if I had a purpose in life?

My server interrupted my dilemma with a frosty mug of beer and the announcement my pretzel would be out in a minute. I sipped and waited for the combo of icy cold, followed by a slow burn. The heat started in my chest and meandered upward until my face warmed.

"How's Mama today?" My waitress set a steaming pretzel on the table.

Her question wasn't merely conversational. Each batch of Hot Mama was different, depending on the potency of the pepper.

I took a gulp of water and croaked, "I'll let you know when the flames die out."

She laughed and left me to my business. The business of not knowing what the hell I should do.

For a brief period after Dad departed, my mother and I operated as a team. Whenever there was a decision to make, like what costume I would wear on Halloween or where we should spend our vacation, we would use colored pens to create a chart of pros and cons. She always let me go first, adding to my list when I ran out of ideas. Then we used a five-star system and awarded each idea its own number of stars. Of course, we weren't bound to the results, and often we would ditch the outcome to do whatever we wanted.

Since I couldn't decide if the risk of introducing myself to Grace was worth it, I hoped the process might help. With my limited supplies, I would have to make do with a black pen and napkins. I laid them side by side, labeling one PRO, the other CON. I switched up the routine Mom and I followed. Instead of filling the one column before attacking the other, I decided to go point by point. For each individual Pro, I provided a related Con.

For the first positive outcome I listed "Not being an only child." I realized the negative aspect was the same, "Not being an only child."

Pen in hand, I considered my next item and came up with "I won't be lonely." Before I could get it down on paper, the table rattled. Beer sloshed onto the napkins and into my lap. I pushed back my chair and bumped into the man who had turned my chart into a sloppy mess.

"I'm so sorry. Here, let me help." He reached over me to pull more napkins from the holder and use them to soak up the liquid. Then he passed a handful to me. "I hope I didn't ruin your sweater."

His voice had a soothing quality, as if he frequently used it to calm children and horses.

"It's okay." I blotted the damp spot and looked up. A glimmer of sunlight haloed his face and blurred his features. I expected to hear the strains of Hallmark movie music that sound at the exact moment the heroine sees the man of her dreams. Instead, someone cranked up the house soundtrack and Chris Stapleton drizzled Tennessee whiskey over us.

"No, it isn't." He motioned to the waitress, held up my half-empty mug and the soggy pretzel, then two fingers.

"Seriously, you don't have to do that."

"I already did. Besides, I'm curious what kind of beer a beautiful woman like you drinks. Might I please sit here until the order comes? I assure you I will be more careful."

Despite the cheesy line, I appreciated he waited for me to nod permission before settling in, unlike some guys who can't imagine any female denying their requests. And when I got a good look at him, I liked what I saw. He wore his dark hair smoothed back from a broad forehead and high cheekbones, tapering into a strong chin, punctuated by a dimple. Thick lashes framed caramel-brown eyes flecked with gold. Rather than detracting from his looks, his crooked nose made him more human and somehow more attractive.

As if he'd read my mind, he said, "Please excuse the cringeworthy pickup line. I promise I am not a creep."

My past romantic experiences gave me doubts about the whole not being a creep thing. But maybe he would prove to be exactly what I needed. A pleasant distraction.

The waitress showed up with our drinks and pretzels. "Two Hot Mamas. Enjoy."

"If you say three hot mamas, I'm out of here."

"I'm crushed you think so little of me." He flashed another smile and another dimple appeared on his right cheek, then he picked up his mug. "To chance meetings and good beer."

I clinked my glass against his and took a healthy sip, watching his lips as he drank.

"Whew. That is one spicy mother."

"It's an acquired taste," I sputtered before taking a drink of water. "Once you get used to it, though, other beers pale in comparison."

"I have a feeling it's true for more than the beer."

I rolled my eyes and said, "You should try the pretzel." I broke off a piece and stuck it in my mouth, hoping eating it would give me time to come up with a snappy retort. It didn't.

"I'm Lorenzo Diez but only to my mother. Everyone else calls me Renzo."

The more I chewed, the bigger the chunk of pastry got, until I was forced to wash it down with more beer. The effect couldn't have been attractive. Instead of recoiling, he kept those incredible eyes laser-focused on mine.

"Okay, Renzo. I'm Natalie Burden."

"Nice to meet you. Wish it had been under drier circumstances." He pointed to my disintegrating napkin, now streaked with rivers of black ink. "May I help you recreate your list?"

"My what? Oh, it can wait. I wasn't accomplishing much anyway."

"So, Ms. Burden. Tell me all about yourself."

Inquiries about my personal history usually turned me off. But the high alcohol content in the drinks loosened me up. Not in a touchy-feely way, but enough to give him an abbreviated account of my life story. I included my parents' divorce without all the daddy-daughter angst and my mother's stroke minus my guilt for having caused it. I mentioned my upcoming graduation, omitting Dr. E's recommendation about an advanced degree.

He pressed for details, but I shifted the subject to him, confident he would leap at the chance to take over the narrative. His story was even shorter than mine. His parents immigrated from Bolivia before he was born. The family settled in San Diego, and he ended up studying engineering at MIT. An opportunity with a tech start-up brought him to Chattanooga and my table at the brewery.

We ordered more beer, abandoning our spicy brews for lagers. He insisted on buying dinner, and I accepted, as much because of hunger as fear of getting schnockered on an empty stomach.

Over Brew Burgers, he got a little looser himself. He elaborated on his history, telling me about growing up in a large family—two brothers and three sisters. Beer spurted out my nose when he told me about the awful things his siblings did to each other—glue on doorknobs, fake love notes, salt instead of sugar. I embellished my role as band manager and rebel without a cause. I stifled the urge to tell him about my secret-sister. The temptation to talk about Grace let me know I had hit my limit.

The city lights outside the window startled me into checking my watch. Four hours since I first sat down.

"How the hell did it get this late?"

Irritation gave the question a sharpness I didn't intend. Everybody knows chance encounters like ours ended in one of two ways. We headed to his place for a slumber party, or I called it quits and went home. Either way, the ultimate outcome would most likely be I'd never hear from him again. If I did, one or both of us would realize we weren't right for each other and pretend we'd be friends. It was up to me to say how I wanted to spend the rest of the night. Alone in my room or alone in his.

No big deal.

He signaled the waitress for the check, and I waited for a sign. One where he suggested we stop by his place or whispered how he hated for the evening to end.

Then I could brush his forearm with my fingertips, look regretful, and say something about having a busy day coming up or needing to help my mother. Or I could ease my foot out of my sandal and run my toes up his calf, consenting without saying a word.

But he ventured off script. "I didn't mean to monopolize so much of your time. Please, allow me to walk with you."

Okay, smoother than the average guy, yet still a guy.

My shoe caught on the uneven sidewalk. I turned the misstep into a stumble and leaned against him. He wrapped an arm around my waist and kept it there until we reached the car. Then he released me and stood there while I fished my keys out of my purse.

"You're sure you are good to drive?"

He had returned to his assigned dialogue and put me in control. All I needed to do was toss my hair and giggle. Or tell the truth and end things before they started. I chose door number two but didn't close it.

"I finished my last beer two hours ago and ate that giant burger. I'm fine." Braced for another round of doubts about my ability to drive, I assured him I was perfectly clear-headed.

Instead of going along with my scenario, he held out his phone. "Would it be too much if I asked for your number? I haven't had this good of a time in I can't remember how long, and I'd really like to see you again."

I could have gone with the popular option and given him a fake, but I tapped my real one into his cell and stepped back, eliminating both the possibility of his kissing me and the embarrassment if he didn't.

"All right, but I must insist on following you to be certain you make it home safely."

A nagging little voice reminded me this could be a serial killer move. I ignored it and gave him the address in case we got separated.

As soon as I drove onto the highway, thoughts of what I would say if he asked to come inside bombarded me. The obvious choice would be to use my mother as an excuse. That would mean admitting I didn't have my own place, wasn't one of the cool girls in on-campus apartments or even a wild sorority girl who could sneak him into my room.

I shook myself to clear my head. What the hell? The evening had ended. I just had to let him know. The moment of truth was coming.

The brilliant glow of our house brought me back to myself. I parked in the driveway and watched as he eased to the curb and cut his engine. I considered making a run for the front door but watching him saunter up the walk stopped me.

"Your outdoor lighting is most impressive," he said as we walked to the postage stamp-sized porch.

I laughed and all the weirdness about not wanting him to know about my living situation disappeared along with my anxiety about how to end something that hadn't really begun.

"What a nice way to put it. We weren't always the brightest bulbs in the box. Before her stroke, my mother was nuts about conserving energy. To her, wasting money on the excessive use of electricity was the eighth deadly sin." I paused to give him time to take in the show, enjoying how his dimples deepened when he smiled.

"I'm totally not kidding. She was obsessed. But as soon as she started getting better — you know, talking and dressing herself — she had me call a company that installed outdoor systems. They suggested we go with a less *impressive* plan, one designed for a smaller property. She wasn't having it. So, voila, welcome to the second city of lights."

"I enjoy people who do it up big. They are more fun." His voice held no hint of mockery, so I broke my rule about oversharing.

"Most nights, like tonight, she leaves every light in the house on, including a unicorn night light my aunt gave me on my eleventh birthday. I'm pretty sure astronauts can spot the blaze from the moon."

I didn't share my fear her insistence on turning our home into a perpetual light show was connected to her illness. And that I'd been concerned enough to mention it to Aunt Char, who offered an explanation.

"If you'd grown up with our daddy, you would understand why the woman became a blackout artist. We called him the Electricity Nazi."

My aunt explained Mom had followed in his poorly lit footsteps. After the brain explosion, her interest in lowering the power bills disappeared along with her ability to add numbers in her head and to remember the names of characters from her favorite HGTV renovation shows.

"There's an almost logical reason, I guess. When I was little, she followed me around the house, shutting off the lights. Now, I do it for her."

"She's lucky to have you." Standing so close to him, I began to doubt who was really in charge. The script I had counted on to guide me had been rewritten, and all my lines had been changed.

"And I am lucky to have met you, Natalie Burden." He lifted my hand to his lips and said, "I will call you."

A cold lump of frustration formed in my chest at the insult of not being given the opportunity to reject his kiss. I unlocked the door without replying. Before shutting it, I risked a last glance and was surprised he was at the end of the walk, watching me back. He waved, but I pretended not to see. When I peeked out the window, he was still there and didn't move for at least five or ten seconds.

My icy irritation melted as I realized he had passed a test I hadn't meant to administer. Renzo waited until I was inside before going. Did that mean he cared about my safety or—as Aunt Char would say—his mother had raised him right? Whichever it was improved his standing as a potential short-term boyfriend.

I remembered my first date with poor Dylan and how he had remained at the end of the drive long after I entered my house. Later, I suspected he had been too stoned to remember where he was going, but at the time I took it as an omen of good things to come.

And look how that turned out.

CHAPTER 21: NATALIE

Despite the unnatural brightness both outside and inside my home, Renzo clouded my judgment with his open charm and overall hotness. Instead of a pleasant distraction, I feared he could become an obsession. I doubted he would call, but if he did, I most definitely would not see him. Hell, I wouldn't even answer.

As I made my way through the house flipping switches, my fear Mom's behavior meant she was morphing into a different person, one I might not recognize, returned. It came to me her inability to illuminate the black places in her mind drove her to seek well-lit spaces with no shadowy corners where monsters lurked.

After restoring an acceptable level of murkiness, I peeked into Mom's room to watch for the rhythmic rise and fall of her blankets. Satisfied she was okay, I washed my face, brushed my teeth, and pulled my comforter over my shoulders. When my phone rang, I picked up automatically.

"I hope you weren't asleep."

"No, I'm awake and tucked in bed safe and sound."

As safe and sound as a woman could be when it came to a man like Renzo Diez.

· · · · ·

I peeked through the rectangular classroom window, waiting for the professor to turn and scribble on the seriously old-school chalkboard. After talking with Renzo for over an hour, I overslept and was late for British Victorian Lit. I had a solid A, and there was no attendance policy, but I didn't want to let my seriously old-school teacher down.

Today, as with most days, the man looked as if he'd stepped out of a mid-19th century British fashion catalogue. He favored fitted vests with a chain for his pocket watch, and although I never saw him wear one, I had no trouble imagining him in a tall black top hat.

Whenever I heard my classmates snickering behind his back or bragging about not reading any of the assignments and still getting C's, I ignored them and kept my inner nerd safely hidden.

The truth was I was a sucker for everything Victorian. My heart beat faster when I read the Brownings's love poetry. I cried over Hardy's Tess and considered *Far from the Madding Crowd*, where the heroine is courted by three men, an early version of *The Bachelorette*.

I got the teacher's jokes. Sadly, I was the only one who did. Leaving him alone with my cold-hearted peers seemed excessively cruel, which is why I stood there, out of breath with no make-up, ten minutes late.

As soon as he picked up the chalk, I eased the door open and darted to an empty seat in the back row. When he faced the class, I gave him an encouraging smile and wondered if he even knew my name.

This morning, it didn't much matter if he'd been thrilled to see me or had no clue I was there. Because for the next eighty minutes, I could have been anywhere at all. While the rest of the students took notes on the hypocrisy of the Victorians, I worked on resisting the temptation to become the heroine of my own modern romance.

My experiences with relationships, both my own and those closest to me, had been dysfunctional. The boy who pretended to be a poet, my parents, Dylan—none provided any guidance in the Lorenzo Diez department.

Don't forget: this is only an attraction.

For emphasis, I wrote it down ten times in my notebook: *Only an attraction.* I used my best penmanship, wishing I had ink and quill handy.

Ten times wasn't enough to dampen my enthusiasm, so I reminded myself of how things had turned out with all the others. Either I would screw it up, or he would come to his senses and head for the open road. The only thing that made sense was to get out before I got in deeper.

I scratched through my previous work and focused on the Brownings.

How he loves me. Hell, I didn't even know if he liked me.

What an idiot. I marked out that line as well.

Then I remembered something Aunt Char said to me when I first started dating Dylan.

"You're driving your mother crazy with this boy. I told her to ease off, that at least going out with bad boys to stick it to your parents is normal. Because, honey, what you've seen with your mom and dad? That's about as far from the norm as there is. Me and your uncle have the kind of relationship you can count on. He may forget to bring me flowers or wine and dine me, but he still floats my boat. And some day you'll have your own Dwight to love. So, go have fun with Dylan. But for God's sake, be careful. You know what I mean, right?"

She kept talking, but her reference to boat floating and my sex life sent me into a fugue state. Later, I sneered to myself at the thought of wanting my own Dwight. After Mom's stroke, I began to see my aunt and uncle in a different light. What I had taken for weakness in the man had been his way of making the woman he loved happy. He had nothing to prove to anyone but her. And she loved him too much to care.

Victorians wouldn't have been impressed, but I was.

·　　·　　·　　·　　·

After four hours of mind-numbing logging of call requests on spreadsheets, I surprised Mom by coming straight home to make ham and cheese sandwiches. And she shocked me by asking how last night's date had gone.

"Date?" I responded in the same guilty squeak I had when she caught me crawling through the window after curfew. "I didn't have a date. I stayed late at the library and picked up a sandwich from Publix."

Where did that come from? I had no reason to keep Renzo a secret. Hell, there was about a fifty-fifty chance she wouldn't remember if I told her the truth. But telling her would make it real. And her memory had improved enough to hit me with a series of follow-up questions. If she applied the right amount of pressure, I might crack and admit I was attracted to him and, later, to explain why things hadn't worked out between us.

"I must have forgotten how long the grocery stays open." Instead of the childlike voice I'd gotten used to during her recovery, her tone had an edge of clarity. And her eyes were clear, with no trace of brain fog.

For a moment, I held my breath, waiting for one of her pre-stroke cross-examinations, but she smiled and returned to her lunch.

At her insistence, I left her to clean up and escaped to my room where I staged an intervention with myself. Standing in front of the mirror, I gazed sternly at my image.

"Snap out of it," I commanded. "You are almost twenty-three years old. Just because a good-looking—okay, gorgeous—guy pays a little attention to you doesn't mean you have to turn into a middle school girl with a crush. You have more important things to do, so do them."

I took my own advice and remembered the resolution I made before Dr. E. declared me a genius. The part about accepting my role as savior of sisterly stuff. All I had to do was behave the way a grown-up would. Not as easy as it sounded. Somehow, I got stuck in an adolescent state. Although taking care of my mother had given me a more mature outlook, I still thought and reacted like a surly, insecure teenager. From fixating on the Burnettes to doubting my potential, I stayed trapped in a prison that was more high school detention than Alcatraz but seemed just as repressive.

The discovery of my sisters should have been a vindication for all those times I had the feeling something was missing in my life. If I only knew what it was, I wouldn't be so out of step with the rest of the world. Most people would laugh at missing what you never knew existed, but not me.

About a year after Dad hit the road, I came up with a complicated theory about alternate timelines. If I experienced a catastrophe—such as, failing a geometry test or having my daddy leave for work and never return—I'd go back to a day or two before the disastrous event and make a list of every decision I made, no matter how seemingly insignificant. Then I would circle the important ones and create a series of events with all the different possible outcomes, all the "if onlys."

Some were logical. If only I had studied for the geometry test instead of watching TV, I might have scored higher. Others depended less on logic and more on wishful thinking. If I'd told my dad I loved him on the morning of his permanent departure, maybe he would have come home for dinner.

I taped all the different scenarios on my wall and spent hours lying on my bed getting lost in those winding roads not taken. The upside of my obsessive fantasies was they drove my mother nuts. That was when she took me to see my first therapist, Dr. Wilde.

Mom ambushed me one day after school under the pretense of shopping for winter clothes. In fairness, we did visit a few stores where she softened me up with trendy outfits she usually refused to buy. Then she said there was a doctor she wanted me to talk to.

"But I'm not sick," I protested.

"Dr. Wilde's not that kind of doctor. He's more about healthy minds than bodies." She kept her eyes on the road as I grew more wary.

"There's nothing wrong with my mind." I fought to keep panic from bubbling to the surface.

"Of course there isn't." She spoke as if she were trying to get a toddler to put on pants. "He just wants to have a little chat." She turned into an office park filled with brick buildings.

"What about what I want? I don't have anything to say. And didn't you tell me I wasn't supposed to talk to strangers?"

She ignored my logical response and dragged me into the vanilla-flavored room. Bright coral shelves were overloaded with books, toys, stuffed animals, puzzles, and games. An almost life-sized giraffe grinned down at me, daring me not to be cheerful.

Even now, I could draw his reception area from memory. But I can't remember much about Dr. Wilde, only his name didn't fit him. He was mild mannered with fluffy white hair and glasses that made his eyes blurry from the outside looking in. I imagine he was used to dealing with reluctant patients, except I was more like a prisoner on probation forced to get help or go back to jail.

The first visit, I sat silent with my arms wrapped across my chest and what I intended to be a bored look on my face. I answered yes or no questions with shrugs and nods, desperate for the hour to end.

I had to hand it to Dr. Not-So-Wild; he hung in there. After the third or fourth excruciating session, I decided to spice things up. Instead of keeping quiet, I would give him what he wanted: deep, dark secrets and desires. At twelve, my desires were pretty tame, so I went all in on the secrets.

I started small, like rewriting the scene when Dad told me he loved me before he left us and graduated to stories of sleep walking and waking up in the neighbor's treehouse. I invented tales of voices in my head urging me to steal pencils from my classmates. And when he asked me if I blamed myself for my father's departure, I assured him I never thought about it all— the biggest lie of all.

I realized there was no way the man believed my tales, but he never called me out. He listened, occasionally probing for details, most likely sifting through those lies in search of the truth hidden behind them.

Then one day, Mom told me we were taking a break from therapy. I should have been relieved but was a little disappointed. I even missed the doctor and wondered if he ever thought of me. The second man in my life to leave me without saying a proper goodbye.

I wasn't about to set myself up for a third.

But I couldn't quite make myself delete Renzo from my phone. So, I got out my calendar and made a schedule for contacting Grace. Tomorrow, I would drive to Atlanta and return to my career as a stalker, just long enough to detect a pattern in her activities. Then I would pick a place and time to establish contact. If she seemed to sense our connection, I would tell her who I was.

Although I was aware my plan sucked, was hardly a plan at all, it was better than nothing. And I would have stuck to it if not for the phone call from Renzo.

CHAPTER 22: NATALIE

"I really appreciate this. My coworkers think I'm some West coast hotshot who doesn't know his ankle from his elbow when it comes to the South."

"Ass," I corrected, then laughed at his puzzled look. "It's doesn't know his *ass* from his elbow, and I'm afraid they may be on to something."

"See how much I need you?" He grinned and kept his eyes on the road, leaving me to wonder if I only imagined the possibilities behind his choice of words.

His ability to speak in a language of emotional ambiguity was the reason I postponed my Atlanta trip.

When Renzo's name popped up on caller ID minutes after I slipped under the covers, I steeled myself to hit ignore. More aluminum than steel, since I answered after the second ring.

"Once again, I hope I am not calling too late. My work here is more challenging than I expected."

"I was just climbing into bed." Shit. Did that sound like a lame attempt at a sex kitten invitation? And did I mean for it to? I cleared my throat and added in my best let's-get-down-to business voice, "I meant I was getting ready to finish the chapter for U.S. history on how the Vietnam War influenced modern policy making."

Nothing sexier than Lyndon Johnson and his lies to the American people.

"I promise I won't keep you too long from such an interesting topic. I have a request to make of you. Of course, you are under no obligation to accept."

Despite the warmth his words brought, I snuggled deeper into my comforter. "I'm not the kind of person who feels obligated easily. What is it you want me to do?" I imitated his polite, formal tone to hide my growing interest in what his needs might be and how he might take care of some of mine.

Instead of an invitation to explore the area of our mutual needs, he requested a crash course in Chattanooga Southern. He wanted to delve into what made it special to the people who lived there. I accepted and suggested we meet at the Chattanooga Choo Choo for coffee. He insisted on picking me up. I prefer taking my car when meeting dates although I wasn't sure being a tour guide qualified as a date. But sitting beside him in the passenger seat would give me the perfect opportunity to observe him in a controlled environment. It also gave me the chance to watch the way his hands held the steering wheel — not viselike, but firm and gentle — and marvel at the length of his thick lashes and the strength of his jawline.

"Turn here." I pointed toward a side street several blocks from the hotel.

"But isn't there an onsite lot?"

"Yes, but it's too pricey. First lesson in basic Southern. Only Yankees pay for parking."

"Technically, I'm not a Yankee. I'm — "

"Doesn't matter. Right there. There's still an hour left on the meter."

We walked the short distance to the front of Terminal Station, a monument to the days when railroad was king, and Chattanooga was her queen. From the outside, the brick building stands tall in the center. The adjoining rectangular structures spread like a Southern belle's hooped skirt, trimmed with decorative arched windows. Another window made of glass and metal crowned the awning covering the entranceway. A little train engine embossed with the words Choo Choo greets people coming from the side.

Neither the majestic nor the tacky prepared visitors for what lay inside.

Renzo stepped through the door and stopped. "Wow," he said, looking up to the sunlight streaming through the domed ceiling. The shimmering light transformed him into the guy on the cover of a romance novel. One where the hot Latin lover tenderly seduces the shy American girl.

"This is incredible." He stood in the middle of what had once been a bustling transportation center and made a three-hundred-and-sixty-degree turn. "The detail on the metalwork is amazing. And this lobby is something from a movie."

Management had gone all out with upholstered furniture arranged in intimate seating areas. Today, a mother of four was wiping ice cream remnants off the kids' faces as they wriggled on a red settee.

"We Chattanoogans love fancy train stations." I tugged on his sleeve and guided him to the coffee bar where I ordered a vanilla cappuccino, and he asked for an espresso that looked like thick, dark mud. I picked up a glossy pamphlet explaining what the place offered.

"If we drink while we walk, we'll have time to check out the gardens."

We wound our way along shrubbery-lined sidewalks where roses bloomed and pansies encircled a little fishpond with a statue of a girl in the middle, her arms extended in joy.

Renzo paused at a sign with Glenn Miller's name on it.

"He came from Chattanooga?"

"No. But he put us on the hit parade when he recorded 'Chattanooga Choo Choo.'"

"You mean a song?"

"Don't tell me you haven't heard it." I sang a line. "Pardon me boy, is that the Chattanooga Choo Choo?"

His face scrunched into an expression of confusion or pain, and I laughed.

"Sorry, but it's a part of Southern culture."

"Quite catchy. Please, sing more."

I stepped in front of him and gave him my most serious look. "I don't think you're being sincere."

"But I am."

"Good because if you were making fun of my heritage, things could get ugly. And speaking of ugly, here's the rest of the song."

I surprised him and myself by belting out all five stanzas while improvising a modest tap dance. By the time we got to the car, he had picked up the tune and most of the lyrics and was singing along as I directed him to Bluff View, a historic bed and breakfast where barges churn up the water of the Tennessee River.

"Sometimes, I close my eyes and imagine canoes sending quiet ripples across it. The inn was built in the early 1800s. They renovated it and turned it commercial about the same time somebody decided Chattanooga should get into the tourist market competition. It's got a fantastic view of the river."

We wandered through the sculpture garden where metal herons peeked from rosy-pink flowers, and a naked youth made of stone forever reaches for a swinging branch and the rushing water below.

I ordered ribs for him at Sugar's, where we sat on the patio overlooking the freeway and the mountains behind it.

"I've never tasted anything like this," Renzo moaned as he pushed away from the table.

"Did you leave room for pie?" The waitress smiled at him and looked genuinely disappointed when he patted his stomach and shook his head.

On the road, I said, "We'll be doing a little backtracking, but I saved the best for last."

We didn't say much on the fifteen-minute ride to one of my favorite places in the world. I hadn't planned to share my feel-good place with him, had intended to go home after our late lunch. Instead, we were headed to Reflection Riding.

"Turn here." The narrow gravel road was lined with stately mansions, out of time and place. It had never seemed fair to me people who could afford to live in luxury should get to plop down their big houses in peaceful, unspoiled spots like this. It was like having hookers show up at your grandmother's funeral. No matter how well dressed they were, they just didn't belong.

"These homes remind me of California. Not the style, but the way the people who build them want to compete with nature. They are, of course, most beautiful, but nature always wins," Renzo said.

I gave him a halfway smile before looking away, fearful he might see how pleased I was with his comment and how much it made me like him.

· · · · ·

"Thank you for sharing your lovely city with me. Other than getting to spend time with you, our last stop was my favorite. It was a magical maze with each turn revealing a different enchantment."

I flushed with unwanted warmth and told myself it was only a physical reaction. But what would have sounded phony coming from anyone else rang with sincerity when he said it. And he was right about the magic part.

We spent over an hour and a half wandering the grounds. The horses on the hill stirred up clouds of dust as they pirouetted around each other while we sat at a pond encircled by wildflowers. I plucked a few and tossed them onto the surface, silently sending a prayer for Stella. When we got tired, we took off our shoes and sat on the riverbank, dangling our toes in the icy water. If the volunteers at the wildlife sanctuary hadn't warned us the park would close soon, there's no telling how long we would have stared at the feisty red fox grinning as he rolled in the dirt, scratching his back. Or at the wolf who lowered his muzzle and focused his glowing yellow eyes on us.

As we pulled onto the main road, I surprised myself again by suggesting we make one more stop.

"Your crash course in Southern stuff wouldn't be complete without a sunset from the patio of the Boat House. But you better step on it."

"Step on what?"

"Go fast, you know, step on it. What part of California are you from?"

He hesitated, then answered, "Northern, of course."

Our Lawton margaritas, complete with fresh lime and slivered ice, arrived minutes before the show began. Named after Lawton Haywood, the owner, they went down way too smooth, and I warned him to sip slowly.

The sky darkened as gray clouds hovered over an explosion of orange and lemon light. A pinkish coral created a rippling border. The still water reflected a mirror image of the display. Then the sun slipped below the line between the river and the sky, and it was all over.

For a moment, I felt as faded as the day and wished we hadn't ordered food, so I could go home. When the waitress brought the queso and chips, I rallied. I offered to share with Renzo, but he was all about the oysters and insisted I try one.

"They're too slimy for me." I shuddered at the thought of swallowing one of the wet blobs.

"You don't know what you're missing." He doused one in cocktail sauce, put the shell to his mouth, and slurped.

"Yuck." Normally, I would have been grossed out, but he ate with such obvious pleasure I enjoyed watching. If he attacked everything with as much gusto as he did those slippery little mollusks, I could only imagine what it would be to have such enthusiastic attention focused on me.

An alcohol insight told me it wasn't a good idea to speculate on something I had no time for. But the margarita buzz urged me to relax and enjoy myself.

CHAPTER 23: NATALIE

If I were the type of girl who kept a diary, my entry for my day with Renzo would have gone something like this.

Dear Diary,

When we were laughing at the three-legged possum eating an apple, Renzo's hand brushed against mine and lingered for several seconds. I wonder if he felt the way I did, as if our hands were meant to cling together. I wonder if the possum misses the leg.

And as we were walking past the aviary trying to spot the resident owl and I stumbled, he wrapped his arm around my waist when it would have been just as easy to hold my elbow. So why, at the end of the evening when he walked me to my door, why didn't he kiss me?

But I'm not the kind of girl who keeps a diary. I never even thought about recording my stupid feelings in some dumb little journal where they would come back to mock me.

When I woke up the morning after sharing my most favorite place in the world with a man who had no interest in me, my head ached from being over-served. I didn't want to get up to take an aspirin because that would signal the start of the long, empty weekend ahead of me. On a branch outside my window, a very loud robin chirped out what I took as a happy bird song, and I wanted to fling my tennis shoe at him.

The temperature in my room signaled Mom was awake and had upped the setting on the air conditioning. Since the stroke, her personal temperature regulator got all wonky, and she ran cold most of the time. My tangled sheets were sweaty and scratched against my thighs.

"Son of a bitch," I grumbled at the universe. "You win. I'm getting out of bed."

I snuck into the hall and adjusted the thermostat to seventy-two. In the bathroom, I swallowed three aspirins before hopping into the shower. Our water heater was a temperamental asshole that took forever to warm up. Today, I didn't mind waiting under the cool spray.

After working shampoo into my matted hair, I replayed the highlights of my day with Renzo, wondering if I had misread the sexy signals that would have been recorded in my diary if I kept one. Was it only me who experienced a little zap of electricity when our fingers touched? Or felt his reluctance to let go of me when he stopped me from falling?

Whatever. He had been a perfect choir boy, and I had no use for that kind of perfection. Unless he didn't want to take advantage of my margarita haze, which meant he was a genuinely nice human being.

Dammit. If I hadn't gotten so buzzed, Mr. Nice Guy might have turned into Mr. Right Guy or at least Mr. Right Now. I rinsed out conditioner, stepped out of the shower, and wrapped a towel around me. I shivered while readjusting the temp, then dressed, dried my hair, and stumbled downstairs for breakfast.

There was no welcoming bacon smell in the air and no Mom in the kitchen. From the window, I saw her kneeling beside a patch of marigolds. Her lips moved as she plucked and pulled, and I imagined her singing "You Are My Sunshine," the way she did when I was a kid.

Since she only sang the chorus, it was years before I heard the entire ballad and learned it was more about loss and less about happy. The melancholy tune matched my mood, and I was unreasonably irritated with my mother for misleading me with the song and for not cooking breakfast.

I grabbed a protein bar from the shelf and ripped it open. My mouth was full when the phone rang. Renzo. I swallowed hard before croaking out a garbled hello.

"Thought I should see how you're doing this morning."

A glob of chocolate and peanuts got stuck in my throat, and I took a long sip of water before responding.

"Not totally horrible, considering the margaritas I threw back." No reason to mention I had no freaking clue how many I had.

"It was impressive, as was your rendition of Taylor Swift singing 'I Did Something Bad.'"

I pretended to remember and was glad I didn't. "Sorry."

"Don't apologize. Your voice is memorable."

"Ha, ha. It's your fault for plying me with alcohol."

"I will accept the responsibility if you agree to join me for lunch. We will eat many carbs to soak up the tequila."

I knew it was a terrible idea, especially after my moment of weakness in the shower. Yes, all that right guy garbage was a joke. But why couldn't we just have some fun? So, I accepted the invitation. He insisted on picking me up.

After popping a few antacids, I walked upstairs to change. Instead of spending time on selecting the perfect outfit, I grabbed a t-shirt and a pair of lightweight denim jeans. Okay, the top was a pale green off-the-shoulder number, and the pants emphasized my curves, but I couldn't be accused of trying too hard.

·   ·   ·   ·   ·

"I'm really glad you agreed to see me again."

Renzo glanced at his side mirror while I checked out his profile, resisting the urge to trace his lips with my fingertips. *Stop it!* I warned and blamed my amorous feelings on the alcohol still in my system.

"Me, too. But I can't be too sure until you tell me where we're going." When he picked me up, I expected him to ask for a restaurant recommendation, but he smiled and told me it was a surprise.

He drove downtown, past my favorite tea shop toward the county government building.

"You're not lost, are you?"

"This is the only part of your beautiful city I'm familiar with. And here we are." He pulled into a spot in front of the St. John's, one of Chattanooga's ritziest restaurants.

"Wow, you must have enjoyed my singing. This place is special-occasion pricey. When did they open for lunch?"

"Technically, they are not open. But the chef is an old friend of my family. He agreed to prepare a take over picnic for us."

"Could it be a *takeout* lunch?"

He laughed. "Yes, of course. Just when I think I've conquered your language, it sneaks up and splats me on the head."

"English can be a real mean head-splatter." I grinned, but the fat raindrops hitting the windshield distracted him.

"Oh, no. It looks as if the weather isn't going to cooperate."

"I'm sure we'll figure something out." His puzzled expression hinted *figuring out* hadn't been included in Business English 101. "I meant we can make a different plan, like finding another spot."

"Ahh, yes, an alternative location. Please don't take this the wrong way, but my apartment is around the corner."

"Well, my house is pretty far away, and the food would get cold, which would be a shame after all the trouble your friend went to making it especially for us."

"Indeed, it would be quite the tragedy. So, shall I go for it? The food, I mean."

"Excellent idea."

I offered to go inside with him, but he insisted I stay dry. A thick drizzle distorted my view of the historic building. I opened my window a few inches to get a clearer sight of the structure that had gone from respectable restaurant to hotel to seedy brothel before being saved from demolition by an architect with a vision. Like Chattanooga herself, the St. Johns had remade itself into a combination of vintage and modern.

Renzo stood under the awning, tapping on his cell phone. Within minutes, lights flickered inside the dining area. White tablecloths gleamed under low-hanging globes, bringing with them the memory of our family's onetime experience at the St. Johns.

It was on my ninth birthday. Thanks to a growth spurt, the shiny black Mary Janes I wore to Sunday school pinched my heels. While dangling them from the tips of my toes, the right shoe sprang loose and flung itself into an empty chair at the table next to us. Dad swore under his breath.

My feet weren't the only things expanding during the year. I sat with my arms wrapped around breast buds struggling against the fabric of the thin taffeta dress at least a full size too small for me.

"For God's sake, Natalie. Sit still." Mom picked up my napkin from the floor and jammed it onto my lap.

"What did you expect?" My father scowled at her. "Bringing a kid to a place like this."

Although his words gave the impression he sympathized with my situation, his tone offered no comfort.

The rest of the dinner blurs for me, but the ride home remains painfully clear. Scrunching tires as dad pulled off. Mom shouting, "Not in the car." The shocking collage of pink and red and burgundy spurting like a fountain as I vomited on the side of the road.

This has got to be better than that.

CHAPTER 24: NATALIE

Renzo exited the restaurant, carrying three oversized plastic bags. I leaned over the seat and opened the door behind the driver side.

"How many people are coming to the picnic? Looks like you have enough to feed a dozen."

He placed the containers on the floor and replied, "We didn't know what you liked, so my friend put something special together."

Within minutes, we pulled into a garage next to another one of Chattanooga's successful make-over stories, The Maclellan. According to an art major I went out with a few times, the blend of Roman and French styles made it an architectural wonder.

"You live here?" I asked on the ride to the top of the thirteen-story building.

"A family friend keeps a place here for when business brings him to the area. He offered it to me." The elevator stopped, and he waited for me to get off before guiding me to an apartment at the end of a long hallway. He ushered me inside.

As if on cue, the rain disappeared. Sunlight streamed through floor to ceiling windows and reflected off gleaming wood beneath my feet. In the distance, clouds hovered above Lookout Mountain, a vast expanse of shimmering green dotted with slate gray rock formations.

"Must be a really good friend." I slipped out of my wet shoes, walked toward the wall opposite the panoramic view of the city, and stopped to admire the three paintings hung there. At first, they were only a mix of vibrant colors refusing to be ignored or forgotten. I recognized the style from an exhibit at Hunter Art Gallery. Mom and my aunt took me to it a few weeks before her stroke.

"See here, honey." Char air-circled a section of the painting. "It's like Where's Waldo only instead of a goofy cartoon guy, you're looking for lady parts." I pretended to be disgusted when she pointed out long legs and bare bosoms and flowering vaginas. The truth was the images fascinated me then and now.

"Lovely, aren't they?" Renzo's voice pulled me out of my search for erotica.

"Incredible. They look like Cecily Browns. Surely, they're not originals."

"You have a very good eye. My landlord is quite the art connoisseur, so my guess is they are."

"Holy shit," I whispered, then covered my mouth.

He smiled. "I am certain both the owner and the artist would appreciate your comment for the high praise it is. Shall I open some wine?"

My stomach lurched at the mention of alcohol, and I asked for ice water. He filled a glass for me and one for him, then invited me to sit while he got lunch ready.

"You were most forceful about not caring for raw fish of any kind. My friend assured me you would love his cooked seafood. But I didn't want to take a chance, so there are land-based options as well. For starters, we have braised sea scallops, trout corn fritters, and heirloom tomato salad."

"This is unbelievable," I mumbled through a mouthful of crunchy fried deliciousness.

He warned me to pace myself for the main course: beef ribeye, Gulf royal red shrimp and sauteed vegetables. Tender enough to cut with a fork, the steak was amazing. The fat crustaceans mimicked lobster with their sweet aftertaste, and I polished off six of the bad boys before I pushed my plate away.

"I can honestly say this is the best picnic I've ever been to. Please tell the chef I ate myself stupid."

"I would never call you that. You are quite intelligent."

I laughed and explained the phrase. He promised he would pass on the praise.

"Did you save room for dessert? There's marshmallow devil cake and a peach inside out cake."

I sorted out his twisted labels—devil's food and upside down—before telling him I couldn't eat another bite.

"Maybe later, then. For now, I will make coffee for us to drink on the balcony."

We sat at a mosaic table tiled in vivid blues and greens of the ocean. I remembered taking care of my mother wasn't the only reason I stayed in my hometown. The combination of the mountains muted and vibrant shades of green against the brilliant blue of the sky made me weightless. It tempted me with the desire to spread my arms and take flight.

The breeze carried away all noises from the street below, and we enjoyed the silence. My city had cast its spell on me again, and I sensed it captured Renzo as well.

I sighed and said, "I forget how beautiful Chattanooga can be."

"The view is most certainly breathtaking. And the town is lovely, too."

His delivery saved the line from being as lame as it should have been. And it kept me from responding with a snarky comeback. What harm was there in accepting him at his word? Just because nobody had described me as breathtaking didn't mean I wasn't, right?

A gust of wind rattled my spoon against the cup before I delved deeper into my powers of attraction. I steadied it and noticed a few dark clouds reflected in my coffee.

"Perhaps we should go inside," Renzo suggested, as fat raindrops plopped onto the table.

He closed the door at the exact moment lightning split the darkening horizon.

"Looks as if our picnic is getting rained out." Thunder rumbled in the distance, and I moved farther from the window.

"I can draw the curtains."

"Storms don't bother me, but I'm glad we're not spread out on a blanket by the river." I blushed at the sudden image of us lying together, his breath warm against the back of my neck.

He sat on the sofa and rearranged the pillows with two on each end and another between us. Then he motioned for me to join him.

"When I was a boy, my mother had to drag me out of the rain. I loved the smell of the earth as it opened to the sky. The way the water poured over my body — sometimes gentle, other times demanding. She would try to frighten me with stories of unsuspecting children struck down by bolts from above. But I never understood how something so spectacularly beautiful could harm me."

I pictured him standing in the storm, only not as a boy. I saw a man with rivulets of rainwater trailing down his naked back, and I longed to trace their paths with my fingertips.

"Natalie, are you all right?" He scooted closer, concern on his face, and I realized he must have said something requiring a response.

"Sorry, I got lost in my thoughts." *And I didn't want to find my way out.* "What were you saying?"

"I asked if you would like a glass of wine. Then I remembered you weren't up for alcohol. How about more coffee?"

"You know what? My hangover disappeared somewhere between the appetizers and the main course. I would love some wine, whatever you have."

He stood and touched my shoulder before walking to the kitchen. Heat rose from the spot where his hand had been.

You barely know him. And there's no point getting attached. His type – all smooth and sophisticated – won't stick around, certainly not for a girl like you.

"I wasn't sure what you prefer, so I brought one of each. Sample both and choose. I'll take the other."

Our fingers touched as he passed the wine. I steadied my trembling hands before tasting it.

"This is perfect." It was so dry I fought to keep my lips from puckering, but I was afraid of what a second touch might bring.

"So, Miss Natalie Burden, tell me something about yourself. What is your passion?"

"My passion?" Just repeating the word sent a shiver through me.

"Yes. What brings you joy?"

No one, including myself, ever asked me that. I thought of the way Dylan's face changed when he played one of his excruciating songs. The scowl lines between his eyes smoothed, and his shoulders relaxed. He jerked along with the beat of those angry lyrics. Despite desperate attempts to fake indifference, he exuded a delirious happiness. He loved what he was doing and it made him loveable. Which is probably why I waited so long to break up with him.

Memories of how Mom looked the first time she managed complete sentences. And Uncle Dwight's expression whenever my aunt entered the room. And my hope Grace would reflect the same delight when we met. These were the things that filled me with warmth.

My passion was seeing other people's joy. Totally lame, so I deflected.

"Tough question. Why don't you go first? What is your passion?"

He circled the rim of the wine glass with his finger, then set it down and moved about an inch closer, setting off a gravitational pull in me. Without realizing it, I leaned into him.

"I would have to say my family brings me joy."

My stomach flipped. When he said family, did he mean parents and siblings, or was he including a wife and kids of his own? I wanted to ask but had no words.

"Sounds like sap, I know, but growing up surrounded by people who care for you gave me a sense of invulnerability. As if I am a member of a tribe and no matter what mistakes I make or goals I fail to accomplish, they will stand by me. And I will always do the same, even when it is most difficult." His upturned lips straightened into a thin, grim line.

"It's been me and Mom for a long time. My aunt and uncle signed on after Mom's stroke. My group is less tribe and more committee."

If Grace and her family accepted me, though, that could change.

"Whatever you call them, your people must be powerful to raise such a strong, beautiful woman. Now it is your turn to share your passion."

He traced my cheek with his index finger. Before he could remove it, I startled him by grabbing his wrist and moving his hand to my chest. It was so quiet I was sure he could hear the pounding of my heart. He pulled away.

"Please, Natalie, there is much you do not know about me."

I drew him closer and trailed kisses from his neck to his jawline.

"Shh." I nibbled on his earlobe. "Remember what you said? It's my turn to share my passion."

CHAPTER 25: NATALIE

My lit professor announced we must turn off our phones and remove them from our desks before he passed out our exams.

Despite my earlier vow not to, I checked to see if Renzo had sent a text in the ten minutes since I last looked. He hadn't, so I tucked my phone away and stared at the blue book lying face down in front of me.

Instead of studying for my midterm in Victorian literature, I spent most of Saturday after Renzo dropped me off and almost all of Sunday replaying our picnic.

A sense of power drove me into his arms. For the first time, I knew what I wanted and how to get it. Even when he guided me to his bed, I was in charge. But the gasp did me in. A quick intake of breath followed by an animal growl. The sound of lost control, and it came from deep within me.

"You may open your test booklet and begin." I bolted upright, startled back to reality.

When I broke the seal on my blue book—regardless of the scorn from his colleagues and frustration from students, my professor swore by pen and paper exams—I experienced another jolt.

Is a strong woman who recklessly throws away her strength worse than a weak woman who has never had any strength to throw away.

Thomas Hardy from *Tess of the D'Urbervilles* spoke directly to me. I stifled a giggle at how my poor teacher's face would look if I personalized my recklessness with details of exactly the way I squandered my strength.

Instead, I spent the next fifty minutes contradicting the statement, arguing strength couldn't be tossed aside. You either had it or you didn't, and who gave Hardy or any man the right to hand down condescending pronouncements about what made a woman better or worse? I included lots of information about Victorian attitudes toward the weaker sex and threw in plenty of more modern opinions—most of them my own.

I nailed it with an A plus or totally bombed. Neither mattered to me because writing it revived my sense of personal control and pride. If Renzo never called, I would be sad but not weakened.

.   .   .   .   .

After three days with no word from him, blasting Hardy offered less comfort and my self-confidence floundered. Until I remembered Grace. Men come and go, but a sister is forever, so I stuck Renzo in a file labeled TBD and renewed my plans for a family reunion.

I made up a story about driving to Atlanta with a friend to do some shopping and have dinner. Before Mom had a chance to ask which of my nonexistent friends would be accompanying me, I grabbed my keys and rushed out the door.

I don't know if I felt better or worse lying to a person who might not remember the lie.

Then I headed south to follow Grace and Emma. And it was a good thing I did. Because if I hadn't, I wouldn't have been there to see my fellow stalker: the man spying on my niece at the playground.

Hypnotized by the child's every move, I wondered what would happen if the little girl recognized me as her aunt. I closed my eyes and pictured her hopping up from the sandbox to run to me. A rustle of leaves close by brought me back to a world where I didn't belong. I glanced toward the sound. He was leaning against the fence, partially hidden by the bushes.

He was totally focused on Emma. While I imagined my expression reflected longing, his was impossible to read. He could have been eating popcorn while watching a lion eat an antelope on *National Geographic* or an episode of *The Price is Right*. Standing motionless like a cobra before it begins its slow dance—one ending badly for the subject of its attention—he struck me as someone who registered no emotional difference between the two.

If he had been aware of me before, he must have written me off as insignificant, a mom or babysitter there to pick up her kid. When our eyes met, he snapped upright before stepping back and disappearing into the greenery.

Without thinking, I darted after him. The underbrush snagged my shoelace, and by the time I untangled it and reached the parking lot, he was gone.

My hands shook as the adrenaline drained from my body. I had no idea why it had been so important I catch up with the weirdo with the cold stare. Or any thought about what might have happened if I caught him.

If this was what motherhood was like—this blind instinct to run toward a burning building to keep your child safe—I wanted no part of it. But I suppose I already was by trying to protect a niece who didn't know I existed. One thing became painfully clear to me. Emma and Grace were in danger. And it was up to me to do something about it.

So, instead of heading home, I called my aunt.

"Hey, it's me. I hate to ask you to do this at the last minute, but I'm stuck in Atlanta."

I explained a friend had invited me to go shopping with her. We were headed back when one of her lights came on and smoke started billowing out from under the hood.

"We made it to the station, but the guy here says he can't get the part until tomorrow morning. Could you please stay with Mom?"

"I'd guess a very good friend if you rode all the way to Atlanta to go shopping, something you've hated like hell ever since you were a kid."

Shit! My mother must have broken her record for sharing speculations about my love life. I ignored the snark.

"If it's too much trouble, we'll rent a car."

"Don't be silly. Aunt Char's got you covered. Oh, and, honey, one more thing." I tapped my finger on the steering wheel, waiting for her parting shot. "No need to rush things. Take it slow and easy."

.   .   .   .   .

I tossed and turned most of the night on a very firm mattress at the Holiday Inn Express. Even though I set the alarm on my phone and put in for a 7:00 wake-up call, I checked the clock every other hour or so. Around 6:45, I gave up, rolled out of bed, and jumped into the shower. In less than forty-five minutes, I paid my bill, then drove to Starbucks for a coffee and muffin. By 8:10, I found a spot on the corner about a block from Grace's place, next to a lawn lined with magnolia trees partially hiding my car, while still giving me a clear view of my sister's house.

My stomach growled, so I scarfed down my muffin but rationed the coffee in case my stake-out dragged on longer, and I needed to pee. Waiting has never been my thing, but that day I didn't mind it so much. After years of making up excuses for not confronting my sibling, I was possibly within hours of accomplishing my mission. And I had no clue what I would say or do.

In my head, I swept in like Wonder Woman, squeezing the truth out of the bad guys with my golden lasso. Then I would dazzle Grace with my story, and we would dispense with the villains and celebrate as a family.

But I had no superpowers or weapons and only a distant relationship with the truth. So, I forgot about the list of pros and cons from the night I met Renzo and began a new one titled *What to Say When You Surprise a Relative with Your Existence.*

I started simple: "Hey, Grace. You don't know me, but we have the same daddy."

I left space beneath it to speculate on positive and negative reactions.

The mechanical whir of a garage door stopped me midway down the page. I saw Grace's car pull out of her driveway. Her windows were darkened, but I made out the outline of a front seat passenger. Probably Justin—funny how his name came naturally to me, as if we hung out together, worked puzzles with Emma, drank beer, shot the shit—although it was unusual for them both to take her to school. I turned the key and eased onto the road after them.

It was after 8:30, thirty minutes past their usual departure time. When she turned in the opposite direction, I guessed she was headed to her mother's house because those were the two places they usually went. According to some old saying, people were supposed to be creatures of habit. I couldn't speak for everybody, but it seemed to be true for Grace, probably because of Emma. Most of the adult population isn't in love with change, but kids really freak out over it.

I kept a discreet distance between her car and mine, hoping I made the right call about her destination since my tailing skills sucked. Relieved when she slowed down at her mom's, I drove past them to my spot behind the house.

Other than a sassy red sportster I'd never seen before, the place looked exactly the way it had the last time I was there, trying to figure out the family's routine.

When I began stalking my sister, I expected to be the outsider. Not a new sensation as I'd played that role most of my life, the one who didn't quite belong. Recently, however, something shifted. Watching them play in the backyard or picnic at the park or shop for Emma's shoes was like following a reality TV show without the drama, until yesterday at the playground.

Grace and Justin stepped out; then she opened the back door to help Emma from the car, the same way she did whenever they visited. A stocky guy in shorts climbed out from behind the driver's seat. Who the hell was he? I reached for the binoculars in the console and zoomed in on the crinkly face of a man who clearly had never been a fan of sunscreen. Either someone dropped him off or he'd spent the night with the family. He might be a relative although he didn't resemble any of them.

Emma skipped around to stand beside him and slipped her hand into his. A bolt of fury almost brought me out of my hiding place. I should be the one holding her hand, not some stranger, who strolled in out of nowhere to become a part of Grace's life.

I was still fuming when the front door opened, and the four of them disappeared inside.

"Stop being an idiot." Pounding the steering wheel for emphasis, I thought about all the things I'd missed. My anger died down as I pictured a future where Emma held onto me.

An urgent message from my bladder interrupted my speculations. No way would I last until they came out even if they were only there to say hello and drop the kid off. If I hurried, I should make it to the gas station down the road, pee, pick up a Red Bull and Cheesey Puffs, and return before they left. If they were there and I saw them leave without Emma, I would hang out for a while until I developed a better idea. If they were already gone, I could always catch up with them later.

Despite the long line at the restroom and an extremely stoned clerk behind the register, I made it back in less than thirty minutes. Grace's SUV and the Mustang had been joined by a black Range Rover.

Another party I wasn't invited to. God, I was getting on my own nerves with all my whining.

Two hours later, I had finished my list of how I might reveal my secret to Grace and read about a third of *Dear Wife*, a very creepy story about a marriage gone terribly wrong. It made Aunt Char and Uncle Dwight look great. I was at the part where the heroine is accused of stealing from a preacher and his congregation when a black car with tinted windows slowed and passed in front of the party house.

I slumped behind the steering wheel as it rolled by me and disappeared.

"Paranoid much?" I asked myself and sat up. Pain shot up my right leg and I squirmed to stretch the cramp from my screaming calf.

"Oh, shit, oh shit, oh shit!" I scrunched my eyes and flexed my foot in agony. Damn those TV cop shows. They never showed this part of a stakeout. Oh, no. That was all suspense and sexual tension between partners. Nobody ever burped or tooted or shrieked over leg cramps.

The worst of it lessened, and I peeked over the headrest to see where the driver had gone. Thank God I had taken a pee break because he parked about ten feet behind me, next to his own clump of magnolia bushes. And, holy crap, he was getting out. I made a dive to the floor of the passenger side, hoping if he saw me, he'd think I dropped my phone or my purse spilled or some other thing that would make him decide I wasn't worth snatching from the car and stuffing into the trunk.

His keys jangled as he passed, and I stayed down until it was quiet enough to hear birds chirping and somebody blowing leaves in the distance. I didn't sit all the way up for what seemed like an hour but was probably about two minutes. Slumped behind the wheel, I watched as he veered off the sidewalk and rushed the house, then ducked underneath an azalea bush and plastered himself against the brick wall.

From the quick look I'd gotten, I could tell the guy was huge — well over six three or four and beefy without being fat. I considered sending Grace a text, but what would I say?

You don't know me, but I've been watching you, and there's a man below your window? Love, your sister

Yes, you idiot. That's exactly what you should do after you call the police. Minus the signature line, of course.

Before I could follow through, a commotion erupted as everyone tumbled out the door and down the walk. My stalker-competitor dashed through the backyard and onto the next street, where he got into his car.I cranked the engine, made a U turn, and left a trail of smoke as I raced away. In my rearview mirror, I saw Grace head in the opposite direction with Mr. Peeping Tom bringing up the rear.

So, what now? I considered joining the parade but decided despite his size he wouldn't be able to overpower Grace's husband and friend. The best way I had to protect them was to text her a warning about the man following her.

It had been a while since I used the hide-number setting. By the time I figured out how to make myself an unknown caller and send a very short, straightforward message — *Look at the car behind you* — everything seemed to have calmed down at the mother's house.

It was almost 1:30 when I drove away. After stopping for a junior burger and fries at Wendy's, I checked in with Mom. She sent Char home and urged me to stay longer because she was fine. There was a slight lilt in her voice, and I suspected my aunt shared her theory shopping was code for having wild sex with a potential husband.

Another night alone in a motel didn't appeal to me, but I wasn't ready to leave. I explained we hadn't hit all the stores we wanted to, so we planned to visit a mall or two and might not get back until after dark.

"Brilliant. Now you have to actually go out and buy something or you'll never hear the end of it."

Char nailed it when she said I didn't enjoy shopping, mostly because my lifestyle didn't require a fancy wardrobe. Other than a couple of decent work pants and blouses, jeans, t-shirts, and tennis shoes were pretty much it. I glanced at my feet and decided the pair I had on were beyond grubby, so I searched in maps for the closest mall and set out.

There weren't many cars in the parking lot, and very few people in the stores. It was as if I were in one of those movies where God or a spaceship or dinosaurs swoop in and take away most of the population, leaving a few lucky losers behind.

It was dusk when I exited with tennis shoes, boots, two pairs of jeans, and a special gift with purchase bag of makeup I would probably never use. If I left for home, it would be after eight when I got there. But instead of texting Mom to tell her when to expect me, I couldn't resist checking in on Grace.

I wondered how my sister had reacted to the message I sent. Had she spotted the thug in the car behind them, or had he abandoned his position by the time she saw my text? Did she think someone was playing a hateful joke on her, or had I frightened her?

I don't know what I expected to find, but everything seemed normal at her house—no weirdos skulking around or police sirens blasting. Still, I sat there for almost half an hour before deciding to check out her mom's place before heading north.

The light was on, but its beam was too weak to pierce the darkness, which made me feel better at parking closer to the front. I could hear one of the old Hank Williams tunes my dad used to play—Senior, not that jackass Junior, he always said—coming from inside the house. I couldn't tell if anyone was home, but everything was quiet and as normal as Grace and her people could be.

The thick, sweet aroma of magnolia blossoms gave me an unexpected attack of claustrophobia, so I opened the door to clear my head before returning to Chattanooga. Halfway out, I heard a noise and saw two women walking in a half-crouch toward the side of the house where a figure dressed in black stood on tiptoe underneath the garage window.

Too small to be the one I'd seen earlier, he stepped back and almost ran into a woman with hair red enough to shimmer in the dim lighting. Her companion jumped in front of her. She waved what looked like a cannister at him. He howled and clutched at his eyes. I recognized Grace's mother as she joined the action by whacking him on the head with a flashlight. He fell to the ground. The redhead sat on him while the other woman yanked his hands behind him and pulled out a length of rope. She must have been a cowboy in a past life because she trussed him up like a calf in a rodeo. Then she took something from her pocket, and the garage door opened. Light flooded the scene, illuminating the unconscious man. Blood trickled down the side of his deathly white face, but there was no mistaking his thick, wavy hair and strong chin. It was Lorenzo Diez.

PART FOUR

CHAPTER 26: GRACE

Rita took a swig of bourbon before repeating for the fourth or fifth time, "I swear to God, Grace, that son of a bitch was right there."

"We're not making this up." My mother stood with her hands on her hips, glaring up at Mike, who somehow kept his face neutral.

"It's not so much we don't believe you," Justin began. I shot him a warning glare.

"Honey, Mom doesn't make stuff up."

"But, Mommy, you said Grandma gets mixed up on her stories. When she forgets about 'xactly what happened, she just starts making stuff up."

Noone noticed Emma stagger into the kitchen, clutching Bunny Foo Foo and the blanket we wrapped around her when we eased her out of bed and into the car.

"Only you didn't say stuff, you said—" I grabbed her and gave her a quick kiss on the lips, avoiding eye contact with her grandmother.

"Justin, could you carry her back to the sofa and get her settled in?"

She seemed torn between returning to the cozy couch and the deep slumber we'd interrupted and participating in our grown-up conversation. Sleep deprivation won out, and she went with her dad.

"Maybe if you describe him again, some details will surface. Try to remember more about his appearance than how you two looked like Wonder Woman and Jessica Jones when you clobbered him."

"Who the hell is Jessica Jones?" Rita asked. "Never mind. The suspect in question had thick, dark hair and beautiful skin. Wasn't his complexion to die for?" She didn't register Mom's eye roll because she was on her own roll. "His eyes were all red and runny from the pepper spray, but they were big and brown and very expressive. And his body, well, let's just say he was nicely put together, not unlike some of you guys."

She smiled at Harry and batted her eyelashes. I had to give the woman credit; once she had a man in her sights, even a peeping tom couldn't distract her.

"What about height?" Justin asked and nodded to Harry. I guessed both men were flashing to the image of the giant on our porch.

"Taller than your cousin but not as tall as Justin. Probably a little under six feet. Wouldn't you say so, Rita?" Mom dropped her defensive posture and took control of the story. "And he was a fighter. I hated whacking him with the flashlight, but sometimes that's what it takes."

I made a mental note to return to the topic and question her reference to "sometimes" since I'd never heard of her whacking anyone with a metallic object. But there was a lot I hadn't known about my mother and most likely a great deal more to learn.

"You're lucky you didn't kill him. What would we do with a dead body in the basement? I guess we could have dumped him in the lake."

"Very funny, dear."

From her slight wince, I determined she caught the reference to the time she helped dispose of Uncle Roy. Her expression, however, offered no clue as to whether her homicidal past troubled her.

"Well, we don't have to worry since somehow the poor guy got away."

"Poor guy! Grace Burnette McElroy. How could you think I would attack an innocent person? That *poor guy* was spying on two helpless women. He very well could have been here to take *you know who*." She cut her eyes in Emma's direction.

Mentioning my daughter was a cheap shot, but it worked. It also reminded me of the anonymous text warning me someone was following us. I had shown it to Harry and Justin while we were driving home. Neither had spotted a tail, but both had taken it seriously.

"Regardless of why he was here, I doubt he'll be back anytime soon after the welcome you two wild women gave him." Harry grinned at Rita and punched her lightly on her upper arm, the male equivalent of eyelash-batting.

"True, but it might be a good idea to step up Operation Emma," Justin said from the doorway. "She's really out this time." He pulled a chair closer to me and joined us at the table.

"What the hell is Operation Emma?" Mom poured herself another finger of bourbon and downed it, then added more and sipped. Rita held out her glass.

They drank while Mike explained the set-up with his friends. When he finished, he suggested we might want to have an adult slumber party since the surveillance team wasn't on duty until tomorrow.

Mom dragged out some old sleeping bags for Justin and me to sleep on the floor next to Emma. Rita fixed up the daybed in Mike's office for Harry and took the nearby guestroom for herself. I resolved to stay out of that part of the house.

·   ·   ·   ·   ·

Justin and I collapsed onto the makeshift bed. We understood each other well enough that there was no reason to talk about the fear we shared. He propped himself on his elbows, leaned over me, and assured me everything would be okay. Then he kissed me and settled in beside me.

Normally, his assurances ease my mind, but I was wired and expected to toss and turn all night. However, the second bourbon and having his arms wrapped around me, worked magic, sending me into a deep state of unconsciousness. I stayed there until images of lurking strangers beating my aunt and mother with giant flashlights thrust me back into a semi-wakefulness lasting until a squirmy little body wedged herself between me and Justin.

"Why didn't Daddy put up the tent?" Emma whispered in my ear.

On special occasions or sometimes just because, Justin set up a tent in the living room and staged a camp out for the two of them.

"Hey, Daddy." My daughter rolled over and shook him. "Where's the tent?" She did not whisper this time.

He grunted. "At home, where we should be."

"Yuck. Your breath is very stinky."

"Stinky, huh? I bet Mr. Tickle Monster won't think it's so bad. Let's ask him and see." He raised his voice. "Mr. Tickle Monster, where are you?"

She squealed in anticipation, and I got up before my mild-mannered husband morphed into a tickling maniac.

Mom and Mike were drinking coffee at the table, while Rita—dressed in form-fitting leggings and matching sweater with her face made up for going out on the town—was at the stove scrambling eggs.

"Morning, sweetheart. Sit down and I'll pour you a cup." Mom stood, touching her husband-to-be on the shoulder as she passed. The worry lines forming an eleven in the middle of her forehead and the dark circles under her eyes told me she hadn't gotten much rest either.

A fresh round of chortles erupting from the den was a sharp contrast to the solemn group at the table. Even the sight of Emma running into the kitchen with Justin close behind failed to lighten the mood.

"No more, Daddy. I'm 'bout out of air." She climbed into her chair and wrapped her arms tightly around her chest.

"Me, too." Justin kissed me on the top of the head and motioned for Mom to keep her seat. "I've got it."

"How about a cup for me?" Harry strolled into the room, freshly shaven with neatly combed hair.

Rita sprang into action, shoving Justin out of the way, while she filled a mug and set it in front of Harry. She scurried back to the stove and removed the still steaming skillet from the burner.

"Have some of my scrambled eggs. I have a secret recipe." She heaped a portion on his plate and beamed at him.

Mom snorted. "She puts cheese in them and thinks she's a world-renowned chef."

"It's not just cheese." She dumped a spoonful on my mother's plate and continued making the rounds until everyone had a serving. "I have several special ingredients. Marilyn's pissed because I won't tell her what they are."

"Aunt Rita said a bad word. Where's your cussing jar, Grandpa?"

"Baby, with your grandmother and her sister here, the sucker got so heavy I had to haul it to the bank in a wheelbarrow. Wait until after lunch, and Rita will write you a check, a deposit on your college fund." Without looking up, Mike shoveled eggs into his mouth.

The sisters exchanged looks and burst out laughing.

Emma took a bite. "These are delicious. But they need something." She nibbled at another morsel, then announced, "Bacon. They need bacon."

Harry laughed, slapped his thighs, and asked where we kept the meat. He insisted on frying it. Normally, the smell sent me into a feeding frenzy. Today, it brought bile to my throat. I reached for a piece of toast and chewed it slowly until the queasiness passed.

Rita's special eggs lost their appeal. I scooted them around on my plate until it looked like some had been eaten, then helped clear the table while Mike got Emma set up in front of the Cartoon Network.

"I tried to get her turned on to Sesame Street, but the kid's all about the sponge," he said when he returned. "I talked to the guy heading up guard duty. They should be outside any minute now. I'll cover things on the inside while you figure out what's going on."

He snatched another slab of bacon. I caught my aunt watching him.

"If you're sure you'll be all right, I need to follow up with my buddy who's been keeping tabs on Adelmo's crew. He's shy about talking on the phone, so I have to meet him in person. Would it be okay if I borrow somebody's car?"

Rita hopped to her feet. "I'll get you my keys—unless you'd like me to be your driver since I'm familiar with the area."

"I appreciate the offer, but my guy spooks easily. And I'm afraid you might be too much of a distraction." He grinned and my aunt giggled. The woman actually giggled and blushed.

Justin said, "I'm going to pay a visit to a former informant. He should know if there's any trouble between suppliers in the area. I'd rather Grace stay put here, but that's a pipe dream. The next best thing is to take her with me. She can charm information out of Lewis. And if that doesn't work, I'll beat it out of him."

Mom pounded her fists on the table. "You are not dragging my daughter to some seedy joint to rough up one of your lowlife criminals."

"They're not Justin's lowlife criminals." I sounded like a petulant teenager defending her wild ass boyfriend.

"I'm sorry, Marilyn. I shouldn't joke around. I promise there will be no low-class bars and absolutely no punches thrown."

I reached for her clinched fists. "I'll be fine."

She shrugged and slipped her hands from underneath mine. It didn't take a rocket scientist to figure out she didn't believe me. I wasn't too sure about it myself.

CHAPTER 27: GRACE

Instead of the back of some seedy bar, we met Lewis Sederman — not his real name — in Banjo Coffee Shop, a trendy breakfast spot in Avondale Estates known for its cold-brew and people watching.

"This isn't exactly what I was expecting." I sipped on a silky-smooth latte while we waited for Justin's dangerous criminal to appear. "You said he chose the place?"

"I'm surprised at you, dear. Profiling someone based solely on his proclivity for illegal activities. Lewis could be a Harvard grad with a mansion in Buckhead." He grinned from behind his mug, then craned his neck and nodded. "Here's our guy, now."

The person moving toward us wore a long sleeve polo shirt with a pricy logo on the pocket and tight-fitting jeans, which were designer or an excellent knock-off. His thinning hair was threaded with gray, but his light-footed gait made him seem younger.

"Long time, J-man."

J-man — Lesroy would get a real kick out of the nickname — stayed seated but shook the hand Lewis offered.

"And this lovely lady must be Grace."

Shocked he knew my name, I hesitated a moment before returning his smile and asking him to please sit.

"Thank you, but I'm going to order something to drink and avocado toast first. Can I bring anything back for you?"

We declined his offer, and I watched him saunter to the counter.

"Avocado toast? What kind of drug lord eats avocado toast? And how did he know who I am?"

"It's not necessary to be a member of the pinkies-out club to enjoy a piece of avocado toast. As for knowing your name, I'm guessing Google. Don't be fooled by all that charm. Before he got out of the business—if he really is out—Lewis Sederman wasn't a very nice guy."

"Well, he reminds me of my physics teacher. Actually, he wasn't all that nice either. He would grin like a fool when he passed out D's and F's."

"Dear God. Lewis was never that bad."

I kicked him under the table at the same moment his informant returned.

"We don't have all day. What did you find out about the Balsutos?"

Lewis frowned and cut his toast into neat little triangles. Only after eating two of them and washing them down with coffee, did he answer.

"Those guys haven't had any product on the street for at least a year and a half. Most of what comes from Ecuador is courtesy of the Castillo family. Of course, I can't personally attest to it." He looked at me and added, "I gave all that up a long time ago."

Justin made a harumphing sound. Our informant ate two more bites and continued. "Word on the street is their stuff isn't up to the standard the Balsutos set."

"So, you're telling me the Castillos have cornered the market?"

"Pretty much."

"I can't see them going after the Balsutos because someone hurt their feelings by calling their product inferior. But if they're not the ones with a grudge against Adelmo, who is?"

"Woah, there. You didn't mention Adelmo specifically. He and Dario Castillo go way back. Nobody's sure how it started, but it had something to do with a cousin of Dario's getting gunned down during a drug deal. The Balsutos insisted they had nothing to do with it. Apparently, the Castillos weren't buying it. Supposedly, they retaliated by kidnapping your friend's sister. She was killed during the transaction, and Adelmo vowed he wouldn't rest until he avenged her death. Dario's lieutenant got whacked, and it looked as if all hell would break loose. But the boys' fathers were practical. They worked out a truce. Nobody expected it to hold up after the two old guys croaked. One had a heart attack; six months later, the other stroked out. Funny, don't you think? It's kinda like those married couples who've been together since the beginning of time. One of them bites it, and the other isn't far behind, as if neither wanted to live without the other."

He paused to allow us to appreciate the depth of his observation, then continued. "Adelmo was out of the picture for a while, in hiding from the cops or possibly from the Castillos. Some people suspected he axed himself because of that hot-as-hell chick."

He looked at me. "Jesus, I'm sorry. I meant hot-as-hell lady."

I nodded and he picked up the story. "Anyway, the Balsutos diversified their interests. Real estate, auto dealerships, even insurance companies. It was clear Adelmo was behind the changes and was serious about getting out of the drug business. Then he came back and started managing the *company*. Pretty impressive."

He speared the last piece of his toast and waved it for emphasis.

"Everybody expected the trouble between the two families to end when Balsutto went legit. And it seemed it had. Of course, there's no doubt if either one of those guys got the chance, they'd slit the other's throat without a second thought.

My latte soured, and I feared I might barf what little I'd eaten of Rita's special scrambled eggs all over Lewis's plate.

It wasn't the image of the two men locked in deadly combat that curdled my coffee. It was the memory of Adelmo standing over the battered, bloody body of Stella's husband, my ex-fiancé. And of how easily I might have put a bullet in the man who killed my sister — without a thought.

.   .   .   .   .

"So, was Lewis telling the truth?" I asked as we merged onto the interstate.

"He had no reason to lie. Which means whatever is going on between Dario and Adelmo doesn't relate directly to drugs, so it must be personal."

"And that means it's much, much worse. Castillo isn't satisfied; he still wants revenge. He wants Emma." I bit my lip to keep from screaming because once I started, I might never stop. My stomach lurched. "Oh, God. I'm going to be sick."

Justin exited and eased off the road. I stumbled from the car and dropped to my knees on the pavement. He raced around to my side and held back my hair.

"It's okay, Babe." He said after handing me his handkerchief. "There's no way to determine what's in Castillo's head. Or in Adelmo's."

But I knew. At least when it came to the man who loved my sister enough to commit murder for her. If Adelmo was in the United States, it was because he was ready to kill again to protect his only remaining piece of Stella. In that, we were alike.

For the first time in well over twenty-four hours, I checked my notifications and saw I had a message from an unknown caller. Before I read it, Justin's phone rang from its spot on the center console. When I picked it up for him, Rita's number flashed on the screen. I answered.

"Oh, Grace." I could barely make out the words through her sobs. "We tried, honey. God knows we tried. But they took her. They took Emma."

CHAPTER 28: GRACE

As soon as we turned down Mom's street, we saw the flashing lights. Police cars blocked oncoming traffic as firemen gathered around a blackened patch of weeds near the sidewalk. Two EMTs were coming out of the house carrying a stretcher. I leaned out the window, straining to see if the person's face was covered.

"Stop," I shouted.

Justin cut the wheel and parked next to a neighbor's Stay off the Grass sign. My hands shook so badly he had my door open before I got my seatbelt undone. I bolted from the car.

A police officer stepped in front of us. "No one's allowed past this point," he said, looking at Justin as if he expected resistance. While my husband explained our connection, I slipped by the cop and was close enough to recognize Mike strapped onto the stretcher.

The good news was no one had completely covered him. The bad news was it looked as if that might happen at any minute. The only color on his face came from the blood-soaked bandage wrapped around his head. If not for the slight rise and fall of his chest, I would have taken him for dead.

And that must have been what my mother thought as she staggered out behind him, holding an ice pack against her forehead. The EMT beside her attempted to take hold of her arm, but she shook her off.

"God damn it. I told you I'm okay. But you're not going to be if you don't move out of my way and let me on the ambulance with him. None of you are." She stopped them and threw herself over Mike, sobbing.

I rushed to her and slipped my arms around her waist, gently loosening her grip on the man she loved. "Mom, they need to get him to the hospital."

"Grace, thank God it's you. Please tell that young woman I do not require her assistance." Her pupils were dilated, and she swayed so far to the right I feared she would topple over.

I kept hold of her, and she didn't resist. "Take it easy, Mom. They just want to make sure you're strong enough to get in the ambulance on your own."

I turned to the attendant. "Is she all right?"

"She has a nasty cut on her cheek and a lump on her temple. We stopped the bleeding, but it's likely she has a concussion. When she saw her husband, she refused to let me continue the examination. Your mother is surprisingly tough for such a small woman."

I didn't bother to explain they were engaged, not married. More because I was afraid they would never make it to the altar now, than because I was concerned they might not let Mom on the ambulance if they knew.

The man trying to load the stretcher said, "We need to get this guy moving. I'll ride with them in the back." He told me the name of the hospital, but for a second, I forgot where I was and why I was there.

"Sorry it took so long. That cop was a stickler for policy, but I finally got him to give me some details." Justin hugged me to his chest and kissed my cheek.

I pulled back. "Where's Emma? Did he say where Emma is?"

He shook his head and caught me when I fell forward.

．　　．　　．　　．　　．

I came to on the living room sofa, the one reserved for visiting royalty. Rita was pressing a cold cloth to my forehead. Angry at myself for being such a wimp, I brushed her off and pushed myself upright.

"Please, honey, stay still. You've had an awful shock." Tear trails lined her face with white streaks where they had washed away her makeup, and her right eye was swollen and discolored.

"From the looks of it, I'm a lot better off than you. Or I will be when you tell me what happened to my daughter."

I heard men talking in the kitchen—Justin, Harry, and someone unfamiliar. But when I tried to stand, I stumbled backward and sank into the cushion.

"Rita. Please. Who took her?" I grabbed her arm and squeezed harder than I intended. My aunt winced slightly but didn't pull away.

"It's like the statement I gave to the cops. Everything happened so fast. First, car alarms started going off. Not ours, I don't think, but from all over the neighborhood. At least, it sounded as if it was all over. Your mom had Emma, and I held onto both of them while Mike unlocked his gun from the safe and duck-walked to the window. By the time he got there, we saw smoke rising outside. He had us lock ourselves in the bedroom and not come out until he said so. We ran toward the back of the house, and all hell broke loose."

I noticed shards of broken glass in the room and the overturned coffee table and coat rack. Rita slumped sideways, resting against the arm of the sofa. I realized I hadn't asked how she'd been injured, and I still didn't. There was no time. I had to find Emma.

"What do you mean?" I nudged.

"What? Oh, sorry." She shook her head as if to clear it and touched her fingertip to her now partially closed eye.

"A man carrying a rifle crashed through the window. Before Mike aimed his gun, another guy smashed the front door and knocked him over, then started beating him with some kind of pipe thing. Emma was screaming. Your mother and I made a run for the bedroom." She stifled a sob.

"I'm so sorry, Grace. So damn sorry. We didn't make it. While all the commotion was going on out here, two more guys broke in through the kitchen. They weren't interested in me, so I got the broom. One of them punched Marilyn in the face and tried to snatch Emma away. But she wouldn't let go until the second guy came up behind her and slammed his gun into her skull. She went down hard, taking Emma with her."

Rita shut her eyes, leaving me with the image of my mother slamming into the floor, unable to get up. My aunt released a shuddering sigh before continuing.

"Then I smacked him over and over on the head with the broom until the cheap-ass handle broke. So I threw it at him and hit him in the crotch. He hollered, grabbed himself, and started coming toward me. He gave me a look that just about made me pee my pants. Honest to God, I thought he was going to kill me. Then the other guy yelled something in Spanish, and he turned around to help his asshole buddy drag Emma to her feet. They headed for the door. I jumped on the back of the son of a bitch who pistol whipped your momma, but he slung me off. He must have popped me in the eye on my way down. The last thing I remember is Emma reaching out her arms to me."

She broke down into gasping sobs while I sat there watching, wanting to comfort her but coming up empty. I tried to stand, but my legs were rubbery and useless, but not as much as I felt.

Get a grip, I told myself. *You can break down after we find Emma.*

A fit of coughing came over my aunt, and she lost her breath. I patted her back, softly at first, then harder when the choking worsened. The spasms eased, but I continued rubbing her shoulder.

"It's not your fault," I said. "We should have never left you all alone."

She stopped crying and ran her fingers through her hair. The gesture reminded me of my cousin. "Have you talked to Lesroy?"

"There wasn't time. Besides, he doesn't need to worry about me."

"If he finds out you got knocked around by gangsters and we didn't call, he'll kill me. And I wouldn't blame him."

My hands shook as I took my phone out of my pocket and tapped on his number. The upbeat rhythm of his voicemail message gave its familiar instruction.

Hello, fellow fabulous person. I'm devastated about missing the chance to talk to you. Identify yourself, so we can right what's wrong.

At the beep, my mind blanked. There was no way to condense the story of how a pair of Ecuadorian thugs had terrorized his mother before punching her in the face into a few sentences. Or that his mom was probably in shock after failing to take down bloodthirsty kidnappers.

Stop by Mom's house. Everything's okay, but it's kind of, um, urgent.

"I wish you hadn't done that, honey. I bet he's in a really important meeting."

"Nothing's as important to him as you are."

Instead of cheering her up, my words started another crying jag. I tried to offer a comforting smile, but my lips quivered as I fought back tears of my own. From the look on Justin's face when he walked through the broken door, I must not have been doing such a great job of hiding my emotions.

"Babe." He dropped to one knee in front of me. "Are you okay?"

His voice came from so far away I could barely hear it. *Why are you whispering?* I wanted to ask but couldn't speak.

He cupped my chin and looked at me. "You're scaring me, Grace. Talk to me."

I attempted to move my head, but his grasp tightened. "Let go," I ordered. He dropped his hand as if my skin burned him. "And no, I'm not okay and never will be without Emma."

"Don't say that." He rose and pulled me up with him. "We'll find her and bring her home. But first, we need to get you warmed up."

At some point, the violent shaking had returned. We went to the kitchen, leaving poor Rita in a soggy heap on the sofa.

Harry and a wiry man with close-cropped hair stood when they saw us. Harry bounded toward me and wrapped me in a bear hug. The heat from his body did nothing to stop my shivering. My iciness originated from terror too deep to melt.

"It's going to be all right," he promised before releasing me.

"The officer Rita talked to said someone from the kidnapping division will be in touch shortly. They're used to this sort of thing, but they don't know the Castillos. Not like my old friend here, Greg Larson. Greg's a member of the FBI's Crimes Against Children Rapid Deployment team. We met in Ecuador when he worked with the locals on a hostage case."

"Nice to meet you." Larson held out his hand, and I stared at it, unable to remember what I was supposed to do. His face remained open and easy when he retracted it. "It's normal to be very frightened right now, but I've had a lot of experience with situations like yours, and much of it has been with the kind of people who took your little girl. Men in the drug business."

I suspected he had a great deal of expertise in dealing with women on the edge of completely losing it because his kind, but businesslike, voice had a reassuring quality that cut through the thick fog in my brain.

"The drug business? Oh, yes. So, you're certain the Castillos took Emma?"

"We can't be positive, but the Bureau has a long history with the family. Kidnappings are their second most lucrative line of work. Plus, the way your kidnappers worked matches the Castillo signature. Creating a distraction by smashing car windows and setting off alarms. Starting fires to increase chaos and panic to force their targets out into the open. Rushing from multiple entry points."

My world tilted, and I fell back against Justin.

"I'll make some tea," he said after leading me to the table.

Seeing my whiskey-drinking husband fussing with tea bags would normally have amused me. Today, it emphasized how losing Emma had flipped our world upside down. I broke through my zombie-state long enough to remember my weeping aunt.

"Harry, why don't you check on Rita? Maybe see if she's up to joining us."

"Good idea." He bounded from the room.

"More coffee, Mr. Larsen?" It struck me I had morphed into my mother when she played the hostess at my sister's funeral — moving stiffly among the mourners, determined to observe the practice of Southern hospitality at any cost.

"It's Greg, please. And thank you, I'm good."

Justin set one of Mom's fancy cups on the table, then spread a selection of teas in front of me. I opened a packet without checking the label and dropped the bag into the hot water.

I was stirring it when Harry appeared, guiding a version of my formerly irrepressible aunt. Her hair was plastered to her scalp, and her injured eye was glued shut and twice its normal size.

"You sit down, Rita, and let me refill your ice pack."

Her glassy-eyed gaze startled me, but by the time I gave her the ice, she seemed to have rallied.

"Since the hospital is limiting visitors, it doesn't make sense to go down there and hang out in the parking lot. I'll call Mrs.

Simons from your momma's church. You know, the big pushy one? She works there in medical records. If anyone can find out what's going on with Marilyn, it's that Bible-loving broad."

Harry walked with her to the hallway, while I asked Larson what we should do next.

"I can't tell you what to do. But if you agree, I'll walk you through the process once you decide on a course of action."

Before he got into details, Rita and her escort returned to the kitchen. I didn't think it was possible, but she was paler than before.

"Aunt Rita, maybe we should get you to the hospital, too," I said.

"To hell with doctors. I'm not leaving until I know where Emma is." Despite the slurred words indicating she needed medical attention, her steely tone made it clear she wasn't going to listen to anyone's advice.

"We all want the same thing," I patted her shoulder, so thin it was birdlike. "Okay, Mr., I mean Greg. Let's hear it."

For about an hour, he laid out scenarios, including who might have taken our daughter, why they had done so, and what they wanted in exchange for her return. Each one began with a ransom demand, delivered within the first twenty-four hours of the kidnapping.

"An entire day," I gasped and squeezed Justin's hand.

"Usually, it's sooner. But if it is Castillo, and I'm certain it is, he enjoys dragging things out."

The idea of Emma being held by vicious strangers for one second longer was a punch in my gut. I swallowed hard to keep from getting sick again.

"There is an upside to it being Dario's men. They're pros, which means they won't panic and risk losing the payoff."

"So, that's it? We sit and wait for the ransom demand?" Justin sounded as defeated as I felt until I remembered the one true friend Stella had in Ecuador—her housekeeper, before Ben fired her, Eva.

"There's another possibility. We—or rather I—reach out to Adelmo. I don't have his number, but Eva will. If he's in the country, he'll know how to get our daughter back."

"I suppose it might work." Larson scratched his head. "But dealing with a man like Balsuto is risky. He is not a guy who inspires trust."

Justin took my hands in his and said, "We're well aware of what's at stake, but it's our best chance."

My husband was right. Adelmo would stop at nothing to get Emma back. He had the same savage love for her as he had for my sister. His savagery outmatched that of our daughter's kidnappers. I had witnessed the warmth drain from his deep brown eyes when he promised he would make my sister's killers pay, and the memory still sent icy daggers through me. He would do anything to ensure Emma's safety. But once he achieved his goal, could we ever be certain our daughter would be safe from him?

CHAPTER 29: GRACE

Larson finished outlining abduction theories — the most common and simplest being the men who had taken Emma wanted money. Harry walked him through the glass strewn living room to the porch where they spoke for a few minutes, leaving the three of us sitting around the kitchen table.

"I don't even know what time it is." The words came out more forceful than I intended as I stared at Mom's stupid grinning daisy clock. The damned thing stopped a few months ago, and no one had replaced the batteries. Under normal circumstances, her disregard for urgency in keeping up with the hours of the day was only moderately annoying. Today, it had the potential to undo me.

"I have no idea if it's too early or too late to call Eva."

"Same time as here. Babe, why don't you let me handle this for you?" He rose and left the room.

Since I was having trouble focusing, I agreed. Then I remembered Mom and Mike in the hospital. What did it say about me that I had forgotten all about them? The dangerous undertow of guilt threatened to drown me. Instead of struggling against it, I swam parallel to the shore.

"Wasn't some doctor supposed to get back to us?"

Rita looked at me as if I were speaking another language. Her lack of comprehension — as if she, too, had forgotten our fallen comrades—made me feel a little better, until I realized how awful it was to be glad my aunt was as bad off as I was.

Was this what senility felt like? Did its victims confuse right and wrong? Forget their moral compass? Or not give a damn one way or the other? If so, losing my mind could be a good thing when dealing with the men who had my child. It meant I wouldn't hesitate to become as vicious as they were. To strike them down without a second thought.

My fury gave me resolve, which countered some of the powerlessness almost overcoming me.

"Well, I'm not waiting any longer. I might not be able to track down the shitheads who took Emma, but I sure as hell can make a doctor talk. Where's the number, Aunt Rita?"

She appeared to be startled. Then she snapped to attention and pulled a slip of paper from her pocket.

"We need something stronger than tea," she said. "I'll fix us coffee with a splash of Irish cream."

While I responded to questions about my identity and purpose for calling, Rita returned with fortified caffeine. My aunt sat beside me as the operator put me on hold for five minutes until another one answered and promised someone would be with me shortly. Then she left me waiting again. An unidentifiable blend of piano and horned instruments made up the never-ending jazz that lulled me into a state of compliance. It seemed I had overestimated my ability to navigate the medical maze.

Seconds after accepting my utter uselessness, the music came to an abrupt stop.

"This is Dr. Azarian. I understand you are Marilyn Burnette's daughter. Other than to say she is resting comfortably after we administered a mild sedative, there isn't a great deal I can tell you about her condition. She is in ICU where we are closely monitoring her. We have eliminated the possibility she had a stroke but are still running tests to determine what is causing her continued confusion."

I wanted to scream maybe her condition had something to do with being beaten up by masked home invaders who knocked her to the floor and ripped her granddaughter from her arms.

He held all the cards, though, so I tried a more tactful approach.

"Is there any way I can see her?" My mother had never been a warm and fuzzy woman, not the kind to kiss booboos. She was more a clean out the wound, slap a Band-Aid on it, and shove you back on the playground gal. But whenever tragedy struck— whether it was the teenage loss of a first love or the death of a sister—her brand of comfort was exactly what I needed. All I wanted was to hear her tell me to stop being dramatic, that Burnette women could handle anything.

The doctor must have registered the catch in my voice, as he answered in a less robotic tone. "Not until we move her out of critical care. Then she can have a visitor."

Heartened at what I took as confidence she wouldn't be in the ICU all that long, I asked about Mike.

"And the man who came in with her? Is he okay?" *Please, God, let him be all right.* Because losing the man she loved might be the one thing this Burnette woman couldn't handle.

"I can only discuss his condition with his immediate family."

"My mother and I are his family, his only family. I'm his stepdaughter."

"His medical history says he is single."

"Because it's a common-law marriage. The kind where they've lived together long enough to be considered legally married." While I don't make lying a practice, once I get going, I'm quite good at it.

"The last time I checked, Georgia was not a common-law marriage state."

Well, shit.

"The only information I can provide is his condition is serious. I will see to it someone contacts you if anything changes with either your mother or your, um, stepfather."

Long after we disconnected, jazz lingered in my ears as my earlier surge of power deserted me.

As clear as if she were standing beside me, my grandmother's advice came.

Snap out of it and stop wallowing, Grace.

And that's what I did.

CHAPTER 30: NATALIE

I couldn't reconcile the idea that the man lolling beside me in a drug-induced stupor was the same one who made love with such gentle fierceness.

When I found him duct-taped to the post with a bag over his head, a machine-gun burst of laughter escaped from a spot deep in my chest. Yes, he looked ridiculous, but that wasn't what amused me. I laughed because of the absurdity of it, like those bizarre plays I studied in my drama as literature class—performances with no logical beginnings or endings and dialogue that made no sense. Theater of the Absurd, written to show how screwed up people were.

I didn't need a college course to tell me that. I needed an explanation. How had my first meaningful connection in forever turned up in the basement of my sister's mother's house?

After my brief spell of hilarity, I pulled myself together and yanked the bag off his head. His silky black hair was matted with blood, and his eyes were red-ringed slits.

"Hey, Renzo. Wake up."

He groaned. "Natalie? Is that you?"

"Shut up. We've got to get this tape off you before those nice little ladies come back and rip you apart." He closed his eyes, and I smacked his cheek. "Do not pass out again, or I'll leave you to them."

I searched for something to cut through the bindings and found a small pair of gardening shears. He mumbled while I sawed through the layers. As soon as they were loose enough, I tugged at the strips. Whenever I tore away bits of hair and skin, he yelped, and it made me smile. Totally sick, of course, but I enjoyed his pain.

I handed him the clippers and said, "Here, you work on your legs while I see if I can find what they did with your jeans."

I let out a few barks of inappropriate laughter at the picture of the neighbors' faces as they watched me lead a pants-less man to my car. He deserved the humiliation, but I didn't want to attract attention to our escape, so I used my flashlight and discovered his clothes draped across the handle of the lawnmower. His wallet fell out. I picked it up, and was surprised his captors left cash and credit cards, but no driver's license. His shoes were nowhere to be found.

I wrestled him into his shirt and pants, then jerked him upright and helped as he hauled himself to his sock feet. With my arm around his waist, we hobbled out of the garage.

"I want to thank you, Natalie. Those women, they are monsters. If you hadn't come—"

"Don't talk. I need to figure out what to do with you."

Taking him home wasn't an option. Mom might have bought a story about him getting mugged, but then she would lose it because I had either been with him when he got beaten up or had picked up the victim of a robbery. Both stories would terrify her, possibly even cause a setback in her recovery. Worse, she would eventually conclude I'd been involved with him, which would lead to questions I couldn't or didn't want to answer.

Aunt Char was a possibility, but she'd never fall for the mugging story. And my exhaustion level had topped the charts, not a good time to match wits with her in an elaborate lie. At least, not in person. But over the phone? I might be able to fool her, especially if I told her something she wanted to accept as true.

While my deceitful passenger moved in and out of consciousness, I called my aunt.

"Natalie Burden. Your mother and I have been worried sick about you."

I hadn't expected that reaction.

"Do you know what time it is?" I didn't but a quick look at the dashboard clock explained her concern. Almost eleven, and I had been due back by seven or eight at the latest. This was going to be harder than I imagined.

"I'm so sorry. Don't freak out, but we had a minor accident."

"Define minor?" She sounded concerned but not panicky, which made her easier to deal with.

"My friend's foot got caught in an escalator at the Marta station. A worker saw it and cut the switch but not before some pretty serious ankle twisting. We're at the ER now. The doctor says it's broken, so there's no telling how long it might take. I hate to ask, but could you possibly be available for one more night?"

"Since I'm at your mother's, it's not an issue. She wants to talk to you, so—"

I raised my voice and half-shouted, "What's that? You need to see an insurance card?"

Renzo started babbling in Spanish. I shushed him and returned to Charlotte.

"I have to go. There's a problem with insurance. I'll text you later to let you know when to expect me."

After his outburst, my passenger fell into what I originally diagnosed as a post-taser condition. Then it occurred to me the Burnette women would take extra precautions to keep their prisoner pliant. The drug of choice for ladies their age was Xanax. A few of those would explain his lingering confusion and grogginess. Without knowing how many he'd taken, I had no way to predict when he might be able to walk on his own, what's less make sense.

I needed to take him somewhere private, fill him up with black coffee, and do whatever I had to squeeze a confession from him about our common interest in the Burnette family. And it was important for me to hear why he had pretended to be interested in me. But had it really been pretense? If so, he deserved an Academy Award. After our afternoon together, I hoped we had a future. Not a married and happily ever after fairytale, just something solid to support my fantasy of a happy-for-a-little-while reality show.

Finding a rich boyfriend never made it to the top of my to-do list, but I appreciated nice things, and I had a Spidey-sense when it came to recognizing wealthy people. From the moment he walked up to me at the restaurant, I knew Lorenzo Diez had money. That night, he wore Ralph Lauren polo and jeans. Not too expensive to stand out, but pricier than the regular clientele could afford. On our tour of the city, he upgraded to a blue and white custom-tailored shirt and khakis with creases sharp enough to slice pepperoni on them.

Since he most definitely had plenty of money, I splurged on the location of my interrogation. I took a chance the Ritz Carlton had a room, and they did. For four hundred dollars, we got a double queen with a marble bathroom and rain showerhead. The shower attachment was especially appealing. If Renzo stayed too dopey to answer my questions, I'd shove him in the shower and douse him with cold water.

Valet parking was tricky since my passenger was so wobbly the attendant had to help him out of the car. "Sorry. Some men just can't hold their liquor."

He glanced at Renzo's bare feet and back at me.

"You can stick him on a luggage rack if you want."

The idea didn't seem to appeal to the poor guy. Together, we supported Renzo to the lobby and propped him against the wall.

"That's okay. I've got it for now." I removed a twenty from Renzo's wallet, put it back, and exchanged it for a fifty. "I'll pay you double if you can find a pair of shoes in whatever size you think will work."

I gave him our room number, and we maneuvered Renzo into the elevator. "Knock three times when you find the shoes."

We stopped at the fourteenth floor. Or was it really the thirteenth? Was this one of those hotels where they mislabel what should be thirteen to keep superstitious people in the dark? Not that I worried about black cats or ladders, but the way things had been going in my life there was no reason to take unnecessary chances.

A look at the man next to me, sliding to the floor reminded me I had no time to worry about it. If I didn't get Renzo to the room, no amount of luck would help.

"Hey, wake up!" I scooted behind him and slid my arms underneath his. I bent my knees and used the wall for support before dragging him into a partially upright position.

"Is it you, my beautiful Natalie?" He straightened himself and flashed me a crooked grin.

Damn it. Even in his pathetic shape, the smile got to me.

"Yes, it's Natalie. And I need you to walk with me to someplace where we can talk."

"Ah, a place to talk. How lovely."

He staggered beside me to our room and leaned against the wall while I stuck the keycard in and shut the door behind us. I flipped on the light switch and tugged him toward the bed, where he landed spreadeagle.

Despite having used the proper form for deadlifting what I guessed was a trim hundred- and-seventy-pound man, my back ached, and my calves burned. No way would I be able to drag him to the shower, so I would have to wait until his drugs wore off.

That gave me time to figure out my onetime lover's identity even though I didn't want to. I should probably be afraid of him because nice guys don't assume a fake name before having sex with you.

But nothing about him frightened me, especially not the way he looked now, wavy hair stiff with blood, a scrape on his cheek the size of a pancake from being dragged across the garage floor. A giant blister formed on his lower lip, the one I nipped gently seconds before he began caressing my body.

I reminded myself only a real asshole would be dishonest enough to seduce an unsuspecting woman like me. Except I made the first move — okay, five or six moves was more accurate. And although I didn't realize it at the time, he tried to warn me when he told me there was much about him I didn't know. I thought he meant stuff like he always left the toilet seat up or he watched live wrestling. Not that he peeped through windows or got the shit beaten out of him by little old ladies.

A wet snort from my semi-conscious ex-lover brought me back to the problem lying on the bed.

"Come on, Natalie. Do something," I whispered to myself. But what? I suppose I could throw cold water on him and make him talk. Only that required energy and enthusiasm, and I had neither, so I lay down beside him and rested my eyes.

·   ·   ·   ·   ·

I was back on the playground where Emma had built castles with her friend. Dark clouds hung low over the empty sandbox. A sudden gust of wind tore blossoms off the trees and scattered them like confetti across the silent park. Behind me, leaves rustled, and I heard muffled cries that could have come from a child or a small animal.

A rapping sound stopped me before I discovered the source of distress.

"Emma!" I pushed myself up onto my elbows and surveyed the darkened room, trying to remember where I was. Another series of knocks—three of them—and I remembered. The bellboy. I stumbled to the entryway and peered through the peephole. The boy from the parking lot stood so close I could see a constellation of pimples on his chin.

Grabbing Renzo's wallet on the way, I eased the door open.

"These should fit." He handed me a pair of mud splattered tennis shoes.

I thanked him and dropped the money into his palm. Cool and calm, as if it was perfectly normal for me to throw hundred-dollar bills around.

Holding the filthy shoes by their strings with one hand, I ran my other over the wall to find the switch for the overhead fixture. So bright, I had to shield my eyes. Once they adjusted I noticed it, the empty spot where Renzo should have been.

CHAPTER 31: GRACE

At the end of my frustrating conversation with the doctor, Rita patted me on the shoulder.

"Too much cream and not enough coffee," she announced. Halfway up, she fell back into her chair.

"Oh, my God!" I jumped to my feet just as she began sliding to the floor.

"Justin," I shouted. "We need some help in here."

Harry and Justin burst into the room, holding firearms in front of them.

In normal times, two men racing through my mother's house with guns drawn would have shocked the hell out of me. Today, I had no illusions we had any chance at all of dealing with Castillo and his team in a peaceful, rational manner. And it worried me. Not that I would find the sight of the kidnappers lying on the ground bleeding from multiple wounds unappealing. It was the image of bullets flying around the people I loved, terrifying me.

"What is it? Are you sick?" Justin lowered his pistol and rushed toward me where I held onto my aunt.

"I'm good. Rita? Not so much."

Harry helped me lay her flat and kneeled beside her, cradling her head and repeating her name over and over.

"Oh, God," I gasped. "Please, wake up."

Justin brought a damp cloth and placed it on her forehead while Harry patted her cheeks.

While I had been trying to swim parallel to the shore, I hadn't noticed how fragile my aunt was. Once again, my grandmother's voice called to me.

"Don't just stand there like a bump on a log. Do something!"

I snapped into action and grabbed my phone. "I'll call 911."

A low moan from the woman on the floor stopped me after the first digit.

"I will not have anybody seeing me in this sorry state, Grace Burnette." Rita slapped Harry's hand away, pushed up with her elbows, and finger-combed her wild hair.

I kneeled and threw my arms around her. "Thank God! You're back," I choked out before breaking down into sobs.

"Holy mother of God! You've killed her." Lesroy dropped to his knees and shoved me off Rita.

"I am not dead, goddammit." She wriggled out from under her son and sat up. "Honey, your momma is finer than frog hair."

Justin pulled me to my feet, and the three of us watched as my cousin stared at my aunt's swollen face.

"Who did this to you?" His words came from a place I recognized from the experience of losing myself to the dark desire for vengeance.

"I'll explain everything later. Right now, we have to concentrate on getting Emma back."

"Emma? Grace, what is she talking about?"

Rita tried to push herself up, moaning at the effort.

Lesroy reached for her, but she shot him a momma-death-stare, and he froze.

"Harry, would you please tell my son, there's nothing seriously wrong with me? Give me a hand, and I'll show him."

He seemed immune to Rita's evil eye. "Not so fast. How many fingers do you see?" He held up two.

"Don't be silly, dear." But her smile was crooked and her eyes unfocused. He moved his hand closer to her face. "Oh, all right. Four. You're holding up four fingers. Is everybody happy now?"

"That's it. We're going to the hospital. Lesroy, you grab an arm. I'll take the other."

I expected a violent reaction from her, but she allowed them to get her upright without a peep.

"I'm coming, too."

"No, Grace. You and Justin stay here. Your cousin and I have got this."

"They only let family in, and it might be a lot for him to handle."

"So, everybody say hello to my hot new stepdad. Isn't he the cutest?" Lesroy pinched Harry's cheek, which turned dark crimson along with the rest of his face.

My aunt glared at her son with glazed eyes. "Stop that this minute. You're embarrassing the poor man." Then she leaned against Harry's chest and murmured, "He's right, though. You are pretty damned adorable."

.   .   .   .   .

"Do you think she'll be okay?" I asked for the fourth time since the newly not-weds and my cousin left for the hospital, and we made it back to our house.

"Are you kidding me? Even half-addled the woman put the moves on him. I'm way more worried about Harry than I am about her. Why don't you settle in on the sofa while I make you a cup of tea?"

I took his advice and wrapped my grandmother's comfort quilt around my shoulders and waited as Justin puttered in the kitchen. The blanket failed to work its magic, and I fidgeted beneath it, wondering what was taking Eva so long to return my call. Then I remembered the voicemail and suspected she had already tried to get in touch.

But it wasn't Eva's soft voice on the recording. It was Adelmo, and he hadn't wasted energy on a lengthy response.

"Do not be fearful. I am coming."

"When?" I shouted.

Justin bounded into the room. "What's wrong?" Once again, he held his gun.

"Put that away, please, and listen." I played the message, made more ominous by its brevity.

"He's something else. Would it have killed him to give a time frame for his arrival?" Justin holstered his weapon. "But it sounds as if he has information about the situation. I guess it's a good thing."

"Maybe," I said. "But somehow him telling me not to be afraid scares me almost as much as Castillo and his men."

From my cell, The Who blasted their iconic question: *Who are you?* My ringtone for unknown callers. The number was blocked. But it was as if Stella had passed on a part of her connection to her dark lover to me. Or was it desperation because I had no doubt Adelmo waited for me on the other end of the line?

"Where are you?" I asked, wasting no time on pleasantries.

"My men and I are outside your home. May we enter?"

CHAPTER 32: NATALIE

I checked the bathroom, the closet, and behind the curtains. Lorenzo Diez had vanished, leaving me holding somebody's nasty tennis shoes. His wallet lay where I dropped it after paying the valet, and his car keys were in my purse. Then I noticed the door to the adjoining room was slightly ajar. I pushed it and it swung open. No one was there.

At three in the morning, the mystery of whether a neighbor had helped Renzo escape or if the maid had forgotten to lock up overwhelmed me. And the prospect of driving randomly around the city, looking who the hell knew where for a man who had set me up — for what I had no clue, except Grace was somehow involved — sucked.

And I was so damn tired the idea of riding the elevator to the parking lot seemed as monumental as climbing Stone Mountain. Maybe if I rested my eyes for a few minutes, something would pop into my exhausted brain.

The rattling of pots and pans jarred me from a dead sleep. Why was Mom up this early? No, not my mother and not cooking utensils — a rolling cart. And the strange bed I finally recognized was the one in my fancy hotel room.

"Of course, you're alone, you idiot." I grabbed the extra pillow, covered my face with it, and screamed. The clock read 6:30 a.m. No brilliant plan surfaced from my muddled mind, which left me with two options: abandon my efforts and head home or drive by Grace's house, woman up, and knock on her door.

After a quick shower, I pulled my wet hair into a ponytail, slapped on some mascara, and checked out of the ritziest place I had ever halfway slept in.

The car hadn't moved from the parking spot. When I turned out of the garage, sunlight reflected on a mixture of what looked like blood and snot smeared on the passenger-side window. Grace's aunt and mother worked Renzo over hard. He might have a concussion or a serious reaction to whatever drugs they gave him. Had he staggered out in search of medical help? If so, had someone taken him to the hospital and left him there lying in a coma or worse?

I pounded the steering wheel.

"Stop feeling sorry for that douche bag and start thinking about what's going on with Grace and her family. Unless you're making up stuff so you can swoop in and save the day."

I shook my head. Who wouldn't want to be a super heroine rather than a throwaway sister and a useless aunt? Except I hadn't imagined the creep in the park, and he had definitely been eyeing Emma. Even if he was an ordinary old pervert, my sister should be aware of the weirdo watching her little girl. It didn't matter if the info came from someone carrying a truth-detecting lasso or from a half-ass sister.

Instead of turning onto Grace's street, I drove around the block to my regular spot to give myself a chance to amp up my nerve for meeting my new relatives. The driver of a long, black car beat me to it. The tinted windows made it impossible to tell if anyone was in it.

This is yet one more attempt to put things off, I scolded myself. What did Hamlet say about screwing your courage to the sticking point? Wait, not Hamlet. Lady Macbeth. Seeing how her story played out, she might not be the best fictional character to take advice from, but hers was all I could come up with.

So, I turned off the engine, slipped my phone into my pocket, hid the keys under the mat in case I needed to make a quick getaway, and got out of the car. I suspected the four-door in front of me was a rental because there was no dealer information on the license plate. The barcode on the back windshield was another clue, both courtesy of my father. He hated getting behind drivers who observed the speed limit or, God forbid, stayed below it.

"Goddamn tourists," he would growl.

When I asked how he knew they were out-of-towners, he told me about the plates and the sticker, information I never expected to need.

Most likely, some grandma and grandpa had come to visit the mother's neighbor. Still, I kept my eye on the backseat. There was no reason for me to suspect it was occupied, but that didn't stop a cold sweat from beading at my hairline. I forced myself to keep a steady pace and stared straight ahead as I got closer to the rear seat windows.

The urge to sprint to the house grew stronger and stronger, and at the last few feet, I bolted. But my foot slipped into one of the root ruts on the sidewalk and I stumbled, jamming my hip against the passenger side. Pain shot through my ankle as it scraped against the curb.

I leaned against the car and bent to check for blood. None yet, but a nasty scratch cut across the top of my foot.

A flurry of movement, like flocks of birds fleeing hunters, startled me, and I turned toward it. The sound of a door opening behind me caught my attention, but before I could turn around, a hand slapped over my mouth, stifling the scream building in my throat. A burning sensation in my nose made it hard to breathe. Then there was nothing.

CHAPTER 33: GRACE

Adelmo left his men outside the house to keep watch, leaving the three of us alone to plan Emma's rescue. The man seated across from me called himself Adelmo Balsuto, but I couldn't reconcile this gaunt stranger with the powerful creature I met on the beach shortly after my sister's murder. His coarse black hair and dark bearded face exuded strength with its square jaw and full lips firm with determination. His shoulders were broad, and his arms roped with muscle. He had a worker's hands with thick fingers and calloused palms.

Today, a bristly gray and white beard shadowed his sagging jawline. Thinning hair in the same faded shade aged him, as did the curvature of his once muscular chest. His expensive looking shirt hung loose on scrawny arms. He cupped his mug of coffee tightly with gnarled fingers.

My sister's death drained his body and spirit, and now he was a sad shadow of the person I had found dangerously attractive.

The only evidence of the fiercely passionate man my sister loved was in his eyes. Although they were sunken in folds of flesh, they blazed with the same cold fury as when he promised revenge against the men who killed Stella. If anything, their fire burned brighter. And, like before, they filled me with terror.

As if reading my mind, he said to Justin, "Time has not been as kind to me as it has to you and your beautiful wife." He smiled at me. "I wish we had more of it to become reacquainted, but I'm certain you will agree we have more pressing matters to discuss."

I shivered at the way his tone hardened when he spoke of *more pressing matters*. No longer pretending to be an old friend who stopped by to chat, Adelmo straightened his back and narrowed his piercing eyes. For a moment, I returned to the filthy trailer where Stella's bloody and broken husband begged for his life, while I decided if I would be the one to take it. My words froze in my throat, and my heartbeat quickened.

Justin put his arm around me. "Grace and I are eager to hear what you have to say."

"I had hoped not to involve you, but Castillo has other plans. And for now, we must go along with the hijo de puta."

He explained Dario Castillo had contacted him. The demand was for $500,000 in cash and an in-person meeting with his nemesis. But Adelmo asserted the kidnapping was about the balance of power, not money. The transaction would be handled as a prisoner exchange. Emma for her father. And he wanted Justin and me there to witness it.

"But isn't that a terrible risk?" I regained my ability to speak but not the capability to understand.

"It is his way of announcing to the world he is in charge."

"More like his way of taking out a competitor." Justin pulled me closer. "And how the hell are we supposed to come up with that much cash on such short notice?"

Adelmo shrugged. "Not a problem. My concern is his insistence the two of you be there. Initially, I refused. But he threatened to end the negotiation, so I agreed. Of course, I have a plan to ensure the safety of your family."

I ignored the catch in his voice when he spoke of *family*. "How exactly?"

"Please, there is no reason for you to worry about those details. We must discuss the ones involving you."

And for the next half hour, that's what we did. Castillo had given instructions to be ready at midnight. He would send a text to Adelmo's phone with the address of where we were to meet. It could only be the three of us. If anyone else showed up, the deal was off. He would take Emma with him to Ecuador, and we would never see her again. All we had to do was walk Adelmo toward Castillo's guys, hand him over, and return with our daughter.

"So that's it?" Justin asked. "You turn yourself over to the man who wants you out of the picture? Out, as in dead."

"I have no death wish, my friend. We shall each wear a tracking device. My men will follow from a distance. After you have Emma in your vehicle and safely away from the location, my team will extract me."

"You make it sound so simple, but I can't believe Dario won't expect it. Why would he let us leave until he had you stashed someplace your men couldn't get to you? Are these the details we don't need to worry about because they don't involve us? Because anything jeopardizing our daughter's life involves us."

"Ah, Grace. You are as fierce as my dear Stella when it comes to protecting our child."

I winced at his choice of words. But whether I liked it or not, Emma didn't just belong to me and Justin. Adelmo's blood ran through her, as did my sister's. And he was right about Stella. She had died to keep her daughter safe.

I would do nothing less.

CHAPTER 34: NATALIE

Flashes of light sent a searing pain into my temples, and my eyes refused to open. A surge of bile singed my throat. *Please don't let me puke all over myself*, I pleaded to whatever force attacked my body. I thought of all the horror stories about kids getting so drunk they drowned in their own vomit and turned my head to the side, hoping to avoid that fate.

Even that slight movement brought a groan of agony at the white-hot lava shooting through my shoulder. When I tried to move my arms, a similar bolt of heat surged from my biceps to my wrist. What the fuck was going on? The contrast of cold metal against my burning hands answered my question. I was handcuffed to the bar above me.

"Somebody let me out of here!" What I'd intended to be a roar came out as a croak. "Water, please," I whispered and was surprised when the tip of a plastic bottle pressed against my cracked lips.

Most of the liquid dribbled down my chin, but I swallowed enough to clear my throat. I opened my eyes to confront the thuggish goon who must have kidnapped—from where I couldn't remember—and bound me to the most uncomfortable cot I'd ever had the bad luck to be stuck on. But there was no crazy-ass serial killer or anyone else lurking over me.

If not for the cooling liquid trickling down my throat, I might have believed the whole thing was a hallucination. That all the crap my health teacher spouted about the long-term effects of drug abuse hadn't been to keep me from having a good time. Even in my confusion, though, I still didn't buy it. At least, not in my case. No, my pot days with Dylan weren't heavy-duty enough to produce this nightmare haze. This was real.

And so was the tiny hand offering another sip of water. My thirst outweighed the shock of the pale face looking up at me from beneath a tangle of dark curls. I killed the rest of the water and stared into the red-rimmed silvery eyes of my niece.

But it couldn't be Emma. She was safe at home with her family. Only I hadn't actually seen her because, uh, because.... Because of the black car outside her house. I almost called her by her name but caught myself. Whoever had taken me must have snatched her, too. She'd experienced enough trauma without someone she never met greeting her by name. I stifled my growing panic and spoke in what I hoped was a calm, grown-up voice.

"Well, hello, there. Thank you for the water. I'm Natalie. What should I call you?"

She narrowed those haunting gray eyes as if considering whether she should trust me, then answered in a tentative tone sounding as if she hadn't quite made up her mind.

"My name is Emma."

"That's a pretty name." I winced at new pain, this time from my throbbing hip, and remembered slamming into the car before everything went dark. An odor similar to the smell of Dylan's garage when he worked on his motorcycle wafted over me. "So, Emma, can you tell me where we are?"

She shrugged and stepped back.

Her retreat scared the shit out of me. This little girl was my only hope of getting us out of here. If she lost interest in my stupid questions, we were screwed.

"Wait. I'm sorry. What a silly question. Let's try this one. Did you see the men who brought us here?"

"Yes, I did." She returned to my side. "There are three of them. They're old and are real stinky like my dog Scarlett when she needs a bath. They talk in Spanish. It's funny because they think I don't know what they're saying. Which is mostly right 'cause I'm only four. But two of my friends are from Mexico, and Miss Casey comes from the kindergarten class to teach us, so we can learn how to make them feel at home."

It didn't seem like the moment for a pop quiz on pre-school be-nice Spanish, so I tried a different tactic.

"You must be very smart." She bobbed her head in agreement. "Do the men come to check on you? To bring you food, maybe?"

"They brought this before you got here." She disappeared from view, and I fought the urge to shout, *Don't leave me.*

She returned with a greasy brown paper bag, took out what looked like a peanut butter and jelly sandwich, and waved it in my face. "Want a bite?"

Stifling my gag reflex, I politely declined. "Did you see them bring me here?"

Emma shook her head. "They locked me in the bathroom. I screamed and screamed. The big crybaby one banged on the door and screamed *Cállate* at me. It means shut up, and Miss Casey says we shouldn't say it even though the Mexico boys do it all the time. Anyways, he yelled it again and I stopped."

By now, the foggy blur had lifted from my eyes but not from my brain, and *crybaby* threw me. I couldn't picture one of Castillo's guys bursting into tears over anything other than missing out on a prison riot.

"What did you call the man who told you to be quiet?"

"He didn't say be quiet. He said *Cállate*. It's okay to ask someone to be quiet. It's not okay to tell them to shut up." She spoke slowly and with more patience than I expected from a four-year-old.

"You're absolutely right. Thank you for reminding me. Now, what was it you called the man who shouted at you?"

"I call him Crybaby because I don't know his name and because of the tears."

A cramp twisted through my calf. I held my breath and tried to relax it.

"What's wrong?" Emma moved closer and patted my hand. I fought back my own tears at her look of concern.

I pasted on a smile and assured her I was fine, then asked why she thought the man was crying.

"Not real tears, silly. They're magic marker fake ones. But he made them black which is really dumb because everybody knows tears don't have a color. If he was at my school, the teacher would have to give him extra help."

One of Dylan's biggest fans was a guy with a teardrop tattoo. My ex warned me not to look because it meant he killed a man. After that, I couldn't stop staring. I concluded his was a fake, possibly drawn with liquid eyeliner. As for Emma's kidnapper, I had no trouble accepting his was the real thing. I didn't want to hang around to test my theory.

While Emma stroked the chipped polish on my fingernails, I noticed my cot was really a workbench set on top of a heavy wooden table in the middle of what must have been a garage at one time. I scanned the cluttered room in search of a tool that might free me from my handcuffs. It was impossible to take it all in from my position.

"I don't much like it here, Emma. What do you say we get out and go home?"

Her face melted, and tears started trickling down her cheeks. If my hands had been free, I would have smacked myself in the head before wrapping her in a hug. Of course, she wanted to go home. I had no way to comfort her, and we didn't have time for a meltdown, so I shifted to a firmer tone.

"All right then. Since we both want to go home, let's figure out how to get these cuffs off me. Does your daddy keep tools at your house, like a hammer or a wrench?"

She swiped at her nose and nodded. "He has a workshop. A hammer has a pointy end and a flat end. I don't know what a wretch is."

"Doesn't matter. Could you please look around the room? If this is a workshop there should be something heavy with a pointed end that might help me take these handcuffs off? Can you do that?"

For the next few minutes, I heard boxes being tossed and metal clanging against the floor.

"I can't find a hammer or pointy things. But what about this?"

She brought her dirty fist forward and opened it.

"Oh, my God. You are freaking amazing! Where did you get this?" Lying in the middle of her grubby little hand was a key. And it looked exactly like the one Dylan had for the pink, fluffy handcuffs he begged me to wear. I never did.

"It fell out of the crying man's pocket, and I stepped on it before he saw. I have to ask Mommy, but I'm pretty sure freaking is a bad word. You might have to stick a dollar in the jar."

"I'll put all the dollars you want wherever you want them if you'll unlock these damned handcuffs."

CHAPTER 35: GRACE

Justin and I discussed whether we should let Greg Larson know what was going on. After all, bringing home kidnapped children was his area of expertise. But most of his cases involved ransom, not a human sacrifice, so we didn't contact him.

We filled the hours waiting for Adelmo to pick us up by getting updates on my family's conditions. I called Mom's doctor and was put on hold, where I paced back and forth until Justin stopped me.

"Try to relax a little. It's going to be okay."

Before I could ask how the hell he knew that, the doctor came to the phone. In my calmest voice, I inquired about changes in my mother's condition and didn't lose it until the end when I shrieked, "For the love of God, man. Tell me the truth. Is my mother going to live or not?"

His answer was noncommittal, and I instantly regretted asking for honesty.

Justin did a better job with his performance as Mike's distraught brother who just discovered his sibling had been seriously injured. He gave the nurse on duty a sob story about how close they were and how his flight got canceled, and no one would tell him how long the delay could be. Like most women, she fell for his charm, making him promise not to say anything before she told him there was no internal head bleeding, and the broken ribs hadn't punctured a lung. She assured him Mike should be there to greet him regardless of how soon Justin's plane took off.

We put the phone on speaker to check in with Harry.

"Lesroy's sitting with her now. The doctors agreed to let us tag team, which is good because your cousin is a hot mess."

It turned out Rita wasn't doing so well. She had a concussion which might have brought on a TIA, accounting for her double vision and lack of balance. Normally, these mini strokes resolve themselves within twenty-four hours, but the head injury complicated my aunt's situation. They were doing tests to determine the damage.

"Lesroy called his buddy Vincent. When he gets here, I'm going to go down the hall and see about your mother and Mike."

We relayed the positive news Justin had wrangled out of his contact. We also shared the vague response about Mom.

Justin filled him in on the meeting with Dario and his insistence that only the three of us come.

"I feel so goddamn useless. Isn't there something I can do?"

"The best way you can help is to make sure the hospital is taking good care of our invalids. We'll call as soon as we have Emma."

.   .   .   .   .

Dario's plan included instructions for Justin to drive with Adelmo in the passenger seat and me in the back. Always prone to motion sickness, I focused directly on the old gravel road in front of us. But the potholes and unexpected curves did a number on my already unsettled stomach.

"Would anyone like a peppermint?" I dug around in my purse, keeping my eyes straight ahead to avoid an attack of vertigo. The men didn't answer, which was good since I only found one piece, and it was half wrapped with a glob of lint stuck to it. I ate it anyway.

KATHERINE NICHOLS 207

We rode underneath a jet-black sky. No moon or stars or man-made lights of any kind to guide the way, and no more words between us. Adelmo stayed fixed on his screen. The GPS lady broke the silence by announcing it was a fourth of a mile to our final turn.

My gut lurched, but the knowledge Emma was at the end of our journey helped me power through the nausea. There would be plenty of time to puke once she was safe.

"Tell me again how this is supposed to work?" I memorized the details but hoped hearing them might steady my shaking hands.

"Justin is to park at the edge of the lot. We all get out of the car where you remain standing beside it. Then I take the money and walk forty steps toward the warehouse, stop and wait for Dario to appear with the child. He will signal for you to join me. When he releases her, I will go with him."

"So, your plan is to just give up?" Part of me was fine with the idea, as long as my daughter came home. There was another part that recalled how Stella had described their relationship and credited him for helping her want to become a better person. "There must be a way to keep Emma safe without letting Dario take you. At least let Justin and me try."

When I turned to my husband, I caught him exchange a look with Adelmo.

"What is it you're not telling me? And don't you dare tell me it's nothing. Remember what we said about not keeping things from each other?"

"It's not like that, babe. I only figured it out a few minutes ago when I overheard Adelmo talking through an earpiece."

"Please, do not be angry, Grace. I told you not to worry. This is merely a—I believe you say—contingency plan. If it appears Dario is not following the actual plan, my men will be there to ensure Emma's safety."

"But he said come alone. What happens when he sees your men?"

"Do you see them?"

I strained my eyes for a sign of life in the crumbling buildings scattered around us. There was nothing but a dark stillness.

"You cannot spot them, nor will Castillo. You have not forgotten how I kept the promise I made to find those who took Stella from us? I must ask you to trust me again."

"What choice do I have?" In Ecuador, I put my faith in my sister's lover, not only to find the men but to bring them to justice. And he delivered on his promise, only not exactly the way I expected. He hadn't relied on the system to dispense punishment. He extracted a violent revenge of his own.

I should have realized a man like him would never go along with a program that ended with his being taken prisoner, most likely to be tortured and killed. I could only hope his love for his child was stronger than his hunger for retribution. Maybe even than his own wish to survive.

Although we stood far from the building, we could see the swap. I suspected the distance reflected Adelmo's concern we might be caught in the crossfire or Dario's worry we would intervene on our friend's behalf.

The image of my ex-fiancé, Stella's husband Ben, came back to me. Bound to a rickety kitchen chair, beaten bloody by Adelmo, he pled with me to save him. I told myself things had gone too far by then. If I could have helped him, I would have. And for a good while after my sister's funeral, I believed my story. But grief is filled with so many long nights, where secrets and shame demand recognition. Eventually, their clamor wore me down, and I faced the truth. I had no desire to save Ben. Worse, the explosion ending his life released a savage satisfaction from within me, and I was glad he was dead.

Accepting my dark side set me free. It forced me to acknowledge if given the chance, I would destroy the man who had taken Emma and delight in his death.

A patch of concrete to our right told us we had arrived at our designated parking spot. Dim lights in the distance marked the location of the only intact warehouse in the area. Justin stopped the car, and I resisted the urge to hurl myself from the vehicle and run toward my daughter.

"Are we sure this is it?" He cut the engine.

"I am certain." Headlights blinked at us in a perverse welcome gesture.

Adelmo's phone buzzed, and he answered with it on speaker.

"Is it you, my old friend?" The false warmth of the voice on the other end sent tremors of terror through me.

"I am here as you wished."

"Perfect. Now, if you and your friends will step from the car, we will begin."

"Not until I know the child is alive."

The steel in his tone was almost as devastating as the suggestion Emma might not be alive.

"I am afraid you will have to take my word the lovely little girl is in the best of health, for now at least."

"Vete a la mierda. I see her now or we leave, and the money goes with us."

"Now, now. What about a compromise? Show yourself. Then I bring the kid out."

Adelmo agreed and ended the call.

"What was all the back and forth about? Didn't we just agree to do what he wanted in the first place?"

He shrugged. "Not exactly. Let's assume he keeps his word. Emma will be there a few minutes before the original plan. And by negotiating, I hope to convince him this is a business transaction. I need him to think yes, I want your daughter returned without his understanding how much she means to me. Also, we have bought time for my men to be in position."

Position to do what? I thought but didn't get the chance to ask.

He opened the door and stepped away from the car. Justin got out and came to my side. I joined him and watched as Adelmo began the long walk toward the warehouse. At what I supposed was forty paces, he stopped and shouted.

"I go no farther until I see the girl."

The only details I made out about the man standing in front of the building were his broad shoulders and a belly hinting he carried at least thirty pounds more than suited his frame. He could have been anyone, but Adelmo had recognized the voice on the phone, and I had to believe he knew what he was doing.

The kidnapper barked orders to someone inside the warehouse before assuring us Emma was on her way.

Justin wrapped his arm around my waist, and I strained to escape his hold.

"Just a few minutes more," he whispered.

A crash sounded, and Castillo turned toward it. Adelmo took the opportunity to remove the pistol hidden in his waistband. His enemy screamed what I guessed were curses at whoever was making all the racket. Rather than quell the confusion, his words brought on another round of thumps and clanging, as if his men were tossing heavy items around in the spot where Emma should have been.

"What the hell is going on? Where is she?" No longer cool and detached. His voice was higher, sharp, almost shrill. But Dario seemed too distracted to notice.

"Stay calm," he responded, sounding anything but. "She is momentarily indisposed."

Justin groaned. Without thinking, I propelled forward and ran toward Adelmo.

My approach went unnoticed because of the physical altercation between Dario and the unlucky thug who approached him with what must have been very bad news.

Footsteps pounded on the broken pavement as my husband rushed past me. Neither of us gained on Adelmo as he, too, raced into the chaos.

"Stop where you are." Dario leveled his gun at us.

Adelmo stopped and spoke softly. "They cannot find her. I have to let my men know the child is not with us."

Shots rang out from both sides of the building. Shadowy figures emerged, firing as they closed in on Castillo's crew.

"Get down," Justin cried out before dragging me off my feet to the gravelly earth.

Adelmo disappeared into the smoke-filled air, but I could hear him as he screamed for his men to hold their fire.

CHAPTER 36: NATALIE

I dangled Emma out the window until her feet hit solid ground, then climbed out. As soon as I landed, a blazing hot pain shot through my knee from the gash I received dismounting the work bench.

"Shit, shit, shit," I said under my breath. She frowned but stayed silent, most likely keeping an ongoing total for the swear jar.

Running blind into the night scared the crap out of me, but not as much as the men chasing us. So, I tried to ignore my injury, took Emma's hand, and sprinted into unknown territory.

We reached a patch of overgrown weeds filled with bags of trash and scattered debris. When my eyes adjusted, I saw the surrounding garbage came from a nearby dumpster. We settled in behind the bulky container seconds before we heard the scrunching of tires on gravel. After a few minutes, two men began a very loud conversation. I couldn't tell how far apart they were, but the way they yelled back and forth in a combination of Spanish and English, the distance must have been significant. Despite the volume, I didn't understand what they were saying in either language. But the air buzzed with the hostility between them.

An unnerving quiet ended when the one closest to us confirmed my guess about their feelings for each other when he blasted his frenemy with a string of Spanish curses. Thanks to

Dylan's crash course in Hispanic cussing, I picked up something about the other dude's mother and hygiene. A third voice entered the discussion, but another round of swearing created a seriously threatening vibe and drowned out the others.

Doors slammed and other men joined in the confusion. As their panicked cries got louder and louder, I put together we were the objects of their search. Their desperation became increasingly clear as they slammed stuff around while screaming for us to come out. And if my translation was accurate, their lives depended on completing that mission. Right or not, it didn't matter because, either way, ours depended on blowing up their plan.

Instead of adding to my fear, their frenzied despair calmed me. The resulting chaos meant they had less energy for me and Emma. I realized they might be playing it by ear. The picture I got from the little girl's description of her guards reassured me, too. We definitely weren't being hunted by the upper five percent of Kidnapper State College.

My fellow escapee didn't feel the same. She shivered beside me and squeaked, "I'm scared."

"Me, too. But it's okay to be scared. It'll help us move faster when we run." Except I had no idea when we'd take off or where we'd land. "For now, let's scootch down behind this dumpster and catch our breath."

Her shaking continued, but she didn't start crying. I took that as a small victory. Because if she did, I would probably collapse into a heap and blubber along with her. Not a great way to come up with an escape strategy.

Without a moon or streetlights, we could have been surrounded by a dense forest or on the edge of a deserted Walmart parking lot. We would have to get closer, which meant we'd have to cross open territory. And that majorly sucked because we couldn't see a damn thing, and our pursuers had flashlights. I thought about hiding Emma under some trash bags and scouting out the area before coming back for her. But even for somebody as totally clueless about how kids operated as I was, one look at her and I knew the idea wouldn't fly.

Then the shit storm started.

I've seen lots of gun battles in the movies and on television. They never bothered me. I always thought they looked fake, even the real ones on the news channels. They bored me with how easy it was to predict who would live or die. Boredom sounded good to me now.

From our hiding place, the sound of gunshots echoed. There were no dramatic close-ups of the good guys returning fire. No angry faces or terrified hostages increased the tension.

Just pop, pop, pop, a super loud version of popcorn in the microwave. Or fireworks at the lake. After a few seconds, the in-between moments got to me. Should I take it out and waste half of the uncooked kernels or leave it in and risk burning the batch? Would the next burst of color outdo its predecessor? If we left, would we miss a more spectacular finale? Or in our case, would we be the finale?

Emma covered her head with her arms and rooted deeper into my lap. I stroked her hair, as much to reassure myself as to soothe her. A drawn-out barrage split the air, followed by a shorter one, then the dreaded silence—longer than the others.

The child peered up at me. "Maybe they ran out of bullets."

"Probably." *Or they're reloading.* I forced a tight smile. "Let's count seconds. If we get to two hundred, we can decide if we want to make a run for it. You start. But be real quiet."

While she whisper-counted, I strained to hear signs of life. Not that it would do me any good since I couldn't tell if the kidnappers were shooting at each other or some other bad guys or, please God, at someone trying to rescue us.

"You're not counting." She gave me a stern look. "Now we have to start over again. This time you—"

Shouts and another volley of gunfire drowned out the rest of her instructions. An unexpected breeze blew a thin layer of smoke in our direction. Not much in the way of cover but better than nothing.

"That's it." I jumped into a crouch and tugged at Emma's arms. "We're getting out of here."

She was surprisingly quick for such a little girl and kept pace with me for the first third of the run. When she slowed, I scooped her up, and she wrapped her legs around my waist. I didn't stop until I reached a wooded area. We were closer to the front of the warehouse at an angle that gave us a clearer view without exposing our location. I picked a sturdy tree with a thick trunk, and we eased down behind it. Emma clung to me like a spider monkey.

My breath came in wheezes, and my ears rang.

"Listen. No more bangs."

She was right. The ceasefire might end at any moment, but now men called out to one another in voices that seemed steadier, less panicked. I peeked around the tree and saw hazy figures rushing into the building. Light beamed through broken windows as they hurried from room to room. Searching for something or someone, most likely Emma.

The question became who the hell were they. They hadn't identified themselves as police or yelled threats through a bullhorn. Would I be putting her in greater danger by bringing her to them?

The face of the empty-eyed man watching her at the playground came to me, and I shuddered. No way would I let him take her. Of course, I had no idea if he was part of the team who kidnapped us, and I didn't care. I would protect her until I could get her back to Grace. And not just because of my feelings for the child. Because any other outcome would destroy my happily-ever-after family fairytale.

For the moment, I would stay put. My entire leg throbbed from what felt like a nasty cut. Now that I had time to check it out, I didn't want to. Finding out how serious it was wouldn't accomplish anything. But I looked anyway. My eyes adjusted enough to make out a rip in my jeans, exposing what was less of the scrape I'd hoped for and more of a deep gash. The good news was the bleeding had stopped. The bad news was when I used my index finger to pull at the torn fabric, a searing pain shot through me, and hot liquid flowed again.

I tried to maneuver myself into a position to elevate my leg, but Emma had me pinned beneath her. The sound of steady breathing and a soft snore stopped me from untangling her from me. Instead, I willed myself to ignore the pain and brushed the hair out of her eyes.

That's when I noticed orange streaks breaking through the pitch-black night. Soon, the decision to stay in hiding would be made for me.

The first explosion woke Emma. The heat from the second one brought me to my feet. When my psychology professor lectured about the fight-or-flight syndrome, I hadn't understood why there wasn't a third option. Like talking your way out of it or stalling until help arrives. But stuck behind a tree with a helpless little girl clinging to me, and crazy people I couldn't see blowing stuff up, I got it.

We had to get out of there even if we ran toward something more dangerous than gunfire and explosions.

"Hold tight," I whispered to the half-awake child, then used the tree to brace myself and stood with Emma in my arms.

Mist rose from the ground beneath us and joined with the smoke to make it difficult to find my bearings. My legs shook and I stumbled, going down on my good knee. I scrambled up, but the dense undergrowth held onto my tennis shoe.

"I have to put you down for just a second. Stand right there."

Another explosion thundered behind us, and Emma whimpered.

No matter how hard I tugged, the ropy vines refused to give. I sat back on my heels and wiggled out of the tangle, leaving my shoe behind. My trembling knocked me off balance, and I had to kneel to jam my foot into it and adjust the laces.

A sliver of sun appeared beyond the trees, revealing a two-lane road ahead.

"Look, honey." I pointed at what had to be a better spot than the one we were in. "We'll go to the highway for help."

But Emma didn't answer because she wasn't there.

CHAPTER 37: GRACE

Either they didn't register his command to stop shooting or were too swept up in the violence to understand, but the gunfire continued.

He screamed a second order for them to cease firing, but everything had spun out of control. He raised his fist to the sky, roared, then bolted toward flying bullets.

"Get down, Grace," Justin shouted before tackling Adelmo and bringing them both to the ground.

I stopped, dropped, and rolled into the fetal position. Lying there with my arms covering my head, I thought of Emma. Whatever comfort I might have taken from the dawning knowledge the Castillos didn't have her shifted into terror. If not them, who had her and what did they want?

It took several moments to take in the quiet. A few feet ahead of me, Adelmo squirmed from beneath my husband, jumped to his feet, and picked up where he left off in his mission to reach the warehouse. As he ran, he called out Emma's name.

Justin helped me stand, then held me back when I tried to follow Adelmo.

"She's not in there, babe."

"You can't be sure. Remember how good she is at hide and seek? I bet she found a really great place. We just have to keep looking."

"Let me do it. You stay here." His expression reminded me no hiding place would have protected her from the onslaught of bullets.

I grasped his hand. "We both have to go."

The first blast shoved us backward, and we stumbled before regaining balance. Heat scorched the air, and fire blazed from the windows.

Adelmo tumbled to his knees. One of his men reached him and dragged him in our direction. The second boom knocked them both to the ground.

"We have to go." Justin took my arm and pulled me into a run.

I screamed for him to let me go, that we couldn't leave our baby. The third eruption ended my protests.

.　　.　　.　　.　　.

Sirens wailed in the distance as a coughing spasm overtook me, and I struggled to sit. Justin got to his feet first and helped me to mine. I focused my stinging eyes on the devastation. Through the pounding in my brain, someone repeated my name, but I couldn't remember how to answer.

Rays of sunlight cut through the blur, and a whirl of wind thinned the blinding smoke enough that I saw a man propping Stella's lover into a sitting position.

The last blast must have rattled my brain because I couldn't understand why Adelmo wasn't where he was supposed to be — in Ecuador minding his own business. And we certainly didn't belong in this place where men lay moaning on the rough concrete and fiery columns enveloped the remains of whatever building had been there. A once deserted spot now filled with fire trucks, ambulances, and police cars.

My ears rang. When I shook my head to clear it, a sharp pain in my neck forced me to gasp and remain still. My husband stood by my side and wrapped an arm around my waist. But all I could manage was to stare at the warehouse. Only it wasn't there anymore.

We were in this hellhole for one reason: to take our baby girl home. But we'd been too late, and now we might never see her again.

"Stop it. You are Grace Burnette, my fearless big sister. And you will find Emma."

I whipped my head to the side, sending another hot bolt from the base of my skull through my shoulder blades. There had been no reason to react as if she might be there, checking up on me. Nevertheless, Stella had spoken to me, probably sent by my grandmother to snap me into action.

Despite the lunacy of it, my sister's voice provided a bizarre comfort. Since she no longer inhabited the world of the living, if she urged me to find her daughter, that meant Emma was alive. Otherwise, she would have been with her mother, a sweet other-worldly concept too unbearable to think about.

"Grace, baby, are you okay?" Justin took me by the shoulders and gently turned me until I faced him.

"A little better now, yes."

"Good. I'm going to see if one of the firemen will talk to me. Promise to wait here until I get back?"

He looked so distraught I nodded, telling myself deceptive head gestures didn't count as lies. Because, surely, he didn't expect me to hang around when Emma was out there somewhere wondering why we hadn't come for her.

Part of the promise was true, though. I wouldn't run toward the building terrified Stella's and my child was in there. Now I knew she wasn't. Somehow, the clever girl had escaped. But that didn't mean she was safe.

Pinks and oranges colored the gray sky with faint light. Through the smoke, I saw the heavily wooded area to the side of the wreckage. A perfect hiding place for the pirate princess Emma often pretended to be.

Shaky at first, my legs steadied as I bolted for the trees. When I reached them, I stopped, surprised at the density of the vegetation. In another year, the lot and everything touching it would be covered in kudzu. Even the charred remains of where Castillo's men held Emma would be threaded with the creeping vine. The image of it sneaking up on my child and strangling her with scraggly, but inhumanly strong, green arms thrust me into the thick of it.

A floating sensation lifted me. If not for Justin calling my name, I might have drifted away. A stab of doubt pierced through me. Had I been wrong about our daughter being alive? The possibility she might be dead, burned beyond recognition, sent a wave of despair over me and anchored me to the ground.

In the stillness, I heard it, a sound so beautifully impossible it sent a chill through me. While I stood there, straining with every fiber in my being to hear it again, my husband caught up with me and threw his arms around me.

Irritated at the interruption, I snapped at him to let go and be quiet. My reaction must have startled him with its intensity because he did as I asked.

"Listen," I whispered. But there was nothing.

"Grace, honey," he began.

I put my hand on his arm and shushed him. And there it was, not as faint as before, still too soft to separate into words, but so familiar.

He squeezed my shoulder, and we stared in the same direction.

"You hear it, too." He understood I wasn't asking a question.

It sounded again, clear enough now to decipher.

"Where are you, Mommy?"

As if we were one person, we flung ourselves toward her voice.

She emerged through the haze, like a forest sprite, and for a second, although she looked solid and real, I shivered in fear this was a dream, conjured by my broken mind.

"Emma." Hearing Justin whisper her name reassured me she was no vision.

I raced to sweep her up and sobbed into her neck.

"It's okay, Mommy. I just had an adventure."

"It was an adventure, all right." Justin gathered us in his arms and held tight.

A little too much so for Emma, who protested and demanded to be set down. I examined her for injuries. Other than a few fresh scrapes and several old bruises, she was physically unharmed. I knew psychologically she might never be the same.

She wriggled away and pointed to Adelmo. "Who's that man?"

While I searched for a way to explain to my daughter who he was, he stepped forward. His gaze was unfocused until he came within a few feet of her.

"It is you," he rasped, reaching toward Emma. "I have waited such a long time to meet you, dear child."

"Who are you?"

"A friend of your lovely mother. And you are just as beautiful as she. I am an old man whose eyes are failing. Come closer, please, so I might see you better."

She stared at him, then gave me a questioning look. The urge to step between them almost overcame me, but I nodded, and watched as she side-stepped toward him. He dropped to his knee. Emma, who had a healthy distrust of strangers, came close enough to touch him. She placed a small hand on his cheek and ran it over his ravaged face. I expected her to say he needed to shave, but she smiled and moved into his waiting arms.

His shoulders shook, but, unlike me, he didn't collapse into sobs. She patted him on the back and murmured reassuring sounds. He straightened and whispered in her ear. I couldn't hear him or see her expression when he spoke.

A surge of panic paralyzed me with an unfathomable dread. Only Justin's presence kept me from falling into the darkness hurtling toward me. He took my shaking hands. "Let's give them more time."

The heavy fear threatening to overcome me subsided. Yes, I would do that. Because it's what Stella would have wanted. She would have wanted Adelmo to have the chance to meet his daughter. To hold her if only for a little while.

Then, as if I had summoned her, my sister emerged from the smokey-gray fog.

Despite the streaks of soot and grime covering it, her pale face cast a ghostly glow. It was the same deadly shade as when I found her lifeless body etched into the sand.

My breath came in shallow gasps, stopping me from screaming her name. I reached for Justin, but he was no longer beside me. He stood next to Adelmo, Emma, and a young man I hadn't noticed during the gun battle. With his back to the spot from which our daughter appeared, he was oblivious to the approaching apparition.

She's not real, I told myself and repeated the statement over and over, as if it were a charm. But this wasn't a fairytale where the evil witch is vanquished with an incantation. This was a flesh and blood woman, and she was calling my daughter's name.

Fury replaced fear, and I shouted, "No, Stella! God help me, I love you, but she's not yours anymore. She's mine."

She stopped and squinted in my direction, then shaded her eyes. I realized the rising sun created a glare, which meant she might not have gotten a clear view of us.

Afraid to look away from the woman, I didn't notice my daughter had stepped away from Adelmo to join me.

She grabbed my hand and squealed, "Look, Mommy. It's the nice lady who saved me."

Before I could stop her, she slipped from my grasp and ran to her rescuer. I watched as her real mother leaned over to greet her.

I started to shout to Justin to grab her before she reached the woman. Then I saw Adelmo, staring statue-still at the scene in front of him. In that moment, it was as if he and I shared a belief in the impossible. We accepted that Emma's nice lady was Stella. For me, the fantasy was fleeting. But not so for her lover. He remained transfixed. Whether frozen in ecstasy or terror or madness, I had no way to know.

A soft breeze ruffled the leaves above us, carrying with it Adelmo's words. "Dios mío. My prayers are answered. My love is returned to me."

He stumbled back into his companion, who eased him to the ground and cradled his head. "Help, please. We need a doctor." He began performing chest compressions.

"I'll get an EMT." Justin broke into a run, oblivious to what had caused Adelmo's collapse. But I understood. He had seen the impossible and accepted it as a blessing. For him, the hateful twist of fate that took Stella from him had been righted. What did it matter if she no longer inhabited the world of the living? He would join her wherever she was, and with Emma, they would be a family again.

His very mortal reaction to the vision of my sister helped me accept the fact it was just that. An illusion, not reality. Unhinged from the trauma of losing Emma, I had succumbed to my terror and assumed my sister had returned from the dead.

The person chatting with my child was not her lost mother. She was younger and softer. She was the version of Stella before Ben came into the picture — the girl Lesroy and I called our Stella Star.

My sister reveled in the spotlight, fully aware of the effect her beauty had on the world. This young woman was reluctant to step into the light, so much so Emma had to pull her by the arm to get her to join our group.

Justin returned with the medic before the girls reached us. She took over the compressions while two other attendants brought a stretcher and loaded Adelmo onto it.

"Mommy, where are they taking Elmo?" Emma tugged at my sleeve.

"He's just feeling a little icky, so they're going to give him a checkup. I'm sure he'll be okay."

Another necessary lie parents tell their kids all the time. No one had told me how bad off Adelmo was. But even if he made a full physical recovery, there was no way back for him. He had experienced the greatest joy of his life when he thought Stella had returned to him. Learning it was only an illusion would destroy him.

And if it hadn't been for Emma, I, too, might have been undone from it. I had been willing to fight my sister to keep her daughter—my daughter. But believing, if only for a few minutes, she was back filled me with a sense of peace like nothing I'd ever felt. Thinking I would get to share with her I forgave her and would never stop loving her flooded me with a childlike happiness I thought was lost to me.

A tug on my sleeve alerted me Emma had been talking to me and was annoyed at being ignored.

"I'm sorry. Mommy's having trouble understanding." The ringing in my ears mitigated this small lie.

"I said I want you to meet my new bestest friend, Natty. The bad men got her, too, but I unlocked her, and she helped us run away." She beamed at me and pointed to the girl standing behind her.

A beautiful blond creature with the eyes of a dead woman.

CHAPTER 38: NATALIE

When I discovered Emma was no longer by my side, I didn't panic. But after two or three minutes of running around in circles, calling her name, I totally lost my shit. It was as if I was in a horror movie, where the smoke from the burning warehouse snuck up and swallowed my niece whole.

I took a deep breath. "Don't be stupid. She's got to be somewhere. Hell, everybody is somewhere, right?"

A gust of wind swirled through the thick haze. A flash of movement in the distance caught my attention. Please be Emma, I prayed and dashed toward the rising sun.

Screaming sirens bore down on me, making it useless to call out her name. So, I kept chasing the vanishing phantom I hoped was my niece. Sunlight cutting through the thinning smoke screen blurred my vision, and I had no idea if I was heading to safety or straight into the arms of our captors.

The presence of emergency vehicles reassured me. The guys who took us wouldn't be eager to hang around to explain things. They most definitely wouldn't want to talk to the authorities. It occurred to me Grace could be in the clearing ahead, and I was tempted to turn and run away. This was not the way I planned to introduce myself to the family I wanted to be a part of.

But what if it wasn't her mother waiting to greet Emma? What if Crybaby or one of those other goons lurked around the corner? I wasn't about to abandon her now. I channeled my inner track star and bolted as if our lives depended on it, which they might if I didn't reach her first.

The worst of the smoke from the blast cleared by the time I got within a few feet of the little girl. I saw a cluster of people in the distance. Beams of light hit me directly in the eyes, so it was impossible to tell who was who.

Even without a clear view, I knew one thing for certain. My sister was among the small group.

A cloud shaded the area, proving my senses were dead on. Grace stood a few steps away from the others, and she was staring in my direction. Her pose reminded me of a boy I had a crush on my freshman year in high school. He wrestled for the team and fluctuated between about one thirty and one forty pounds. But when he hovered at the edge of the mat, fiercely assessing his opponent, he gave off a much bigger vibe, kind of like the Hulk only better looking. Grace's position mimicked his but scored at least three times higher on the *Scare the Shit out of You* meter.

Before I began stalking her family, I might have taken her hostility personally. After getting to know her daughter, I got it. If someone with her hair practically on fire was chasing my child, I would Hulk up, too.

While my niece rushed to her mother, several men walked behind a stretcher carried by paramedics. They headed toward one of the ambulances. I recognized Justin and ignored the other at first, deciding he was probably a paramedic or a good Samaritan. Or worse, some freak who showed up at disasters for fun. Then I caught a look at his profile and realized he was my deceitful lover. Instead of being flooded with righteous anger, the need to rush to him was so strong it almost knocked me off my feet. I'm not sure if I would have been able to resist it if Emma hadn't skipped over to me and grabbed my arm.

"Come on, Natty. I want to show you to Mommy."

Nothing appealed to me less than being put on display in the middle of this terrible chaos. Not to mention I looked like shit on a cracker. But I had waited too long to make a run for it, so I let myself be dragged along.

Emma introduced me as her new best friend and her rescuer. Grace never took her eyes off me. Drained of the superpowers her rage and fear provided, she had turned a frightening shade of beige and seemed as frail as my mother when she came home from the hospital. I remembered how shocked I'd been when I found the photo of Stella on Facebook and discovered how much alike we looked. I gave myself a mental smack on the head for not considering Grace's reaction when I popped up without warning.

It wasn't until Emma repeated her introduction that her mother reacted by extending a shaking hand.

"It's Grace McElroy. Thank you for bringing her back."

Her married name confused me for a second, and I hesitated before offering her my own unsteady one.

I identified myself as Natalie Burden and could think of nothing else to add. She didn't let go of my now very sweaty hand or break eye contact. Her grip grew tighter, and her glassy-eyed stare changed into something that made me want to follow my original impulse to get the hell away from her. I imagined the color draining from my face at the same time it returned to hers.

"Well, Natalie." The way she said my name sounded as if she were testing it on her tongue. "The police have agreed to come to my home to fill out their reports. I volunteered to give you a ride if that's all right with you?"

Emma clapped her hands and jumped up and down. "Oh, yes, please. Pretty please. You can meet Scarlett, and I'll paint your picture after you wash your face and comb your hair." She yawned and swayed. "Maybe after we take a nap."

Despite the girl's enthusiasm, I realized the request was less an invitation and more of an expectation. Strange, but only a few days ago, I would have been thrilled at being asked to go to her home. How many times had I pictured the two of us sitting at her kitchen table chatting the way sisters do? Or the way I assumed they did. In my dreams, it was a reunion because hadn't we known deep down there were more than two Burnette girls?

But instead of going to a celebration of new beginnings, I would be attending a funeral mourning the end of a relationship that had never existed.

Even following her to the car seemed like a death march. Grace slowed her pace to match Emma's while I limped along behind them. Justin waited in the spot where the ambulance had been. We stopped to wait for him as he approached us with a puzzled expression.

He swooped his daughter up and gathered his wife close to him in their version of a Hallmark movie ad. The picture of family bliss, still perfect after the worst time of their lives. Something like longing wrapped in bitterness or bitterness wrapped in longing came over me.

Grace explained I was the one who helped Emma get away from her kidnappers and would go with them to answer questions from the police.

"And a few of ours as well," she added in an icy tone. Unless I was projecting, which from Justin's raised eyebrows, I didn't think I was.

"I asked the cops to give us a few hours to clean up before they come. No offense, Natalie, but you're welcome to take a shower if you want. I'm sure Grace has some clothes she can lend you."

This time it was his wife who raised her brows.

·　　·　　·　　·　　·

On the drive home, Emma demanded to tune in the radio to the kid channel. She insisted I hold her hand. The space between her car seat and mine behind the driver made it awkward, but I didn't mind. She fell asleep to a kiddie bop version of Taylor Swift's "Bad Blood," and I pretended to sleep, too.

Justin and Grace whispered to each other, too low for me to pick up anything. I guessed she was sharing her suspicions with her husband and tried to imagine what they might be. Did she think I was involved with our captors and had used Emma to escape when things went wrong? And how had she explained my obvious resemblance to Stella?

I took a breath and told myself to settle down and stop expecting the worst.

Instead of doubting me, had she shared the pull I experienced when I learned of her existence? Losing Stella must have left her with the sense of being incomplete, the same sensation I'd had for most of my life. Wasn't it possible finding me would give her some comfort? Not the relief of completeness it gave me, but a little joy from being a part of something special because it was too happily unexpected not to matter.

Don't kid yourself, I warned.

Grace had been complete as Stella's sister. Selfishly, I wished her death would bring more than simple grief from the loss of a loved one. I wanted it to leave her as adrift as I was, so she would be driven to seek another connection. And I would be that connection.

The way she and Emma were together showed me how foolish I'd been. Like the one she had with Stella, their bond was too strong for an inconsequential event like dying to break. Her sister would always be part of her. I had been an idiot to hope I might fill an empty spot in her life.

When we got to the house, Justin carried Emma inside, where a giant-size Doberman rushed to greet her. She sniffed at the girl's tangled curls and licked her cheek. Emma responded with a moan, and the dog went dead still.

"It's okay, Scarlett. She's just sleeping." He reassured her, but she refused to move until Emma snuffled softly. Then she gave her another lick before letting them pass.

They put her to bed, filthy clothes and all. Grace led me to the guest room and explained a friend had been staying with them, but I should find everything I needed. She would lay out some clean underwear and outfits for me to choose from.

The idea of borrowing from my older sister warmed me, as if I received the gift of acceptance. Another dumbass delusion that would soon be ripped from me. I wasn't a treasured younger sibling to be loved and fussed over. I was a stalker who might have put an end to the kidnapper's plans before they started if only I'd come forward and told them about the guy at the park and that I knew their peeping tom.

In the middle of rinsing the conditioner out of my hair, I thought about my mother. The thugs had taken my cell phone, which meant she and my aunt would be flipping out about being sent to voicemail over and over. They would suspect the worst. That some vicious criminal had kidnapped me. I burst out laughing. How many times had Mom warned me about awful degenerates hiding in the bushes, ready to pounce on helpless girls on their way home from choir practice? And every single instance, I sneered at her melodrama. Finally, she was right. It seemed cruel not to give her the credit she was due. But crueler to tell her how close her daughter had come to extinction.

Instead of leisurely strolling through the walk-in closet to select the perfect outfit to wear during my audition to be a member of the family, I threw on a pair of leggings and a tunic top. I finger-combed my wet hair and rushed down the hallway to the stairs leading to the kitchen, where I'd noticed a landline. On the way, I passed the Doberman sprawled in front of the door to what had to be Emma's room. She lifted her head as I got closer.

"Good girl," I whispered, hoping she cared about my opinion. I skirted around her and felt her sharp eyes on my back as I took the steps two at a time.

I dreaded the call but made it anyway. "Hey, Mom. It's me, and I'm fine."

She burst into tears, and I waited for a break in the sobs before telling her my friend's injury had required surgery, and I lost my cell phone, and wasn't sure when I'd be home and not to worry. I heard Char mumbling curse words but hung up before she could take over the conversation.

Once, I was proud of THE creative lies I spewed to my mother. Now, they made me feel like shit. If that was a result of becoming an adult, it sucked, and I wanted no part of it.

Footsteps interrupted my frustration about being a member of the sorry world of grown-ups.

Grace rounded the corner, also in leggings and a loose top. Damp curls framed her face. Without makeup, she was a much younger version of herself. I had been so focused on the missing sister I hadn't registered the beauty of the one she left behind. Although there were dark shadows under them, her silvery gray eyes stunned me. She possessed a quiet kind of elegance, reminding me of a starlet from a black and white movie. I pictured her standing beside Stella, happy to fade into the background and give her the spotlight. But Grace had no need of special lighting. She glowed on her own.

"I didn't hear you come down. Have a seat while I fix us some coffee."

Her voice was soft and a little raspy, probably from all the smoke. It was also weirdly familiar. Except it really couldn't be since I'd only heard it once in person at the boutique. But she had spoken to me many times in my dreams.

I watched as she moved from sink to counter in that calm, confident way people do when they're performing the same mundane tasks as they did the day before and the day before and backward to infinity. Yet we both knew this was no ordinary occasion.

"It'll be easier to talk with just the two of us."

Nothing in the world would make this conversation anywhere close to easy, but I nodded as if my agreement mattered.

She got straight to the point. "I checked you out online to be certain you are who you claimed to be. Justin is running a more thorough background check right now."

"I understand."

"Perfect. So, Natalie Burden, how did you end up being kidnapped by the same people who stole my daughter?"

"My name is as good a place as any to start. Officially, it's Burden. Or it is if my father legally changed his name. From what I learned about him, I doubt he even bothered. His real name is Jack Burnette."

Grace choked on her coffee and began coughing and sputtering. After a few seconds, she went completely quiet and sat there staring, those weird eyes piercing through me.

The heavy silence between us made me want to scream, but I waited it out.

Finally, she spoke, so softly I had to lean closer. "Of course. It's why you look so much like her." Then louder, "How could I be such an idiot?"

"Well, you kind of had a lot going on."

She snorted with amusement, and I laughed along with her. Our hilarity didn't last long.

"So, we've clarified your identity. That doesn't explain why you were here."

Starting with the night I found out Stella died, before I was aware she'd lived, I told her everything. I hadn't intended to include how finding out about the two of them filled me with emotions I still couldn't name. Or how connected I felt the moment I saw Emma on the playground. But I did.

Her expression never wavered as she let me ramble on without interrupting until I reached the point in the story where Emma and I ran away from the building moments before it caught fire. When I described how frightened we were, my voice broke, and Grace took my hand.

"Emma's right. You saved her, and I'll spend the rest of my life thanking you."

Without hesitation, I replied, "She's my niece. I'd do anything for her."

CHAPTER 39: NATALIE

Both Justin and Grace tried to get me to rest before I headed home, but the thought of Mom wringing her hands and working herself up for another stroke was too scary. He packed snacks and drinks for me while she explained how the Castillo gang smacked her mother and aunt around and gave her soon-to-be stepfather a serious head injury. I learned Aunt Rita— technically, the title didn't fit, but I liked the sound of it— had been coerced into going to the hospital with her son and a family friend.

"You and I have so much to catch up on, but everything is such a mess. I called Mom's and Mike's doctors before I came downstairs. Thank God, they're out of intensive care. They both have concussions, and he has a couple of broken ribs and a bruised kidney. Hard to believe, but neither of them seemed to have any permanent damage. I should be able to talk to them later today. No news on Rita. Neither Lesroy nor Harry are answering their phones, and it's driving me crazy."

I wanted to say something reassuring to make her feel better, but I've never been good at quick comfort. A commotion at the front door saved me. Scarlett whined and sped to the hallway, growling as she went. Her snarls turned to yelps of joy when I heard a man call out, "Hello, you crazy bitch."

"Get ready. You're about to meet the slightly bent branch of the family tree," Justin said. I relocated to the corner, hoping to be less noticeable when the trio stepped into the kitchen.

Grace ran to them and gave Rita a gentle hug. "I don't understand. They said you had a stroke."

The man I resented, because he got to hang out with Grace and her family and I didn't, looped an arm around the waist of the redhead I pretended was my aunt.

"I most certainly did not. I just got discombobulated. Nothing worse than when your Uncle Roy smacked me up the side of the head."

A younger man with the same bright blue eyes as Rita winced, then put his hand on her shoulder. "Momma, calm down. You remember what you promised the doctor about taking it easy."

"I thought we agreed the doctor was an idiot."

"No. You agreed with yourself, as usual. Truth is, she got pissed off when he told her when geriatrics go up against drug dealers and gangsters, they should expect to spend a night or two in the hospital. The remark about geriatrics made her so mad, she threw him out of the room and bullied us into bringing her home. That's right, isn't it, Momma?"

"Now, honey, be patient. I'm still having a little memory loss." She grinned at him.

"Too soon. And this is serious. Just because —" His face froze when he saw me.

Rita noticed and turned in my direction. She emitted a cry somewhere between a shriek and a yelp, then covered her mouth with her hands and sunk into the older guy.

"It's okay. This is Natalie. She's not a ghost. She's my sister."

• • • • •

Those words danced around in my head on the drive home. Our meeting hadn't resembled any of my fantasies. It had almost been anticlimactic, like a series finale where the serial killer gets whacked by his son, and nobody cares.

But those three words, *She's my sister*, marked a beginning, not an ending. They didn't signal a happy-ever-after fairytale. They were the start of a future filled with the stuff that happens in real families.

And this time, I wasn't fantasizing because Grace had promised to call me when her mother and Mike were out of the hospital. We would all sit down for dinner together like those seventies TV shows.

An immediate twinge of guilt hit me when I thought of how my excitement over the future would affect me and Mom. Not that she and Aunt Char and even good old Dwight weren't real or family. They just weren't Burnettes. And, despite my legal name, I was.

I didn't look forward to reassuring Mom my having a sister wouldn't change things between us. It would be especially tricky because I had resented her for keeping Grace and Stella from me, but now I understood she had been protecting me from the possibility they wouldn't have welcomed me into their lives.

My guilt turned into fear when it hit me that I would have to fill Mom and Char in on all that happened on my trip. What exactly is the best way to tell your mother you were kidnapped by Ecuadorian gang members after rescuing my almost boyfriend from two little old ladies and then losing track of him? And how should I phrase it when I told them the same guy showed up at the warehouse that blew up minutes after my niece and I escaped from it?

Keeping my involvement in the fire and rescue of Emma secret made more sense than spilling the frightening details. And it's what I would have done if not for the certainty the events would be on the eleven o'clock news with a follow-up the next morning and a first page spread in the local paper.

The image of my mother clutching her heart—or whatever a person grabs when having a stroke—came to me. If I wanted to avoid killing her, I had to stay calm, to project a maturity I didn't feel and a sincerity I did.

Any possibility of handling myself in a cool and collected manner disappeared when I saw my aunt's car at the curb. How stupid was I to think Char would leave without all the dirt on her irresponsible niece? No. It would be the Charlotte Shit Show with me as the guest shit.

I took a few deep breaths before getting out of the car. Then I straightened my shoulders, tossed my hair back, and headed for my close-up.

.   .   .   .   .

The hours I spent summarizing my time in Atlanta began and ended with an apology. The first for lying about the trip; the second for underestimating the two most important women in my life and Dwight.

Apparently, my uncle—God love him—had plied the gals with booze because neither of them were coherent enough to do more than throw their arms around me and sob. He settled everybody down with coffee for them, vodka tonic for me.

I expected a barrage of interruptions in the form of expletives and questions, but they were so quiet it gave me the creeps. Except for Dwight refilling cups, no one moved until I got to the part when the warehouse exploded. Then Char broke the spell.

"Son of a bitch! Here I worried those assholes were going to rape you but no. Rape would have been a hell of a lot better than getting blown into tiny pieces and disappearing in the wind."

"Please, Char." My mother put her trembling hand on her sister's. "Let her finish."

I skipped all the parts about Renzo, included a health update on the injured senior citizens, and ended with Emma being safe.

We all started crying, including Dwight. When we stopped, I delivered the second apology.

"I was afraid to tell you all everything because it would upset you. Guess I forgot how tough my family is."

More tears ensued before my uncle announced he was taking his wife home to rest. She let him guide her from the room, leaving me and Mom alone.

"I sure wish you'd told me what was going on, but I get it. You didn't want to upset me. Now you know I'm not made of glass, and I want you to promise you'll come to me when you need help."

I nodded and started to speak, but she stopped me.

"When you're ready, I expect to hear all about this boy you've been so careful not to mention and what he did to hurt you."

.   .   .   .   .

Other than soaking in a hot tub, nursing my scrapes and bruises, and stumbling to the table for dinner, I stayed in bed the next day. Mom gave me the space I needed without asking more questions about the man who stomped on my heart,

But I had to have answers for myself. What exactly had Renzo done? From the beginning he shied away from getting close to me. He warned me his time in the city was limited. It was me who pushed for more. But he was the one who pretended to be someone else, making me into a fool for caring.

Worse, I didn't understand why. Obviously, it had something to do with Adelmo Balsuto or he wouldn't have been at the fire. But I hadn't even known the guy was still alive. I fell asleep trying to come to terms with the likelihood I might never find out who Lorenzo Diez really was or ever see him again.

CHAPTER 40: GRACE

When the shock of seeing Stella's doppelgänger wore off, I compiled a list in my head of all the ways Natalie Burden was different. Her full lips might remind me of my sister's, but unlike Stella, she projected a shy, sad vibe, as if she were constantly on the verge of apologizing. Her sea-blue eyes were wide with no hint of subterfuge or mystery. Taller than our lost sister, her willowy frame was softer, lighter, which made her rescue of my daughter more impressive.

The sight of Emma sprawled out in her car seat, an exhausted dancer in a Toulouse-Lautrec painting, eased my mind. Her hand in Natalie's both pleased and disturbed me. I had fallen into the kind of relationship where one member wants to settle down and start a family while the other is only just considering getting a cat together. The question was which of the two was I.

Despite my suspicions regarding her sudden appearance in our lives, my new half-sister had formed a bond with my daughter, and Emma was an excellent judge of character. She had instantly disliked Justin's tech guy, who ended up going to jail for beating his wife.

And when we brought Natalie home to interrogate, she passed the Scarlett test. The dog pressed against her, demanding to be petted.

Could I welcome this young woman into my life without giving up something of myself? And if she wasn't as genuine as she seemed, if — God help me — she was more like Stella than I assumed? What then?

Justin understood my reluctance. After we put Emma, dirty clothes and all, to bed and got Natalie situated, he suggested I speak to her alone.

"Remember, you don't have to decide anything until you get a better feel for the situation." He kissed me as I headed to the kitchen to fix coffee.

The sight of her sitting at the table jolted me, but I kept my cool.

I had no doubts concerning her story of my father's second family and none about him deserting that one as well as ours. The perverse satisfaction I had at his abandonment of them shamed me but established common ground between me and the girl. But I wasn't ready to acknowledge it, which was also shameful, since I saw how much she wanted me to accept her. From the way she leaned in when I spoke and glanced away when I caught her staring at me, she radiated the desperate need to be a part of our lives.

While she might long to be someone's sister, I didn't. Losing Stella had changed me in ways I was still discovering. I missed her every day but not the person I was when she was alive. That woman let herself be so consumed by sisterhood it became her only identity. My sister's death forced me to recognize I was more than the older sibling, had a purpose greater than smoothing the way for Stella at the expense of my own happiness.

The sudden appearance of Lesroy with Rita and Harry bought me time to determine how to respond to the vulnerable young woman whose presence had both saved and upended my family.

Their arrival had an adverse effect on my intent to remain detached from Natalie until I made a rational decision about what our relationship would be. Relief that Rita's condition hadn't been as bad as expected and the fear Mom's or Mike's might be worse wore at me. And I let down my guard when I introduced the girl as my sister. As soon as the words left my lips, I knew I was in trouble.

. . . . .

Lesroy tried to get his mother to leave at the same time as Natalie, but short of a blast of dynamite, she wouldn't budge before we dished the dirt on the Stella-lookalike in our house.

Justin gave her an abbreviated account of the events at the warehouse, glossing over as much of the terror as possible. Despite her slightly addled condition, my aunt was no fool. Her side-eyed looks toward Harry made me pity him. As soon as they were alone, she would demand he get the whole story from my husband and relay every single detail to her. I didn't blame her and wasn't worried if the woman who so fiercely defended my daughter and maimed one of her attackers could handle it.

Vincent showed up with chicken biscuits and hash browns. I hadn't realized how hungry I was and gorged myself before hitting a wall of exhaustion too high and wide to ignore. I excused myself to leave the group to their cross-examination of Justin.

Rita stopped me." You look all pale and done in. Get yourself to bed and stay there awhile."

Sometime after one, I woke up. Other than the comforting sound of Justin's whistle-snore, the house was quiet. Much too quiet.

I bolted upright, stumbling over Scarlett, who snorted but refused to budge. A growing terror tightened my throat. If the dog was here, that meant Emma wasn't asleep in her room.

"Wake up, Justin," I shouted. Like our brave watchdog, he groaned but didn't move.

I threw open the door and raced down the hall, shouting our daughter's name as I ran. Her empty room heightened my growing hysteria as I neared the stairs. By now, my decibel level had climbed to an extreme neither man nor beast could ignore.

"Babe," Justin came up behind me and put his hands on my shoulders. Scarlett nudged me and whined. "Emma's fine. Vincent and Lesroy took her to their house to hang out while we rested."

I sank to the floor and burst into tears. He sat beside me while the dog covered me with concerned kisses. If not for the insistence of my bladder, I could have curled into the fetal position and stayed there.

Instead, I rushed to the bathroom, then collapsed onto the bed where my husband commanded I remain. Thanks to the combination of adrenaline letdown and my crying jag, I didn't have the strength to argue.

"Hey, Scarlett. Let's let Mom rest some more."

She scooted closer and refused to move until he went to the kitchen and banged on her food bowl. Even then, she waited for me to give the go-ahead before galloping downstairs.

For the next several hours, I floated in a black hole of sleep. Snippets of conversations from unrecognizable voices drifted past in invisible thought bubbles. What dreams I might have had were forgotten before completion. They weren't bad or good; they simply were until they weren't.

Whispers from someone I recognized woke me. I felt her solid little body welded to my own and discovered Emma watching me with her shining silver-gray eyes. With one hand, she twirled a strand of my hair. She was vigorously sucking the thumb of the other, something she hadn't done for years.

"Daddy said I could come up to see if you were still sleeping. You're not anymore, right?"

"If I were asleep, could I do this?" I raised on my elbow and tickled her under armpits. Justin found her in a fit of giggles while I blew on her belly, and Scarlett, her heavy paws on the edge of the bed, watched with doggy concern.

He yelled, "Incoming!" and jumped onboard. The dog joined him, barking and nuzzling each of us.

We stopped when Emma gasped for air and insisted we were making her not breathe.

"Whew. I don't know about you two, but all that laughing made me hungry. Who's ready for pizza?"

She wriggled out of bed. "We got the meat lubbers for me and Daddy and a veggie for you."

Over dinner, Justin told me Mom was out of critical care but needed to stay overnight for observation. Mike's heartbeat had returned to normal, and his head injury was less serious than the doctor had thought. He had pain medication for the broken ribs but had been cleared for check-out. He informed the hospital he had no intention of leaving without his wife and was firmly planted by her bedside. The doctor must have forgotten Georgia's stance on common-law marriage. More likely, he decided going up against the two of them wasn't worth the time and energy.

I wanted to call, but Justin convinced me they might be asleep or high on drugs. He said we would go to the hospital in the morning so I could talk Mike into swapping places with me.

Because the police had Adelmo in custody, my husband hadn't been able to get an update on his condition. From his appearance in the ambulance, we agreed it had to be serious. I reminded Justin it wasn't the first time he'd walked away from an explosion.

"True, but even if he does fully recover, he won't get out of this. The Feds will probably extradite him."

"Is that so bad? The Balsutos are used to bribing their way out of worse situations than this." My visit to Ecuador had been an education in tropical corruption.

"The legal system isn't what worries me. It's the Castillo family. No amount of money can keep them from going after revenge. Adelmo will be a dead man walking."

Despite my fear of his reclaiming Emma, I didn't want her father murdered. The person I was before my sister's death wouldn't have understood there was nothing we could do to change a fate chosen for him when he took over his family business. The Grace I had become learned how futile it was to try to save someone from themselves.

Later, when Emma fell asleep lying between us, we let her stay there. Scarlett draped herself across the foot of the bed, ignoring Justin's commands to get off the damn bed. We let her stay, too.

"Just this once," I promised. He rolled his eyes.

.   .   .   .   .

We were eating Justin's special blueberry pancakes when the phone rang. When I answered, a young man identified himself as Adelmo's nephew.

"I am sorry to disturb you so early, but my uncle's condition has improved. If he remains stable for the next few hours, he will be transferred to a detention center until your government determines what to do with him. A friend at our embassy in Washington has secured permission for him to have one visitor before he is relocated. He requested I contact you to see if you might find it in your heart to let him say goodbye to your daughter."

The concern on Emma's face when Adelmo disappeared, how easily she had gone to him, and his willingness to sacrifice his life for hers signaled their undeniable connection. It was almost as if she recognized him on some primitive level. If I denied them the chance to be together, would she resent me for it later?

"We'll bring her, but one of us must be in the room with the two of them. And if she doesn't want to come, forget it."

He put me on hold, supposedly to clear it with the doctor, but I suspected he spoke directly to Adelmo.

"Anything that makes you comfortable."

Since time was running out for his uncle, I agreed to ask Emma right away. If she seemed the least bit anxious, I would call it off. Otherwise, he should expect us in a little over an hour.

"You are most kind. I wish I could be there when you and the child arrive. Unfortunately, I have a most important meeting, but someone will be there to greet you in the lobby."

Justin wasn't happy I hadn't run the plan by him but shared my belief Adelmo would eventually show up in our lives again.

"But if she hesitates at all, it's a no go."

I assured him we were on the same page. "But you know Emma's always up for socializing."

She was coloring in her room when we asked if she wanted to visit her new friend in the hospital.

"So, that's where Elmo went. Is he very sick?"

"Not so much now. He's doing so well he gets to go home soon. And he wants to see you." My voice trembled when I got to the part about him leaving.

She returned to her drawing, scribbling furiously with a gray crayon. I wondered if we'd been wrong about her interest in seeing him. Then she stopped and, with a proud smile on her face, held up her work for me to admire.

"I was going to send this to him, but now I get to give it to him in person."

In the midst of a flurry of grayish and black swirls, a halo of yellow surrounded a dark man with a brown and white beard. He holds the hand of a curly-haired child with silver eyes. His lips are set in a straight line, but the little girl—my little girl—smiles with her head tilted toward him.

My throat filled with a bitter taste, and my expression must have shown my distress because Emma's grin disappeared.

"What's wrong, Mommy? Don't you like it?"

I swooped her into my arms. "It's beautiful, baby. He's going to love it."

My initial reaction seemed to make her doubt my reassurance. She wriggled away and turned to Justin.

"I want him to keep it forever and ever."

"Your mom's right. He'll be crazy about it."

We exchanged looks, and his conveyed he was as disturbed by the image as I was. But he hadn't been lying when he said Adelmo would treasure the drawing. What father wouldn't save a picture of his daughter gazing at him with what could only be seen as adoration? Especially when he thought he'd lost her forever and ever.

.   .   .   .   .

Emma played hopscotch on the hospital tiles while we waited for Justin to speak to the guard stationed in the corridor.

"You're cleared to go in. I'll wait out here. Yell if you need me."

The heaviness settling in my stomach as soon as I saw my daughter's drawing expanded to the size of a small boulder. It pressed the air from my lungs. On the way to the hospital, Justin reassured me that her artwork was nothing more than get-well wishes, but we both knew it was more.

"It's not like Emma to become so invested in someone she just met. What if he tries to take her away from us?"

"No judge is going to be influenced by a kid's coloring. Besides, he gave you custody. He has no legal standing. Oh, and he's a notorious drug lord."

I snorted but didn't bother to point out I hadn't said anything about custody. Adelmo Balsuto had no respect for legalities. If he wanted our child, he would take her.

Before I could knock, Emma pushed the door open and skipped into the room, waving her drawing ahead of her like a flag leading her onto the battlefield. I hurried after her but stopped when I saw the shriveled figure on the bed. Adelmo's initial appearance in my kitchen a few nights ago had surprised me with how much he had aged. This man was unrecognizable. His eyes almost disappeared into the folds of flesh surrounding them. The high cheekbones that made him so imposing gave him a skeletal look despite the sagging skin.

When he saw Emma, he sat upright, transforming into at least a shadow of my sister's devoted lover. Instead of hesitating with fearfulness over his diminished appearance, Emma broke into a short run to reach him.

"My beautiful child. I was afraid you would not come." He held out his hand, and she took it with her free one before scrambling onto the bed.

The sight of them so close together chilled me. Not because it hinted at something unnatural. More that it was too natural. I rushed to stand beside them.

"It's okay, Mommy. Elmo and I are friends, so can we have a little piracy?"

He flashed a crooked smile, but tears welled in his eyes. His breath caught in a wheeze before he could clear his throat. "I think you mean privacy, do you not? Your mother is also my friend and is welcome to stay, should she wish to do so."

Emma squinted at me, her expression so like Stella's as a child when things weren't going according to her plan. For whatever reason, my daughter wanted to be alone with this almost-stranger.

"I'll tell you what. We can move this chair into the hallway and sit there with the door open."

She sighed and rolled her eyes, also Stella-like.

"Or I can stand right here."

"Okay. The hallway."

When I pushed the door, it bumped against Justin's shoulder as he scrambled out of the way.

"Emma wanted a little piracy," I whispered. He gave me a puzzled look. Then, louder, I added, "The door stays open."

My husband stood behind me while I watched them from my seat. Emma leaned over the patient, her curls hiding half her face. Her head bobbed up and down in an unrecognizable rhythm with one of her many tall tales. Every three or four seconds, he fell against the pillow, laughing at what I was sure were most colorful details.

When she stopped for a breath, he began to talk. I clenched my fists, panicked at where all this would lead. Justin put his hands on my shoulders, and I eased back down. Adelmo might be many things, but he would never do or say anything that might hurt his daughter.

·   ·   ·   ·   ·

Emma remained quiet on the way to the car. I was dying to find out what she and Adelmo had talked about but knew better than to come right out and ask. I took a less direct approach. "So, how was your private talk with your new friend?"

She swung her legs and kicked the back of my seat without answering. I ignored it and waited. When I didn't react, she stopped and stared out the window before she responded to my question. "We laughed a lot, but I think he's very, very sad."

"Maybe it's because he doesn't feel so good," Justin offered.

"I guess."

Time to give up on the subtle approach. "You must have cheered him up, the way he was laughing." I pivoted to gauge her reaction.

She shrugged. "Not really."

"Well, it sounded like he enjoyed it a whole lot. Which one did you tell him?"

Instead of her usual enthusiastic performance in response to a special request, she discovered a loose thread on her shirt and pulled it. I curled my fingers into fists but kept my mouth shut.

Justin broke first. "Was it the one about the boy who stole the little girl's lunch and how she followed all the clues until she tracked him down and took his sandwich, which was way better than the one her mother packed?"

"She didn't track him down. Duh. He was sitting right next to her. And no. Not that one. It was a new one, just for him."

Being snubbed for a man my child barely knew stung, but I refused to exhibit weakness in what had become a battle of wits, or a game of who blinks first, or no-show and no-tell. Whatever it was, the parents needed the win.

"I'm sure he liked it. What about the one he told you? I thought I heard him mention a unicorn?"

"Not a unicorn. A mermaid. His story was about a beautiful princess who changes herself into a mermaid to save her little girl from evil warriors."

I shuddered, and Justin reached over to hold my hand. Stella had lost her life keeping Emma safe. But her journey to the sea didn't turn her into a magical creature. It turned her into dead.

"Sounds exciting," he said. "But also kind of scary."

"I wasn't scared because the mermaid swims close to the beach where her little girl plays. And once a year, on the girl's birthday, she turns back into a princess to visit. But even when she's not a human person, she's always there, to watch after her and keep her safe."

My husband squeezed my hand a little tighter but didn't look at me. I bit my lip, unable to speak.

After a few minutes, Emma piped up to ask for a juice box. Comforted by the appearance of normal, I found the snack bag and handed her an Arty Apple, 100 per cent real fruit. Her slurps from the back seat were oddly reassuring. We had faced almost losing her twice — once to the kidnappers, once to her biological father. And our little family had survived.

This knowledge filled me with a calm confidence. Emma tossed me the empty box, burped, and giggled at her grossness.

"I told Elmo how it would be fun to have my very own mermaid. We could go swimming, and when I got tired, I could ride on her back. It made him laugh but not happy. He's sad because he has to go away. That makes me sad, too."

"Just because he has to leave doesn't mean you'll never see him again," I lied like any good parent would. But Emma wasn't buying it.

"No, he won't be back. Not 'xactly."

"Not exactly? So, he might come back?" I asked, unsure what it would mean if she answered yes.

"He said all I had to do was close my eyes, and he would be there, same as the mermaid. That made me laugh 'cause that stuff only happens in fairytales. But he wasn't joking. He told me when you love somebody, it's magic. And anything can happen with magic."

I wondered if the spell he planned to cast was for good or evil. "What did you say then?"

"I told him I believed him."

"But you don't think your friend was talking about popping up out of nowhere like a cartoon genie. That would be crazy. Right, Daddy?"

"Absolutely nuts. Emma gets that. Don't you, baby?"

"Duh. Elmo's magic is real."

"How do you know?" My words came out interrogation-style, clipped and a little hostile.

"You know. Not imaginary. He'll be there, but he'll be indivisible."

"You mean *invisible?*"

She gave me a pained look. "Yes, Mommy. Like he's there only nobody can see or hear him. Nobody 'cept me."

I should have let it go as another fantasy friend. But Emma had grown out of the stage after the disappearance of Mr. Sassypants, a make-believe buddy of hers who spilled milk on the counter and ate Scarlett's dog food. And Adelmo Balsuto wasn't imaginary. Any sympathy I had for him being shipped back to Ecuador vanished.

"Honey, you know how grown-ups are. They play pretend games with kids all the time." My neck ached from craning it toward her, but I had to watch her reactions.

She shook her head hard enough to send her curls swirling. "Elmo wasn't playing a game. But don't worry, he is going away soon."

I sighed in relief. "Yes, he has to return to Ecuador. That's why we took you to say goodbye."

"Not there. Somewhere else."

"No, Emma. He has to go to his own country. And he won't be back. You tell her, Daddy." Frustration and a growing unease with the conversation demanded I call in reinforcements.

"Mommy's right. When he said he'd come whenever you need him, he was talking about seeing him in your mind, like a dream, not in real life."

I swiveled my shoulders around to get a better view and watched as she scrunched her eyes shut before she nodded and scooted as far to the right as her seatbelt allowed. A slow smile lit her face as she tilted her head to the empty space behind my seat.

CHAPTER 41: NATALIE

I woke with the worst kind of hangover a little before eight—a dry one, the result of physical and emotional exhaustion and confusion combined with frustration. Determined to forget about Renzo, I bounded down the stairs with false cheerfulness. Other than a slightly shocked look, Mom acted as if my quick recovery from being kidnapped and heart-broken was completely normal. I volunteered to clean, but she didn't want me to work.

"Honey, you've been through hell and back. Why don't you give yourself another day to recover?"

"After lounging in bed yesterday, I can't take any more rest. I'm so hyper I am about to jump out of my skin."

Mom laughed. "You sound like your Aunt Charlotte. Go ahead and clean to your heart's desire."

Mindlessly spraying lemon mist on the furniture and humming tunelessly as I ran the vacuum calmed my nerves and mostly kept my mind off Renzo. After adding a shine to the woodwork and smoothing the trace marks out of the carpet, I trudged upstairs to straighten my room.

When we finished a lunch of Mom's homemade pimento cheese, I grabbed her sun hat and gloves and walked outside to pull weeds. Renzo's face popped up on every dandelion and clover I snatched from the ground. The poor little things never had a chance.

By dinnertime, my frenzy of energy evaporated, and I was almost too tired to eat. I settled in early and slept dreamlessly until a familiar voice seeped through one of those vague dreams you're sure you had but can't remember. Sunlight through the blinds striped the bright orange rug beside the bed. My old clock radio read 12:16.

"Screw you, Renzo Diez," I said aloud and thought of my new sister instead. What would Grace be doing right now? Would she be on the phone with the hospital trying to get more information on her mother and Mike? And what should I call them? Mrs. Burnette and Mr. Whatever or Marilyn and Mike? Hell, would they even want to meet me? I'd be a painful reminder of all they lost. As for him, why should he give two flying fucks about me?

I made a mental note to clean up my language in case Grace some day decided to introduce me to them, then dashed for the bathroom. On the way, I heard it again. The voice from my dreams, only it didn't make sense because I was awake, wasn't I? A splash of cold water assured me I was.

Footsteps on the stairway filled me with a combination of dread and excitement.

"Natalie, it's after noon. Are you up?"

"I am. I'll be down in a minute."

I waited for her to ask what I wanted for breakfast, or would it be lunch? It didn't matter to me because I was starving. She knocked on the door before opening it a crack. Instead of asking about breakfast, she said, "You might want to get dressed before you come down. We have a visitor."

Half an hour later, Renzo and I sat in the living room, him staring at me; me refusing to look at him. I'm not sure what he told my mother, but she made an excuse about needing groceries and rushed out of the house.

"I understand you may never wish to see me again, but I would not leave without speaking with you."

When I didn't respond, he reached for my hand. I kept it in a tight fist, more because I was afraid of what I might do if his fingers touched mine.

"Please, Natalie. Do not shut me out."

"How can I possibly do anything to you when I don't even know who the hell you are?" I startled myself with the extent of my fury but didn't try to rein it in. I wanted to unleash it, to hurt him like he hurt me. No, I wanted to hurt him more. But it's impossible to inflict emotional damage on a stranger. This added to my anger, making me want to throw him out before he said another word. But I had to find out what kind of person I'd fallen in love with.

He ran his fingers through his hair, then placed his palms on the table. After examining them for a few seconds, he looked at me through lowered lashes. I sat on my own to keep from reaching out to him.

"My name is Roberto Balsuto. Adelmo is my uncle. More like a father after mine died. When he met your sister, I was at university, so I never got to see them together. But I can tell from his gentle change in tone when he speaks of her how much he adored her. And his transformation after her death has been remarkable. When he disappeared after he lost her, he contacted me to say he hadn't been killed in the explosion. He advised me on how to set up a legitimate real estate company designed to help poor families improve their housing situations. He named it La Estrella, The Star."

"That's so beautiful." My words slipped out before I remembered how much I hated both Renzo and Roberto.

"As was the love they shared. I can only hope I will someday experience the passion my uncle had with his Stella."

Okay, now he was really pouring it on, and I was way too close to falling for it. "Right. Maybe you should get on with why you lied to me about who you are."

"Yes, yes, of course. It is important you understand my relationship with the family business. All of my cousins and I were sheltered from it. We were sent to boarding schools with children of varied backgrounds. It wasn't until my last year in high school I started piecing together the Balsuto story. By then, my father had been killed and avenged by his brothers. When I confronted Adelmo about my suspicions, he was honest although I'm certain he glossed over some of the more egregious sins of the family. He shared his vision of shifting into legitimacy and enlisted my help." He cleared his throat. "May I have some water, please?"

Thankful for the chance to digest what he'd told me, I nodded, then took a glass from the cabinet, and filled it. So far, everything synced with what I learned from my research about my sisters, especially Grace's trip to Ecuador. And while there was no reason for him to keep lying, I still didn't know why he had to lie in the first place.

He took a sip and thanked me before picking up where he left off.

"I began working for Adelmo, setting up various corporations. Gradually, he brought several of my cousins onboard. Word got out the Balsutos were no longer dealing in the drug trade. Most of his competitors celebrated the news since it meant more money for them. But Dario Castillo refused to accept it was true. He spread the rumor Adelmo was covering up a plan to take over the drug business. When no one showed interest in his theory, he sent a warning to my uncle that he was wise to his real intent and would stop him at any cost."

"This is all very interesting. But what does it have to do with me?"

"Not you. His daughter, all that remained of the woman he loved. You see, he had been keeping track of Emma and her aunt to make sure they were safe but also to have some small part in her life. He stationed people here in the States to follow them from time to time and take pictures of the child he could never acknowledge. Somehow, Dario discovered this weakness and sent men of his own with a very different purpose. Then you came into the picture."

"Me? How did anyone even know I existed?"

Instead of answering, he stared into my eyes, waiting for it to come to me. And it did.

Stalking Grace at the mall, following her home and to her mother's and to the school and the playground.

"They saw me watching Emma while they were doing the same thing."

"Yes, and we couldn't decide whose side you were on. My uncle sent me to find out."

"So, he had you figure out if I was a danger to his little girl. Did he suggest the best way to do that would be to get me to fall into your bed, or was it your idea?"

"It was my—no, it was not like that. I had no intention of seducing you. The plan was for me to follow you closely to understand why you were interested in Emma at all. That night I bumped into your table wasn't supposed to happen. But watching you go to class and to work and seeing you with your mother made it impossible for me not to at least speak with you. I promised myself we would only talk one time, then I would disappear from your life. I broke that promise, but I never meant to hurt you."

"Don't be ridiculous. You didn't hurt me. You pissed me off because I hate being lied to. There are plenty of guys who'll do that."

"I hated myself for telling you so many untruths. But you must believe me. What happened between us was real. I care deeply for you. You have to allow me to prove myself because, Natalie Burden, I'm falling in love with you."

He lifted my hand to his lips and kissed it. The logical side of my brain insisted only a fool would accept his words as truthful.

Every other part of me jumped at the chance to be that fool. To throw myself at him and drag him to my bed.

The buzzing from his pocket saved me. He glanced at his phone and frowned.

"I'm sorry, but it could be news of my uncle," he said before learning Adelmo Balsutto was dead.

CHAPTER 42: GRACE

Emma and Justin were walking Scarlett when my phone rang. It was Adelmo's nephew calling to tell us his uncle had died. The doctors surmised a blood clot from the impact of the explosion migrated to his brain. He'd been in the middle of a conversation with his nurse one minute and was gone the next. Because of his background, the authorities requested an autopsy but didn't suspect foul play.

I relayed the information to Justin while Emma got ready for bed. We waited until the morning to tell her Elmo had passed away although I had the uncomfortable suspicion she already knew.

Her reaction to the news supported my theory. After her dad and I stumbled through a child approved account of her biological father's last few minutes on earth, she listened but said nothing. When we finished, she asked if she could go outside. Her lack of emotion should have eased my mind about the strength of the bond between the two of them. Instead, it unsettled me.

"So, should we worry she might be a sociopath or be glad she's not upset?" I joined him where he stood, watching Emma kneeling at the edge of our goldfish pond.

"Beats me. Maybe we should take her to a counselor or something?"

Before we could discuss getting psychiatric help for our daughter, she bounded into the room with her arms outstretched.

"We need another memory rock like Tina's."

Tina was a small box turtle who crawled into our yard with a broken shell. At Emma's insistence, we took her to the vet. He wasn't hopeful but taped her up and sent us home with special food. Poor Tina lasted a month before she went belly-up, devastating Emma. We staged an elaborate funeral for the unfortunate reptile. Lesroy and Vincent wore matching t-shirts and ties, Mike brought a miniature U.S. flag to drape over her shoebox, and Justin delivered a moving eulogy. We buried her by the pond and painted her special sunning rock to serve as her headstone. In tiny letters, I printed a tribute dictated by my daughter.

Tina was a very good turtle.

After the service, we ate Mom's homemade pound cake with fresh strawberries, Tina's favorite fruit.

For weeks, Emma placed flowers on the sad little monument daily. The floral deliveries grew fewer and farther apart, but she still remembered Tina from time to time and always on holidays.

"Elmo needs his own special place."

Justin brought the stone to her. He cleared a spot on the kitchen table for her art supplies, and they began painting the rock. While they worked, I prayed she wouldn't insist on a turtle-style send off for the man who had been both a blessing and a curse in our lives. Then I moved to the window to stare at our expanding memorial garden.

·   ·   ·   ·   ·

According to my GPS, the drive to Destin should have been a little over six hours. Of course, that's without stops and assuming traffic is normal. Since there's no such thing as non-stop with an almost five-year-old child and an almost seven-year-old Doberman and normal traffic out of Atlanta is a joke, it took us eight hours and thirty minutes to reach the beach house we had rented.

With ten adults, one kid, and a dog, family wasn't a big enough word for our group. If you counted the urns tucked safely inside a gym bag in the back of our SUV, we numbered twelve adults. But in death as in life, Adelmo and Stella existed in their own space and time. We planned this trip to let the wind take their ashes across the sea to a place they would be together forever.

But with the addition of Natalie and her mother, our gathering was more than a formal goodbye. It was a celebration of new beginnings.

.　　.　　.　　.　　.

A week after Adelmo's death, I arranged to meet my newfound sister at a restaurant in Calhoun, Georgia, the halfway point between Atlanta and Chattanooga. I arrived fifteen minutes early to have the advantage of checking her out as she entered. Natalie was already there.

With her blonde hair smoothed into a low ponytail and very little makeup, she was easily mistakable for Stella before her glamor days. But her smile when she waved to me from the booth transformed her into a different person, one who didn't use it to manipulate or deceive.

She fidgeted in her seat as if deciding whether to stand. I dropped into my spot hard enough to rattle the table. Neither of us knew the proper greeting for stranger-sisters.

"I hope a booth is okay." She shredded pieces of a torn napkin and gulped down half of her glass of water.

"It's perfect." I stared at a spot over her head, pretending to scan the area for our server.

"I'm so glad you called."

The slight tremor in her voice touched me. For the first time, I looked at her and didn't see Stella at all. I saw a young woman willing to risk rejection to be part of something bigger than herself. Justin's research revealed she and her mother had been on their own for years. I learned about her mother's illness and tried to imagine how someone her age had stepped into the role of caregiver, wondering how I might have handled the situation. Unlike me, Natalie had no strong, loving grandmother, only an aunt and uncle, who came across as decent people.

"I'm really glad, too."

·　　·　　·　　·　　·

Lesroy and Vincent arrived before us. A six-foot banner reading *Welcome, Emma and the Beast* hung over the garage. Before Justin killed the engine, my cousin bounded out the front door wearing a grass skirt over floral shorts, a coconut bra, and a wig featuring shiny black locks tumbling over his shoulders and down his back.

He screamed *Aloha* while Vincent followed in a knee-length bathing suit. He carried a pineapple drink in each hand.

"Sorry. I tried to rein him in, but that only made him worse."

Lesroy danced around the car and opened the door, leaving plenty of room between him and a visibly confused Scarlett.

"It's me, you crazy mongrel. I come to set you and your princess free."

Emma giggled and the dog wagged her tail. In seconds, they were racing toward the back yard and the ocean behind it.

"You go with them. Vincent and I can unload."

I grabbed a pineapple from Vincent's hand and rushed to the three escapees. Scarlett's bark led me to the trio, who were splashing in the surf. Lesroy's skirt rested low on his slender hips, and his wig had slipped across his forehead.

"Emma, I think your mom's entirely too dry. What do you think?"

"Don't you dare," I warned. As expected, he completely ignored me, so I swallowed as much of the drink as I could before he attacked.

When we returned, soaking wet and covered with sand, Mom's car was parked beside ours. Mike sat on the steps, holding a hose.

"My instructions are to clean you up before you're allowed inside."

"Well, shit. If this isn't adding insult to injury."

"That's a dollar in the jar for you." Lesroy cackled until Mike blasted him with water.

After we were hosed down and toweled off, we changed into dry clothes and joined everyone on the lower deck. Rita and Harry shared a lounger while Mom and Mike rocked back and forth in the glider. The table was loaded with watermelon, strawberries, and pineapple, along with an assortment of Emma's favorite unhealthy snacks.

"So, you and Natalie really hit it off?" Rita asked.

"I guess you could say that." The truth was I had grown much fonder of my half-sister than I'd expected but hated to admit it. Whether it was from loyalty or guilt, I couldn't shake the feeling my relationship with Natalie shouldn't be going so well, so fast.

"I more than guess you could." Lesroy, his mouth full of chips and salsa, called me on my hesitancy. "But you know our Grace. She's highly suspicious of anything that makes her happy."

"You leave her alone. Sister stuff can be delicate." His mother defended me.

Lesroy snorted. "Delicate, my ass." He paused, probably expecting a reminder about the swear jar, but Emma was arranging shells on the railing.

My mom chimed in. "Rita's right. But Natalie seems like a good kid. And, Grace, honey, it's okay if you decide to love her."

Decide to love her? I thought. Was it that simple?

Scarlett barked at the commotion out front, and I guessed I would soon discover the answer to my question.

•   •   •   •   •

Even though Vincent and Lesroy had arrived before us, they insisted we have the master bedroom.

"It's the least we can do since you're picking up the tab for this swanky place."

After learning Adelmo had appointed us to oversee the trust fund he set up for Emma, we splurged on a rental nicer than our own home. As trustees, we received an allowance, and he left Eva enough money to run the Stella Burnette Women's Shelter, a charity he started before coming to the states. He named me as chairman of the board with generous salaries for Eva and a yearly stipend for me.

Justin and I were still processing what these changes meant for us as a family. I hadn't shared it with him yet, but I'd been thinking how the extra money might free me up to write Stella's book if I could bring myself to do it.

Tonight I was content to lie beside him listening to the waves crashing against the shore.

"I could get used to this." He wrapped his arm around my shoulders and leaned his head against mine. "Hmm, your hair smells great."

"I call it Eau de Sand Castle and Doberman."

"My favorite." He nuzzled my neck, sniffing like Scarlett searching for a hidden treat.

Much later, after Justin found the treat he was looking for, he asked me if the big send-off we scheduled for our last day at the beach had gone the way I expected.

"I'm not sure. Not about spreading their ashes together. I'm sure that's what they both would have wanted. And it's been great getting to know Natalie and her mother."

"I can't believe how well Olivia gets along with your mom and Rita. They had me cracking up talking about setting her up on a geriatric dating site."

"You better not let them hear you call it that."

"No worries. I don't have a death wish."

"They were funny, especially when they started in on what terrible ex-husbands they had. I guess being divorced from the same son-of-a-bitch creates a special bond."

"I'm just glad they didn't get into too many details about how crappy your dad was in bed. That kinda made me sweat."

"That wasn't the part that got to me. It was when they started in on Uncle Roy that scared the bejesus out of me."

"It would have been awkward for Olivia to learn she was hanging out with a couple of killers."

"Shhh. Don't even say it out loud, please." I poked him in the side with my elbow.

"Ouch! So, are you still worried about Emma?"

We stuck as close to the truth as possible by telling her the urns were filled with the ashes of love letters between Adelmo and the woman he loved.

"No. I think she took it pretty well."

"All right. If you're not worried about Natalie or Emma, what is bothering you?"

"Nothing I can put into words." Because there were none to describe the place between learning to live with a loss you thought would kill you and letting go of it enough to celebrate the good things coming your way.

·　　·　　·　　·　　·

We had waited until sunset to gather at the shoreline. The wind whipped off and on during our last day at the beach but had lessened into a soft breeze. It ruffled Mom's curls, hiding the lines that had deepened since her hospital stay. Wrapped in Mike's arms, she seemed light and small enough for a more serious gust to carry her away with the remains of her lost daughter. But more than a force of nature was necessary to stop the woman who had both given and taken life.

Justin held Emma on his shoulders, Adelmo's urn in his hands. The shiny bronze container with all that was left of my beautiful Stella seemed to weigh more than she had in life. I kept her close to my chest.

Lesroy stood beside me and whispered his request to offer his goodbye last. And I agreed.

Rita put her arm around Mom, and the sisters sobbed quietly together. Mike wiped tears from his eyes, and Vincent placed his hand on Lesroy's shoulder.

I looked to the sky and said, "You'll always be our Stella Star. I hope happiness finds you and your one true love." Then I nodded to my cousin.

"When I remember her, I see roses. Because it's what I thought she was when Aunt Marilyn brought her home from the hospital snuggled in a pale pink blanket. But she was more beautiful than flowers and shone brighter than the stars. She is never sad when she visits me in my dreams. She is running on the beach, trying to keep up with Grace and me. Or dancing on the porch in her nightgown. She stands in front of the mirror waving a curling iron like a magic wand. And we laugh at our reflections." His voice broke, and Vincent spoke to him, too softly for us to hear.

Lesroy shook his head and swiped as if angry at the tears on his cheeks. "Stella lost her way for a time. But we never lost her. She left us with the greatest gift imaginable. We'll always be grateful, and never, ever stop loving our beautiful Stella Star." He closed his eyes and Vincent pulled him close and held him.

Justin lifted Emma down and led her into the surf. I joined them. With our daughter between us, we opened the urns and gave up the contents to the gentle ocean breeze. Within seconds, the ashy clouds merged into one.

We returned to our family on the shore. The water was deeper than when we waded in, but the surface was smooth and still. Mom ran to me and hugged me. Scarlett broke free from Harry's hold on her leash and scampered into the rising tide toward Emma, who sloshed her way to me.

"Don't cry, Mommy. Remember, they're not really gone." She looked over my shoulder and called out, "Natty, come here. I've got something special to show you."

Natalie reached Emma as the waves rolled quietly in. The rest of the family clustered around us waiting for the announcement. Before my daughter could speak, a rogue wave rose from the smooth surface and exploded, leaving everyone drenched and knocking Lesroy onto his behind.

He scrambled to his feet and shook his fist at the sky. "Damn you, lady! You always have to have the last word."

After relocating to drier land, Emma tugged at my shirt and gave me her *excuse me, I was talking* look.

I apologized to her before addressing the family. "Listen up, please. Emma has something to say."

"Not say, show." She took her hand and placed it on my belly. I flushed with the possibility she was about to proclaim it was time for me to go back to the gym. Instead, she smiled and placed her cheek on my stomach. Then she spoke the words I'd been too afraid to let myself acknowledge.

"Look, guys. We're having a baby sister."

EPILOGUE

Natalie's hair curtained her face as she gazed at the sleeping infant. I thought of Stella and the short time she'd had with her baby. But the pain was less sharp thanks to the gratitude Lesroy spoke of and the child Justin and I had been blessed with.

"Oh, my God. Those tiny little fingers. And those itty-bitty toes. What is it about baby digits that makes adults go stupid?"

Emma piped up from her spot behind the sofa where she was reading a book to Scarlett. "They look like regular old feet to me."

"No progress in the sibling love department?" Natalie asked.

I whispered, "At least she stopped insisting we take *that thing* back to the hospital. And she tolerates being in the same room now. We're not worried, though. Being a big sister just isn't what she expected."

"She'll come around. How's the book going?"

When Emma announced my pregnancy, I was four months along. The doctor feared the trauma from the kidnapping and Adelmo's death could have an adverse effect on the baby and insisted I take it easy.

I finished ongoing projects for my freelance business, stopped taking new clients, and tried to relax. But Stella had other ideas. During quiet morning moments after Justin left for work and throughout the day, she came to me.

Sometimes her voice was a sweet whisper.

Please, Grace. I want Emma to know the truth about me – the good and the bad.

Other times, it had the edge of frustration.

What are you waiting for? Me to write the damn thing for you?

So, I began my sister's story. I completed the final chapter two days before I went into labor.

"My editor has it. She plans to send it to an agent she works with. I'll believe it when I see it, but she thinks we have a good chance of signing with the friend. Fingers crossed. So, what's going on with your love life?"

Natalie had shared her anguish over discovering the man she considered relationship material wasn't who he claimed to be. Despite her insistence it was no big deal, I could tell his deception – although understandable – had devastated her.

"He keeps calling, and I keep hanging up. Mom says I should talk to him before he goes back to Ecuador, but why drag it out?"

"If he takes the job with Justin's security company, he won't be there forever. And just because you agree to talk to him doesn't mean you're getting married. From what you've told me, it's clear he has feelings for you."

"I don't know if I can forgive him for making such a fool out of me."

"How does caring about someone make you a fool?"

"Who's a fool?" Emma had crept up on us when we weren't looking.

"Nobody's a fool, honey. Aunt Natty has a big decision to make, and she's not sure what to do."

A grunt signaled the baby was stirring. Emma rolled her eyes.

"It's awake. Probably pooped again." She wrinkled her nose.

Determined not to rise to the bait and remind her *it* had a name, I ignored the comment.

She seemed not to notice and asked Natalie, "What do you have to decide?"

I could see my new sister was at a loss and rescued her. "Your Aunt Natty has a friend who didn't tell her the truth about himself."

"You mean he lied to you?" She put her hand on Natalie's shoulder.

"Yes, but not about the important things."

"What important things?" She moved closer to Natalie and stared into her face.

"The way he feels, stuff like that."

"How does he feel about you?"

"He says he loves me."

"Do you love him back?"

A soft whimper followed by a single bleat saved her from answering.

Whether it was from irritation at the interruption or a moment of forgetfulness about her disdain for the child, Emma pivoted from her aunt and leaned over the bassinet. Fearful she might try to smother the baby with the blanket, I inched closer.

"What's the matter with you?" Instead of the angry tone she normally used, she turned the question into a melody.

Finn's eyes popped open, and he began flailing his arms as if reaching for his sister. She tickled the bottom of his foot, and his gurgle became something very much like a giggle.

"Emma!" Natalie squealed. "We just heard Finn Burnette McElroy's very first laugh. And you made it happen."

"Did I, Mommy? Did I really make him laugh?"

"You most certainly did." I sniffed back tears. Careful not to sound too desperate, I asked, for at least the tenth time since we brought her brother home from the hospital, if she wanted to hold him. She squirmed into the rocker and held out her arms.

I eased her brother into her lap, and she grinned down at him. He wrapped a finger around one of hers and nuzzled her chest. "Look, Natty. Finn's just like Daddy—a boob man."

I covered my mouth and vowed to have a talk with Justin. My sister laughed out loud.

"Most men are," she said.

Emma kissed Finn's fuzzy head.

"So, maybe brothers aren't so bad?" Natalie asked.

"Maybe. But I still want a sister." She pointed to her lap and added, "He wants one, too. Don't you, Finny?"

The little traitor gurgled a smile. I promised we would try.

Later, while I nursed the baby, Emma and Natalie worked on a puzzle together, their foreheads almost touching. They shared Stella's delicate profile and heart-shaped face. Instead of filling me with sadness, the resemblance comforted me as did the differences.

"You forgot to answer me." Emma placed a corner piece before peering at her aunt.

Natalie pretended to be confused, but we all knew what my daughter referred to.

"You never told me if you loved him back."

"It's not that easy. I care a lot about him, but what if he lies to me again?"

"What if he doesn't?" She patted her aunt's hand. "Just do what I did with Finn."

We exchanged perplexed glances over her head.

"And what did you do with Finn?"

"I decided to love him. Like Mommy and Daddy decided to love me."

Someday Justin and I would tell Emma the story of her birth. We would explain to her how many people loved her before and after she was born. We would make her understand our love for her came instantly and would never die.

But for now, I decided that loving her was enough.

THE END

ABOUT THE AUTHOR

Katherine Nichols is a writer of suspense with heart and humor. Her books include *The Sometime Sister*, *The Unreliables*, and *Trust Issues*. She serves as vice president of the Atlanta Writers Club and is on the board of Sisters in Crime Atlanta. A strong advocate of women authors supporting one another, she co-hosts the podcast, Wild Women Who Write Take Flight. When she isn't spending time with her children and grandchildren, Katherine loves to read, walk, and travel. She lives in Lilburn, Georgia with her husband, two rescue dogs, and two rescue cats.

NOTE FROM THE AUTHOR

Word-of-mouth is crucial for any author to succeed. If you enjoyed *The Substitute Sister*, please leave a review online — anywhere you are able. Even if it's just a sentence or two. It would make all the difference and would be very much appreciated.

Thanks!
Katherine Nichols

We hope you enjoyed reading this title from:

www.blackrosewriting.com

Subscribe to our mailing list – *The Rosevine* – and receive **FREE** books, daily deals, and stay current with news about upcoming releases and our hottest authors.
Scan the QR code below to sign up.

Already a subscriber? Please accept a sincere thank you for being a fan of Black Rose Writing authors.

View other Black Rose Writing titles at
www.blackrosewriting.com/books and use promo code
PRINT to receive a **20% discount** when purchasing.

CPSIA information can be obtained
at www.ICGtesting.com
Printed in the USA
JSHW020004030423
39736JS00007B/8